LOST GIRLS

When **EVERYTHING**
YOU'VE FORGOTTEN
IS WHAT **YOU NEED**
TO SURVIVE.

LOST GIRLS

MERRIE DESTEFANO

Entangled Publishing, LLC
2614 South Timberline Road
Suite 109
Fort Collins, CO 80525

Entangled Teen is an imprint of Entangled Publishing, LLC.

Visit our website at www.entangledpublishing.com.

Edited by Heather Howland
Cover design by Louisa Maggio
Interior design by Toni Kerr

ISBN: 9781633756052
Ebook ISBN: 9781633756069

Manufactured in the United States of America
First Edition January 2017

10 9 8 7 6 5 4 3 2 1

*Dedicated to my friend, Rachel Marks,
who believed in this book from Day One, Page One.*

PART ONE

Peace. LOVE. Unity
Respect. Party.

CHAPTER ONE

I remember last night perfectly.

I know what we ate for dinner. I know my little brother didn't do his homework. I know Dad drove me to my ballet lessons, then waited for me in the Starbucks across the street.

I know that, later in the evening, I fell asleep when I was supposed to be studying geometry, my earbuds in while I listened to Taylor Swift's latest album.

That was my yesterday.

The problem is, everyone, from my parents to my teachers to the police, says that stuff didn't happen yesterday.

It happened last year.

I went to sleep with music playing, curled up on my bed, and wrapped in the afghan Grams knitted for me when she was on chemo.

I woke up in a ditch, half-buried in a pile of leaves. I was shivering and wet, a soft rain falling, icy drops hitting me in the face and running down my neck. Trees towered overhead, black branches scratching the sky, wind howling, and from somewhere nearby came the muted sounds of traffic.

I sat up, confused and scared, grogginess giving way to an intense adrenaline rush.

Then I screamed, louder than I thought I could. The sound ripped out of my lungs and wouldn't stop; it went on and on until I thought I would collapse because I knew I couldn't breathe and scream at the same time. And then— when I was sure I would fall forward, bent over at the waist, my lungs empty and spots dancing before my eyes—*then* I found some way to yell again. At first my shouts were primal and there were no words, just terror and pain and a black pit in my stomach that wouldn't allow me to have conscious thoughts.

I began to cry the same thing, over and over.

"Help! Somebody help me!"

I tried to stand, but the gully was so slanted that I kept falling back to my knees, every stumble forcing me to become aware of another injury—the raw skin on my wrists and ankles, covered with dried blood and stinging with each drop of rain; the muscles in my legs sore and weak, like I'd been running for days; the soles of my feet aching, my tennis shoes ripped and stained with mud.

I stretched out my arms, latching onto tree roots to gain my balance, and I pulled myself up the incline, foot by foot. Fingers now coated with mud, I perched on the edge of a highway, nearly blinded by headlights whenever a car sped past.

There I stood, waving my arms and screaming again, not knowing that my hair was matted or that there was blood and dirt on my clothes or that my photo had been on the news for the past two weeks.

Lost girl. Disappeared on her way home from school. Anyone with information, please contact the Santa Madre police department.

Two cars drove past, headlights splashing me with brilliant light. I hadn't realized until now that the sun tipped on the edge of the world, ready to disappear, or that twilight shadows were already stretching across the horizon. Great pockets of violet darkness yawned between each pair of lights that hurtled toward me, greedy fingers of darkness that wanted me to tumble back into that gully and remain hidden.

Please, somebody stop and help me.

I was screaming again and some sort of weird survival panic took over.

I walked into the middle of the two-lane southbound road and stood there.

Go ahead, run me over. I dare you.

Wait, what was I doing?

Several cars spun to a stop, skidding sideways, tires squealing, metal crashing metal and rubber burning. The old me, the girl who fell asleep listening to Taylor sing about a broken heart, never would have done this. What was wrong with me?

My heart thundered in my chest, but I refused to move, even when the wreckage screeched closer and closer, fenders crunching, bumpers twisting, windshields shattering. I stared all the passengers in the eye, glancing from one face to the next, coolly noting that none of them were hurt—nothing beyond a bump or a bruise.

You. Will. Stop. And. Help. Me.

Still the wreckage surged forward. I merely lifted one hand, palm up, signaling for them to stop. Like I was a traffic cop or something.

Everything finally slid to a stop, a few feet away from me.

Tears coursed down my cheeks and I began to shake

uncontrollably. I sank to my knees, truly myself again. Frightened and alone and lost.

"Help me," I begged, then buried my face in my hands.

Car doors opened. A strange cacophony of voices tumbled out, some yelling, some speaking in hushed tones.

"What's going on?"

"Is that the missing girl from the news?"

"9-1-1, we have an emergency here—"

"Honey, you're gonna be okay, don't worry—"

An elderly woman with white hair and bright, pink lipstick pulled me close and draped her coat over me. When I glanced up I saw blood on her forehead, but she didn't seem worried about herself. She smiled down at me, her face a map of connected wrinkles.

"We're gonna get you home to your parents," she said. "Do you want to call them?" She handed me her cell phone, but my fingers were shaking too much to dial. I told her the number and she punched it in, waiting while it rang. When a voice answered on the other end, the white-haired woman said, "I have someone who wants to talk to you." Then she handed me the phone.

"Hello? Who is this?" It was my mom, a frantic tone in her voice that brought fresh tears to my eyes.

My voice came out shakier than I expected.

"Mom?"

Neither one of us could talk, not for a long time, because we were both crying. Then she finally whispered my name, like it was a magical word that could change the world.

"Rachel? Rachel, baby, where are you?"

I looked around. "I don't know."

"You're on the 39, just north of Azusa," the white-haired woman told me.

Flashing lights spun in the distance and sirens blared.

An ambulance and a fire truck and two police cars were headed toward us. I blinked at the brightness, shielding my eyes with one hand.

"Rachel? Are you still there?" It was my father's voice now, calling me back to the cell phone.

I pressed it against my ear. "Daddy?"

"Honey, when the ambulance gets there, you get inside and you stay there. Do you hear me? Don't get in a car with anyone else!"

"I will—I mean, I won't. I'll go with the paramedics." My teeth were chattering and I was shivering so much I could hardly hold the phone. I think I may have started talking gibberish, half-sentences with little meaning. I remember saying something about my geometry test and worrying that I wouldn't make it to class tomorrow and I may have mentioned something about my biology class, too, because Dad interrupted me.

"Rachel, are you talking about the class you took with Miss Wallace?"

"Yeah. She always gives exams on Wednesday."

There was a long silence. I wondered if we had gotten cut off. Meanwhile, the ambulance doors opened and someone wheeled a stretcher toward me.

"Honey, you had geometry with Miss Wallace last year. When you were a sophomore."

I frowned. "But I'm a sophomore *now*."

"Baby girl, you're a junior. Don't worry about it. All this will get straightened out when you get home—"

I dropped the phone. My hands were shaking too much to hold it. I glanced down at my hands, at the chipped red nail polish. But I hadn't been wearing nail polish last night and I never use this color. I turned my hands over and discovered a tattoo on my inner wrist.

A tattoo?

Always and forever. That's what it said. But there was no redness or swelling. I didn't get this tattoo anytime recently.

The paramedics helped me onto the stretcher, and then the world was rushing past me, rain falling on my face, people staring down at me as the stretcher wheeled by, the air thick with the smell of oil and gasoline and burned rubber. Then another smell came suddenly and violently—a memory.

A thick, cloying scent of pine and cedar.

My stomach lurched and I couldn't stop.

I started screaming again.

CHAPTER TWO

I didn't recognize myself.

When I went to sleep last night, my hair had been dark brown and shoulder-length. Now it was cropped short and dyed platinum blond. My face looked longer and thinner, my cheekbones more pronounced. I looked away from the mirrored wall on my left and focused on the man sitting across from me instead.

FBI agent Ryan Bennet.

Any other time I would have thought it was cool to be alone with a guy like this. About ten years older than me, he looked like a stunt double for Channing Tatum. Cool green eyes studied me, a pensive expression on his face. He glanced down at his notes, tapping his pen on the table between us.

"You don't remember anything about where you were for the past two weeks?"

He'd asked this before. I'd already answered it.

I sighed. I wanted to go home.

"There was a smell. Like a forest, maybe. Pine and cedar. That's all."

"Could that smell have been a man's cologne?"

I shrugged. "Maybe."

"The last thing you remember is…"

"Going to bed and listening to music."

"And your current class schedule is…" He began naming all my sophomore classes, reading a list I had written down a few minutes ago.

I nodded.

"You don't remember taking chemistry or Algebra II?"

"Are you kidding?" There's no way I was in Algebra II. I hadn't even mastered geometry yet. I was still worried Miss Wallace was going to flunk me.

He shifted in his chair, then shot a quick glance at the mirror, maybe wishing he could talk to whoever was on the other side. "There's one other thing we haven't discussed yet."

An unwelcome shudder raced over me. I already knew that I hadn't been raped. I'd spent hours with a woman doctor while she gently poked and prodded me, asking me questions. When she was drawing my blood, both of us had been puzzled by the marks on my inner arms.

Needle marks.

Either I was a druggie, which just couldn't be true, or someone had been injecting something into me. The tricky thing was, some of those track marks looked a lot older than two weeks. Now I had a possible threat of withdrawal hanging over my head, with symptoms that could range from headaches to night terrors to tremors.

Across from me, Agent Bennet opened a large manila envelope, one that had been sitting conspicuously beside him throughout our interview. He slid out several photographs, all eight-by-ten glossies—each one catching his attention for a moment and causing his brow to lower—

and then he slapped them down on the table, lining them up in a row so they faced me. They were all shots of girls about my age, each one with different hair and eye and skin color, each one smiling into the camera, like they were expecting something wonderful to happen. These had to be yearbook photos, because every hair was perfect, every girl was staring right at me.

All of them waiting for something.

I glanced up at Agent Bennet, wondering what he wanted.

"Do you know any of these girls?" he asked.

I ran a gaze over them again, imagining them stretching on the barre, wearing one-piece black leotards, or running down the hall at Lincoln High, wearing jeans and T-shirts, backpacks slung over their shoulders. Six girls looked up at me, wanting me to know their names, but I was lucky to remember my own name right now.

I shook my head. "Who are they?"

He started listing them off as if they were his younger sisters; every time he touched a photo he would say the girl's name and his jaw would shift, just a fraction, as if the muscle was working too hard. As I expected, he said six names I didn't recognize—Emily, Hannah, Madison, Nicole, Haley, and Brooke—then he spoke again, still staring down at their faces.

"All these girls have gone missing within the past three months. Two of them disappeared after school, like you did. Three left home for sporting events but never came back. One girl told her mother she was spending the weekend with a friend, but the friend waited and waited. The girl never showed up."

He paused, then looked directly into my eyes, watching me so closely that a trickle of sweat began to run down my neck. "You're the only girl who has come back," he said, leaning forward. "How did you get away?"

How was I supposed to know? My skin started to heat up, a feeling of being trapped started to overwhelm me, and my breathing turned ragged and raw. I needed to get out of here.

I shook my head, my stomach roiling. "I don't remember."

"There were pine needles stuck to your clothes, Rachel, and seedpods that can only be found in the San Gabriel Mountains. Could someone have been holding you captive in the mountains?"

That smell of cedar and pine came back, as if he had conjured it. It wafted around me, oozing out of the floorboards and the seams where the walls met. It curled like smoke away from the mirror until foggy clouds covered the floor. I fought a gag reflex, holding my right hand over my mouth. Without realizing it, I pushed my chair backward, accidentally knocking it to the floor with a loud crash. I struggled to my feet.

At the same time, the door behind me clicked and swung open. A woman dressed in a navy blue suit looked in at us, a stern expression on her face as she glanced from me to Agent Bennet. "That's enough for today, Bennet. In fact, it's enough, period. Miss Evans can go home now. Her parents have been waiting for more than an hour."

One hand still over my mouth and nose, trying to block out the stench of pine and cedar, I stumbled past her, heading down the hallway. But no matter how fast I walked, I could still hear the two of them arguing.

"You will not follow this line of questioning any further, do you understand, Bennet?" the woman was saying. "This girl has been traumatized enough."

"But there's something here that connects these cases. I'm sure of it. Something we're overlooking—"

"Half of these girls are probably runaways. There's not enough evidence to prove they fall into the category of Violent Crimes Against Children, or that these cases are related—"

The farther I walked away from them, the more their voices faded, which was what I wanted. I could see Mom and Dad and Kyle through a large glass window up ahead, all of them waving at me, big smiles on their faces like we were going to Disneyland.

The two agents behind me probably hadn't realized that I could still hear them. It was like I was invisible. I tried to ignore them and forget about what might have happened during that two-week period when I was lost.

Except now, after talking to that FBI agent, I knew that I wasn't the only one. There were other girls out there who had gone missing, too.

And they were still lost.

Chapter Three

We all piled into Dad's SUV and headed away from the FBI's Los Angeles Field Office. Dad drove while Mom sat in the front passenger seat, chewing her fingernails, staring out the window, occasionally saying something overly cheerful like, *we need to take a family vacation* or *isn't the weather gorgeous today?* Dad didn't say much. He'd been a lot quieter since his last tour in Afghanistan, right before he retired from the Navy last year. A new Taylor Swift song played on the radio, one I didn't recognize—apparently she'd released another album during my missing year. Cars drove past that I'd never seen before, some new model of Mini-Coop and a sporty-looking Kia.

It felt like I'd been to Mars and back since I went to sleep last night.

Even worse, I didn't fit in with my family.

I was as tall as Mom now, but I used to be two inches shorter. Kyle, my little brother, wasn't little anymore. He towered over both me and Mom.

Dad was the same. Almost.

There were worry lines on his forehead and around his eyes, an expression of dread that never seemed to leave him. I was used to him making me feel safe. Now something about me put him on edge.

It was weird, but I could remember almost anything, as long as it had happened more than a year ago. It felt like someone had erased the hard drive in my brain, leaving a handful of important folders empty. It didn't make sense to me. Why had I only been gone for two weeks, but my memories of the whole last *year* were gone? The therapist had tried to explain it, saying that I had a form of retrograde amnesia, possibly combined with PTSD, and that it would take a while before my memories came back—if ever.

In the meantime, I was left with a family that all stared at me when they thought I wasn't looking, like I was made out of porcelain and was about to break.

I missed how things used to be.

Sighing, I pressed my forehead against the cool window. The San Gabriel Mountains curved beside us as we drove— all the way from L.A. to Santa Madre—a massive chain of peaks that bordered the suburban sprawl, purple and hazy in the smog. Mount Harvard, Mount Wilson, San Gabriel Peak, Mount Lawlor, Monrovia Peak, and Strawberry Peak, all of them linking hands across the valleys and gaps.

Was that where I'd been for the past two weeks, wandering through the Angeles National Forest, forging a path down the mountains, trying to find my way home after being kidnapped? It reminded me of the survival training Dad always drilled into us every time he took Kyle and me backpacking. Since we were about five years old, he'd been taking us into deep forests, teaching us how to find our way back to the main trail, even if it took us days to get there.

But Dad hadn't been there when I went missing, and I wasn't five. And there were more things to be afraid of now than tree spiders or empty canteens.

Except for the landscaping, our house looked almost exactly the same. Living room, family room, dining room...all decorated in muted tones that said Nothing Very Exciting Ever Happens Here. As soon as we got in the door, Kyle nose-dived into the sofa, flipped on the big-screen TV, and launched Halo 4. Mom and Dad watched me as they pretended to go about normal activities: her making a grocery list even though the pantry door hung open and it was fully stocked, him flipping through a recent *Sunset* magazine, zeroing in on the garden section.

I wanted to be alone, so I jogged upstairs and headed toward my room.

But once my door swung open, I wasn't sure if I was in the right house.

My room looked like it belonged to someone else. The pale yellow walls had been repainted dark burgundy and all my Taylor Swift posters were gone, replaced by Amy Winehouse, The Cure, and Marilyn Manson. My glitter eye shadows and pale pink lipsticks had been traded in for dark, somber shades—grays, browns, and burgundies. Apparently Mom had left my room just as it had been right before I disappeared. Black shirts and skirts and pants were draped over everything.

Had I gone Goth?

This wasn't right, this wasn't me.

I tore down the posters one by one, my fingernails

scratching the wall. By the time I was done, Amy, Marilyn, and The Cure lay in a tattered pile on the floor. I opened the curtains to let in more light, then lifted the window and gulped in fresh air. After that, I rooted through my top drawer looking for my iPod, and found a pack of condoms instead.

I was a virgin.

Wasn't I?

Behind me, the closet door swung open with a lazy creak and I flinched at the sound. That door never stayed closed. Humidity would make it stick, and then, when the weather was dry, the door would unlatch and creep open. It used to scare the crap out of me when I was a kid, and it was the main reason my best friend Molly refused to spend the night. We both used to worry that a monster or a serial killer was going to spring out, right when we fell asleep and were defenseless.

Apparently that invisible monster in the closet finally got me.

Beads of sweat slicked my forehead and upper lip.

I stared at my bed. At the neatly folded afghan blanket. I had fallen asleep *right there*, in that exact spot, and that was the last thing I remembered. But then I woke up a different person, alone in a ditch.

I sank onto my bed, suddenly exhausted.

I pulled my new iPhone from my jacket pocket. Dad had given me this when I got out of the hospital, knowing my old one had gotten lost when I went missing. I cradled it in my hand for a moment, almost as if I expected it to burn my fingers, then I started thumbing in Molly's number. At least I remembered *that*. I'd wanted to talk to her since I woke up in that ditch, but when I got to the last digit, I panicked and hung up. What was I supposed to say when she answered? *Hi, did you notice I was gone for two weeks?*

Yeah, I was kidnapped, but I don't remember anything, it's like I've forgotten a whole year.

How could I tell anyone that? I couldn't even think it without wanting to clench my fists so tight that my fingernails cut into my palms and made them bleed.

That was *not* like me.

The phone awkwardly slid from my fingers onto the bed. A series of unexpected images began to flash through my mind, all the colors wrong, like I was watching a video that had been manipulated and altered. Without realizing it, I stood up and backed across the room, retreating as far from my iPhone as I could.

My back slammed against the wall and my room disappeared—

I was standing in a corner, trying to make a phone call, hoping no one would notice me, my fingers trying to punch in 9-1-1. But I only made it to the first two numbers before someone knocked the cell phone out of my hand. It clattered to the ground, a cement floor spattered with glowing paint, the phone casing shattering, the face cracking, and the battery flying out. I tried to speak, but someone grabbed me and tied a gag around my mouth—

I sank to the floor, shivering.

Was this my first memory of the kidnapping? It was awful, like plugging my finger in an electrical outlet until my insides were charred.

I didn't know if I'd ever be able to pick up my phone again.

Instead, I crawled into my bed and wrapped myself in the afghan Grams made me. Cocooned in darkness, I clutched my pillow tight against my stomach.

I tossed and turned while the sky outside my window burned bright and brighter, until finally it faded to murky gray. Night blossomed around me, the air turning chill, before I finally fell asleep. But my dreams never fully matured, as if they couldn't decide whether or not they should be nightmares.

CHAPTER FOUR

The sun came up in the morning as if nothing had changed, thin April beams pouring in my open window through the smog that had collected at the base of the mountains. Sunlight glinted off bottles of perfume on my dresser, and carried the pattern of the lace curtains that hung on my window, big flowers that changed shape with each breath of wind.

Air filled my lungs and I remembered.

I was home. I was finally home.

Mom and Dad were chattering downstairs, their voices hushed as if they didn't want to wake me, the rich aroma of scrambled eggs and turkey bacon and pancakes drifting up to my room. I dressed quickly, ready to head downstairs, although I wasn't sure if I felt like eating.

My fingers ran through my hair—a reflex after tugging a shirt over my head—brushing my bangs out of my eyes. I vowed to dye my hair back to dark brown later today. Every time I saw myself, it caught me by surprise. I looked like someone else, my limbs too long and skinny. Granted,

I had more muscles than before, but it looked like I never ate. Last year I had weighed a hundred and thirty pounds. I hadn't been fat, not exactly, since I was five foot seven and danced about twenty hours a week. But I'd never looked like this.

Now, I was a hundred and eighteen. Maybe I was anorexic. Maybe that was why I didn't have an appetite.

The smell of cedar and pine washed over me again.

My stomach twisted. My skin prickled. I felt trapped, like my hands and legs were bound. I needed to break free, to get outside, go for a run. I grabbed a sweatshirt and headed out the door of my room. Down the stairs, through the family room where Kyle slouched on the sofa, once again playing video games.

"I'm going for a run," I said.

He glanced up and gave me a strange look.

My parents paused in the kitchen, Mom setting plates on the table, Dad in front of the stove, spatula in hand. Yesterday, I'd gone upstairs like I never wanted to see the world again. Now I was racing out into it.

"Rachel," Mom called, her voice louder and sharper than I think she expected. "Don't you want some breakfast?"

"Maybe later."

She gave my father a look.

"Kyle, go with her," Dad said, taking charge of the situation. Like he always did. "You've got your tennis shoes on and you could use some exercise."

Kyle started to argue, but stopped. Like he realized he didn't want to lose me again. He jumped up, right in the middle of a Spartan Op, and joined me at the door. I didn't really want company, but if it had to be someone, my little brother was a good choice.

I was already out the door and jogging across our lawn

toward the sidewalk by the time he caught up with me. I tugged on the jacket I was carrying, realizing it was one of Dad's old sweatshirts. Even though it had been washed a hundred times, it still smelled like his aftershave. Wearing this always made me feel warm and safe, so I'd stolen it from the Goodwill bin when he was getting rid of it.

But when was that? Last month or last year?

The landscape of suburbia fell away behind us. Nothing looked familiar. There were more houses here than I remembered, the suburban sprawl reaching toward the 210 and then back toward the foothills. The Keefers must have remodeled their house, because it was almost twice as big as it had been last year. Every block we passed had countless foreclosure signs stuck in brown grass, houses abandoned.

"Did the Taylors move?" I asked, noting that the swing set in their front yard was gone and there was a FOR SALE sign in its place. I used to babysit their kids.

"Yup."

I wondered if I'd had a chance to say good-bye.

I forced my attention on the road, knowing that the houses of Santa Madre would thin out eventually. My feet slammed pavement, Kyle keeping pace with me, as familiar hills rose around us. On our right, tangles of wild morning glory dotted the foothills with white blossoms, while flowering yucca spikes towered above them, waving in the breeze.

A trail appeared to our left.

"This way," I said, jogging across the street toward a path that snaked up a San Gabriel foothill. We continued to run side by side, higher and higher, our pace slowing as we struggled to get up the switchbacks, until finally we were surrounded by trees that pushed the sky away, branches like thick arms with clawed fingers, pine needles on the ground and a sharp fragrance in the air.

This used to be one of my favorite places. Whenever I wanted to be alone, I'd hike up here. Half an hour in these wooded trails and I'd feel better, no matter what had been bothering me.

It wasn't long before I realized I'd made a huge mistake.

Every step I took kicked up the smell of pine needles, making a fine cloud of dust that hung in the air, while my hands started to shake. The trees were pinning me in, blocking out the rest of the world.

I started running faster. Off the trail and into the forest, wending a crooked path through the trees, darting first one way then another, as if trying to get away from someone.

I forgot all about Kyle and the fact that my home was just a quarter mile away—

I was trying to escape and someone was chasing me, matching me step for step through the woods. He'd been after me all day, through shadowed thickets and sun-dappled vales, both of us with chests heaving and skin glistening with sweat. My only advantage was the fact that I knew the mountains better than he did. If I could keep up this pace until nightfall, I'd lose him. He wouldn't be able to see in the dark—

A hand reached out and grabbed me by the arm, pulling me to a stop.

"Rachel!"

I spun around, temporarily not recognizing the person

who stood behind me.

"We should go back," he said, tugging at my arm.

The image of my brother faded away, turning into someone taller, heavier, stronger, older. The man's face wasn't clear, but that didn't matter.

It was him or me.

With a couple of moves I'd only seen in films, I flipped him over and pinned him to the ground, my knee in his back, his face in the dirt. He chuffed, a long thud of air coming out of his lungs, unable to talk because I'd knocked the wind out of him.

"Hey!" he said, spitting out pine needles and twigs with each syllable. "What the hell, Rachel? Let me go!"

The image of the man faded away, changing back into that of my brother. I gasped and released Kyle, stumbling away, my hands reaching for whatever might be behind me. Finally, I latched onto the bark of a nearby tree.

"Oh my God." That was all I could say.

Kyle brushed himself off and rubbed his neck as he climbed to his feet. "Son of a bitch!"

I crossed my arms over my chest, so tight it felt like I was wearing a straitjacket.

"Did you think I was gonna hurt you? You *know* I'd never do anything like that." Then he paused. "When the hell did you learn to fight?"

I leaned against that tree until the bark pressed into my back, the pain forcing me to stay focused. "I don't know," I confessed. "Every time I smell pine or cedar, it triggers something. Then, when you grabbed me, your face disappeared—you turned into somebody else."

A silence stretched between us, until finally the sounds of the wood swelled, revealing the hiss from a waterfall up the trail and the chatter of birds in a nearby meadow.

"My sister, the assassin," Kyle said at last, a grin teasing his lips.

"You have to promise not to tell Mom or Dad what happened," I said. I took a step closer, my feet crunching over pine needles, stirring the scent that made my stomach knot up. "My therapist wanted to keep me in the hospital longer. I was worried I'd never go home again." My voice was shaking. "*Please* don't tell them."

"It's okay. But what you don't know is, I was *this close*"—he held up his thumb and forefinger, spread an inch apart—"from showing you *my* Wild Ninja Skills." He grinned, shaggy brown hair hanging in his eyes. "I'm not gonna tell anyone you tried to kill me. Your secret's safe."

I sat awkwardly on a nearby rock, hands on my knees. "What happened to me, Kyle?" I ran my fingers through my short hair. "I dyed my hair, got a tattoo, and the only clothes I own are black."

He frowned. "So?"

"So, that's not *me*. I like pastels and miniskirts, not long dresses and ripped jeans. I was trying to grow my hair long, but then I just chopped it all off?"

Kyle stared at the ground, rubbing one finger over his lip. He always did that when he had something to say that he knew I didn't want to hear.

"Spill," I said. "Now."

He took a deep breath then looked me in the eyes, a hesitant expression on his face. "You *have* been different this past year, Rach. Kind of a bitch, if you really wanna know. Short-tempered. Sneaking out at night to hang with your friends. Then coming home either high or drunk—"

I frowned, not sure I wanted to hear this.

"The weird part is, you started doing really well in school. It made me a little mad that you could act out so much and then do better in your classes. Like you've been getting straight As in everything—"

"That's not possible," I interrupted, thinking about how hard I struggled in some subjects. I wasn't stupid, but I wasn't an A student, either.

"It's possible, all right. On top of that, you got the lead role in one of the ballets your class put on, *Swan Lake*—"

"Seriously?"

He didn't argue. He just pulled an iPhone from his pocket, scrolled through some screens, punched a button, then held it up for me to see. It was a video of me dancing. There I was in a tutu and slippers, my hair pinned back, my chin raised, and all of my body poised on the toes of my left foot, my right leg extended behind me, my left arm reaching up as if it could pluck clouds from the sky. Then I started to leap across the stage, my body hovering in the air, like I was flying. I stared at the screen, astonished. I'd been taking ballet lessons since I was six, but I'd never gotten a lead role and I'd never been able to dance like this, no matter how hard I practiced.

"I really did that?" It was like watching a movie of someone else. "Can you send me this video?"

"Yeah," he said, punching a few buttons before he slid his phone back in his pocket.

Apparently I'd gotten some mad skills in the past year.

"Look, I won't tell Mom or Dad what you did. But could you teach me that move, the one where you flattened me and pinned me to the ground?" Kyle asked, his eyebrows raised.

"No."

He had that look on his face—the one he used when he wanted the last bowl of ice cream or when he wanted the whole family to watch one of his Bruce Lee DVDs on movie night. Half his life he'd been the brat I had to babysit, and the other half he'd been a video-game-addicted, bad-joke-telling best friend. But that look of his wouldn't work, not this time.

"No way, I don't know how I did that, but I never want to do it again. Okay?"

He shrugged, and we both pretended as if what had just happened was no big deal.

CHAPTER FIVE

I scrolled through my phone, staring down at my new obsession—a collection of ballet videos, performances by the greatest ballerinas in the world. My breath caught in my chest and I imagined my back arched, my head held high as I leaped across a stage, all lights focused on me. I could hear the whisper of ballet slippers scuffing the floor, then the music rose and everything was drowned out, everything except the applause.

Something about it both frightened and excited me.

"Are you sure you want to do this?" Dad asked.

We both sat in the Starbucks across the street from my old dance studio. I lifted my gaze to stare at him, hoping he didn't notice that my hands trembled in my lap.

"Yes." But my mouth was dry and that single word sounded more like *no*. I glanced across the street, at the bank of windows that revealed girls and boys in unitards, all of them stretching, all with serious expressions on their faces. I recognized most of them, but would they be glad to see me? Sometime in the past six months, I'd dropped out of class, right when we were in the middle of practicing *The Nutcracker Suite* and I'd gotten the role of the Sugar Plum Fairy.

I was surprised that my teacher, Ms. Petrova, was willing to take me back. But then, money opened a lot of doors. I had a feeling that my parents' generous offer to replace the studio's worn flooring was what finally convinced her.

"We can come back next week, if you don't want to start class now," Dad said. His eyes met mine, eyes so dark you could barely see the pupils, just like mine.

Someone walked past our table then, some guy a few years older than me, wearing a woodsy cologne with faint notes of cedar and pine. For a second, I was back in the mountains, fighting some unknown assailant who had no face. I struggled against tears, my chin quivering.

"Rachel?"

I shook my head. I wasn't going to give in to the fear. Instead, an unexpected determination began to grow in my chest. More than anything, I wanted to fly across the dance floor right now, to push myself as hard and as fast as I could. I wanted the freedom and release that I only knew how to find in one place.

"I *do* want to go back to ballet," I said, my words thick with emotion, my hands still and calm. "Tonight."

He gave me a thin smile and a nod. "I know, sweetheart. I was just waiting for you to figure that out. Let's go."

We left the coffee shop together, but I walked through the door to the dance studio alone, not sure how my classmates would react, and realizing that I didn't care.

All I wanted was to erase the fragrance of the forest that seemed to permeate my clothes and my hair. I wanted to feel myself flying through the air, my muscles responding to every step of the dance, and my blood pumping fast through my veins.

I wanted—no, *I needed*—to feel free.

Chapter Six

My dreams changed that night. Up until this point, every time I fell asleep I had the same nightmare, over and over. I woke up in that gully and couldn't remember who I was or where I lived.

It was horrible.

Tonight was different. As soon as I closed my eyes I was in the woods, somewhere in the San Gabriel Mountains. And I was trying to find my way home—

A cabin stood on a ridge behind me, silhouetted by the sky and a countless army of ponderosa pines. I knew the walls, floors, and ceilings of that lodge were made of cedar, but I couldn't remember what was inside. All I knew was I had to get away.

I had to run.

Birdsong filled the woods, robins and sparrows and mockingbirds, and a worn footpath led away from the cabin.

In my left hand I carried a bottle of water, as I ran down a steep incline that opened up onto a clearing. From here I could see ridge after ridge of the San Gabriel mountain range, folding and refolding, slopes that led both up and down, all covered with trees, so many you could only see the tops, crests of green that bowed and swooped with every whisper of wind. There was no road in sight, no switchback highway to aim for, but hopefully I would find one later.

Feet sliding, I left the path, jogging as fast as I could, my tennis shoes skating over gravel and tripping over tree roots; down and ever down I went. Sunlight couldn't cut through the branches that laced overhead as I took the fork to the right, through pine-scented darkness, sweat staining my shirt and dampening my brow. A peak appeared up ahead, a rocky outcropping that jutted out over a spruce-filled vale, an expanse of sun and green.

Hands gripping rock and crawling up like a crab, I headed toward the summit, knowing I would be exposed. I tried to keep to the shadows, my body flat against the rock as I inched forward until, at last, I could peer over. My breath came out in a loud gasp when I saw what lay to the left, to the right, and straight ahead. It was all yet another vast expanse of green vales folding into green peaks, all of them extending toward the horizon. I was heading away from civilization, not back toward it. If I continued in this direction it would lead to starvation and exposure and death from thirst.

I was going to have to double back, skirt around the cabin and go a different way.

I was going to have to head back toward something even more dangerous than the vast wilderness that stretched as far as I could see…

...

I woke, covered with sweat, a thin whine coming from my throat, not sure where I was. A long moment passed before I realized that I'd been sleepwalking—a possible drug withdrawal symptom, just like that doctor had predicted. I must have crawled into my closet and now that damned afghan was tangled around me. It took a while to wrestle my way free, to throw the blanket to the floor and push the closet door open. For several minutes, I crouched beside my bed, gulping mouthfuls of air, trying to steady my hands, wondering if I'd had a drug-induced nightmare or an actual memory.

Could that be how I had escaped? Why could I only remember part of it? A cool breeze toyed with the curtains and I uneasily walked across the room toward the window, until my fingertips rested on the sill and my lungs filled and emptied at least three times.

Something wasn't right on the street below.

It was more than the fact that the Robinsons had ripped out their white picket fence, replacing it with cinder block, or the fact that the bulb in the streetlight was burned out, casting unwelcome shadows on our front lawn.

There was a buzz in the air, a hum that vibrated against my skin, saying *something's wrong, something's wrong, something's horribly wrong*.

Then I saw it. A gray Toyota rumbling at the curb, halfway down the block. Lights turned off, a faceless, shapeless person inside, just sitting there, staring up at my window.

A chill shivered over me and I stepped back, hiding behind the curtains. I could still see out, but I hoped that whoever was down in that car couldn't see me. Was it my kidnapper, should I go wake up Dad, should I call the police? I froze, forgetting about simple things like breathing or self-preservation or calling for help.

In that instant, while I stood frozen, the car flared to life, headlights blinding me before the Toyota sped off, taking away any chance I had of seeing the person's face.

He was there and then he was gone.

Just like I'd been.

CHAPTER SEVEN

I hadn't planned my grand entrance back into high school very well. All I had to wear were black Gothic shirts, ripped black jeans, heavy black boots, and dark, brooding makeup. I'd been rooting unsuccessfully through my closet for half an hour, hoping to find some of my old clothes, digging my way through a pile of dirty shirts and ripped fishnet stockings.

A week had passed since I'd had that nightmare and spotted that car parked on the street. Mom had been more worried about the nightmare. Dad was more concerned about the car. Neither one of them wanted me to go back to school. The only place I'd been allowed to go was ballet class, and even that had been chaperoned by either Mom or Dad. There'd been long discussions about whether I should be allowed to live like a normal teenager or whether I should stay home and work with a tutor until I started to remember my class work.

Mom did most of the talking, while Dad looked like he was never going to let me leave the house again. Like that monster in my closet was now living in the shrubs outside the front door and was counting the minutes until I was dumb enough to walk past.

Surprisingly, it had been my therapist who convinced them to let me go.

Two points for Dr. Rivera.

Even this morning, Mom was talking to my therapist on the phone downstairs, trying to change the doctor's mind. She was saying things like *mmm-hmm* and *yes, but,* and *I know.* Mom was used to dealing with doctors, since she was a nurse, so this was how she was helping me. I mainly hoped she didn't schedule me another appointment. Having my memory, or my lack of a memory, examined more than once a week was more than I could handle. Dr. Rivera would stare at me, her lips smiling but her eyes cold, her manicured fingers steepled in front of her on the desk while she listened, whether I talked or not. Sometimes I just sat there, wordlessly studying her office, the tastefully decorated tables and bookcases, all filled with vases and paperweights, none of which contained sharp, pointy edges.

Apparently, sharp edges were frowned upon by psychiatrists.

She was convinced a major meltdown was coming.

My therapist—I still couldn't get used to those words—had told us all that something was going to trigger my memory. It could be something as small and inconsequential as a song, or it could be something big, but unfortunately she didn't give us any examples of what a big trigger could be. I'd imagined them, though.

A car crash. A major illness. A death.

As if losing my memory or being kidnapped wasn't bad enough, now there was a looming Big Trigger out there with my name on it, waiting for just the right moment to leap out at me.

Life had definitely taken a sudden turn for the creepy.

I kept digging through my closet, trying to find a decent outfit to wear, until piles of shoes and rumpled clothes were strewn all around me. That was when I discovered something tucked behind my laundry basket—a purple box decorated with hearts and glitter. I vaguely remembered this. It was something I'd made for an art project back in seventh grade. I was about to toss it aside when I realized how heavy it was.

With trepidation I pulled off the lid. I didn't have much time left. I had to leave within five minutes, and even then, I still might be late for school.

The box opened and everything inside was lovely—silk flower barrettes, a handful of elastic kandi bracelets with brightly colored pony beads, a pair of silver ballet slippers, several neon glow sticks, a sequined bikini top, a couple of lacy white tank tops, and a zippered makeup case filled with foundation, blush, lipsticks, and eye shadows. I didn't have time to go through it all, so I grabbed the top of the box, ready to put the stuff away and go through it later.

The lid flipped upside down, revealing a note taped on the inside.

I peeled it off, recognizing my own handwriting.

The new, strange Gothic Me had left herself a note.

Peace. Love. Unity. Respect. And party like there's no tomorrow.

Two ticket stubs were taped to the note with the words "PREMIERE" and "BY INVITATION ONLY" and "PHASE TWO" written in a vintage-looking typeface and surrounded by elaborate scrollwork.

Phase Two?

I sat back on my heels, my thoughts spinning. The kandi bracelets and bikini top and glow sticks looked like rave gear, although I'd never been to one. Still, I knew about PLUR, the motto most ravers claimed to live by. They downed tabs of Ecstasy like other teens downed shots of espresso. They met in secret underground clubs and danced all night long. The thought of dancing crowds brought a chill to my skin. I loved to dance, and not just ballet.

Was Phase Two some kind of street dance competition? Is that what I'd been doing for the past year? As exciting as it sounded, I had a feeling I'd been involved in something much darker and more dangerous.

I realized there was something written on the back, dark letters bleeding through as I held the paper up to the light. I turned it over and discovered a list of names, all girls I'd never heard of before.

Janie Deluca.

Alexis Cartwright.

Nicole Hernandez.

Shelby Lee.

Lacy Allen.

None of these names sounded familiar, but my eyes kept flicking to one over and over. Nicole Hernandez. I didn't remember who she was—still, her first name sounded an alarm in my brain.

Nicole. *Nicole*.

That was the name of one of the missing girls Agent Bennet had talked to me about.

Who were these girls, and why were their names hidden where no one but me would find them?

How did I know them?

I felt like I was sitting in a snowbank, all of me starting

to go numb. I couldn't move for a long time, my thoughts slow and sluggish. My mind kept searching for some connection but I couldn't find one. All I could do was stare at that list of names.

What if I never found the answers, what if I never remembered the past year? Would I spend the rest of my life stumbling over things like this—puzzles I couldn't solve?

Mom called out my name from the bottom of the stairs. Her voice startled me and forced me back to reality. No matter what secrets I discovered in my closet, I didn't want to stay home anymore.

Right now, I wanted out of here—even more than before.

I shot a quick glance around my room, settled on an outfit and a pair of shoes, ran my fingers through my hair, and slid lip gloss on my lips.

Then I jogged down the stairs, as ready as I'd ever be to face the crowds at Lincoln High.

Kyle and Mom stood in the garage, waiting for me. He texted someone and chuckled. I glanced at his screen and saw *Halo 4* and *play online during 4th period* and *gotta go*.

"You sure you don't want me to drive you?" Mom asked, her voice an octave higher than normal.

"We practiced, remember?" I said. "Just like Dr. Rivera suggested. All week long I drove Kyle to school and you rode with us. I even picked him up yesterday. By myself."

"But your doctor warned us that almost anything could trigger your memory—"

"*I'll* be there, Mom," Kyle interrupted. "If she snaps, I'll—I'll—I don't know. I'll chase her until I catch her. You know I can run faster than she can. Or I'll call the cops. Look." Kyle held up his phone. "I got them on speed dial. Just in case."

Mom gave us a shaky grin. "Did you give your sister that paper yet?"

"Paper? What paper?" He gave us both his best thickheaded look, eyes half-closed. "Oh, yeah, *this* paper." He rummaged through his backpack, unzipping one pocket after another before finally locating a folded sheet of paper, with two columns of computer text. "Here," he said as he handed it to me.

"What is this?"

He pointed at the column on the left. "Those are your classes." Then he pointed to the right-hand column. "Those are mine. And that number at the bottom is my cell. I'll, uh, keep it turned on all day, in case you need to call me or something. Even though Mr. Reed will have a mutant cow if he finds out." He directed the last sentence at Mom, who shook her head. "Oh, and this is your locker number and combination. It's on the second floor. I think."

"Thanks," I said. "Do I need a note or something?" I asked Mom. "For being out several weeks and for being late today?" I wanted to add, *and for not knowing anything about Algebra II or chemistry or any of my other classes.*

"I had a long talk with the principal and the counselor last week. All your teachers know that you might not be participating in class discussions for a while," she said. "And the counselor, you know her? Mrs. Jenkins? She said you can come in her office anytime, if you want to talk or just kind of catch your breath."

I held my bottom lip between my teeth, knowing

that—no matter what happened—there was no way I was hanging out in the school counselor's office today.

Kyle and I headed through the garage toward a gorgeous, lime-green Bug that I still couldn't believe belonged to me. We both slid into my car, the drive to Lincoln High surreal, like I was cruising through a movie set instead of living a day in my real life. Houses slipped past, one street bled into another, me on autopilot, not even thinking about which way to turn or how long to wait at each light. I automatically knew when the lights would turn green and that if I turned left a block before the school, I'd miss the clogged traffic from a line of school buses and parents dropping off students.

Then we pulled into the student parking lot and Kyle swung his door open and all the noise from outside poured in, packs of students running and laughing and yelling, boys flirting with girls and girls teasing each other, a whole social hierarchy that I didn't fit into anymore.

I got out of the car, backpack on my shoulder, and walked toward the building, forgetting to lock my doors or say good-bye to Kyle.

"Go ahead, pretend you don't know me. Like usual," he said, following behind me. "Remember, I'm watching you."

He jogged past me, turning around briefly to wave and stick out his tongue, before disappearing inside the school building.

A long hallway and cool darkness waited inside. All the voices of the other students narrowed down to a whisper as I tried to listen for what was up ahead, but I couldn't hear anything. There were no clues as to whether I would fit in or whether I would recognize anyone.

Up ahead of me stood a pair of doors that led into the unknown.

CHAPTER EIGHT

I felt like one of those fish that glow in the dark, noticeably different from everyone else. People whispered when I walked past. *She's that girl who went missing last month* and *she doesn't remember anything that happened in the past year, she doesn't even remember her name.* I wanted to correct that last comment. *Of course I remember my name*, I wanted to say. *I just don't know who the heck you* are.

It was true, too. Even the students I should have recognized looked different. They'd grown taller, fatter, skinnier, prettier, uglier since last year. They'd dyed their hair and gotten braces, they'd gotten tattoos and piercings, they'd grown their hair long or cut it short. The girls had discovered the miracle of makeup and the boys had mastered the art of hair gel.

And some of the boys had discovered the magic of working out.

Guys who used to be thin and geeky now sported six-packs that rippled beneath tight T-shirts.

And one boy who had been gorgeous since seventh

grade, Dylan McCarthy, caught me in a mesmerizing gaze from the moment I walked through the front door. His mouth dropped open half an inch, just enough to make him look even hotter—if that was possible—and for a moment I thought I heard him whisper my name. I stared back at him, slightly perplexed, knowing that I was blushing but unable to stop myself. Black hair and cool gray eyes, his skin just pale enough to make him look like the poet that he secretly was. The other kids in Lincoln High might not remember, but he had sat beside me in seventh grade English class and he'd even made our teacher swoon with the stuff he'd written.

It was lame, but I never forgot the time I'd dropped my pen and he'd picked it up for me, his hand brushing mine in the process, his eyes focused on mine for a long second, his full lips tilting up in a half-smile.

And then the bell rang. In my seventh-grade memory and now.

I glanced at that paper Kyle had given me, a quick panic in my throat and a feeling like the flutter of birds' wings in my chest. Room 126. That's where I needed to be, but it was where, on this side of the building or over in the other wing?

"Are you lost, little girl?"

Dylan was standing beside me. I took a deep breath, inhaling the scent of him. He'd never been this close before and had definitely never spoken an entire sentence to me. If I couldn't talk before, I certainly couldn't now.

"I've been sick worrying about you," he said, his gaze on my lips. "I haven't slept since you went missing."

"You're kidding, right?" I asked. I couldn't tell him that I'd had a crush on him for years and that this wasn't a funny prank.

He cocked his head, studying my face, maybe looking

for a clue or a tell. His voice lowered until it was barely above a whisper, almost as if he was talking to himself. "You don't remember me, do you?"

"No—I—" I answered too quickly. "I mean, everyone knows who you are."

He gave me a shy grin, but then his gaze traveled back to my lips and his smile broadened. For a moment, I thought he was going to lean closer and I was hoping he would.

Instead he rubbed a finger over his lower lip, a simple gesture that I thought, maybe, I'd seen before.

"You need to get to algebra."

"How did you know?"

Another long smile followed, making me wish we weren't at school, that we were anywhere else but here. "Because you're in my class. Come on." He held out his hand, one eyebrow raised, almost like a challenge.

I took his hand and a warm tingle flowed up my arm.

"We better hurry," he said and then we both ran down the hall, hands locked like we were little kids heading out for recess, him grinning and me fighting the urge to giggle.

I never expected my first class to begin like this. A rabble of papers shuffling, backpacks slamming to the floor, desks creaking as people sat down, mumbling, giggling, whispering, a teacher scrambling to write something on a whiteboard, his back turned. Me entering the room and then a hush descending, all sound disappearing as heads lifted to look at me, until all I could hear were my own footsteps, my own breathing.

Each time, I forced my shoulders back and my head to stay high, although I wanted to cringe.

Everyone was staring at me, open-mouthed, just like Dylan had a few moments ago. I could practically hear their thoughts.

So glad it wasn't me that went missing.

Thought she was dead.

Wonder what happened to her.

Eyes traveled over me, brushed me and unwrapped me, searching for hidden scars and broken places. I tried to push my lips into a smile, but it hurt too much. So I settled for a stoic expression, one that I hoped communicated strength.

And, right about then, when I was searching for my seat and Dylan pointed toward an empty place—the empty place in the room that belonged to me—right then, the teacher noticed the unnatural silence and turned around. He spotted me, the smile on his face fading and a sorrowful look filling his eyes.

I was stealing everyone's words today, like this was my new super power.

Finally, the teacher woke up. "Welcome back, Rachel. You've been in our thoughts and prayers, and we're all very glad you're back."

And then a really bizarre thing happened. The whole class started clapping. I never thought applause would feel so good, but it was like a drug I'd been craving, like I was an addict and didn't even know it. Girls got up from their seats and gave me hugs or hastily written notes or a small favor, something they'd been carrying with them for two weeks. Soon my desk was covered with pink wristbands that said, FIND RACHEL. The boys stood awkwardly, trying to see over the girls, giving me a nod and a shy grin, lifting their wrists to show that they were wearing the bands, too. Even my teacher was wearing one.

Dylan came over to my desk then, pushing his way through the cluster of sad-faced girls and making me blush when he rolled up his cuff and showed that he was wearing *three* wristbands.

I couldn't speak. It was more than I could take in, that all these kids had been looking for me. It overshadowed everything and gave me hope. I still didn't know who I could trust or who my real friends were, but I knew I would find out soon enough.

You always find out who your true friends are at lunch.

The cafeteria looked the same. Big enough to swallow us all, to contain all of our laughter and teenage angst, to make us feel small and insignificant. I already had my lunch, so I stood in line to buy some chocolate milk, part of me wondering where I was going to sit, the other part wondering where my best friend, Molly, was. I hadn't seen her yet, but it was possible she was out sick today. She had a problem with asthma, and spring was the worst season of the year for her.

Kyle slid past me then, joking with a group of his soccer/video game buddies. He paused to lean toward me and asked, "Doing okay? Remember, you've got my class schedule if you need me."

I wanted to ask him where Molly was or why he hadn't told me about those wristbands—and why he didn't have one, the jerk—and what the heck was going on with Dylan. But my brother just breezed away, laughing when one of his friends tripped and almost fell.

"Little brothers. You can't live with them and you can't hang them upside down from the goalposts—even though you want to," a girl behind me said with a toss of her head. She grinned, waist-long, blond hair falling over one shoulder. Her smile looked different from the sad-girl grins I'd been getting all day. She had on one of those pink wristbands, but she didn't point it out and she didn't take it off. Lauren Maxwell, head cheerleader. Not someone who would have talked to me last year and, judging by my behavior this year, not someone I would have expected to be my friend now, either.

"I know you don't remember me," she said.

We inched past the glass-covered case, past meat loaf sandwiches and veggie burgers, when she held up her hand, pointing toward a spinach salad.

"Lauren. Yeah, I think we had PE together last year." *And you're the girl every boy in school wants to hook up with in the janitor's closet.*

She paused, as if fumbling for words. "Dylan said you didn't remember him, so I guess I should have expected you wouldn't remember me, either." She had that sad-girl expression in her eyes now. "We were friends, Rach. *Really* good friends. I stopped by your house almost every day when you were gone. And I've texted you about a hundred times since you got back."

"My phone got lost when I was—" I could never finish that sentence.

She bit her lip and looked away. Her voice shattered, just a bit, when she tugged at the wristband she wore. "I had everyone looking for you," she said. "We'd all go out for a couple hours every day after school. And you probably haven't seen it, but we have a memorial out by the student parking lot, the last place anybody saw you."

I didn't know what to say. It seemed like a weird way to prove she was my friend, but she'd always been one of those girls who lived by committee, either running for class secretary or organizing a blood drive. *Thank you* didn't feel like the right thing to say, so I just nodded and paid for my milk and a bag of Cheetos that looked too good to pass up. And then it happened again. When I turned around, heads lifted, eyes stared, people stopped talking. It spread across the room from where I stood to the far side of the cafeteria, a soul-stealing hush, one that could make your skin crawl. Whispers started.

It's Rachel, that girl who went missing.

I thought she was dead.

Well, she's obviously not dead now.

Lauren laid a cool hand on my arm, and spoke softly in my ear. "Why don't you come eat with me and my friends? They're *your* friends, too."

I took a deep breath and followed her across the lunchroom.

"Look who's here," she said with enthusiasm when we reached a table of kids I couldn't imagine all hanging out together. Besides Lauren, there was another rich, college-bound girl, with glossy brown hair and expensive designer jeans. Next to her sat a shaggy-haired guy wearing horn-rimmed glasses who looked both half-asleep and scarily alert, and another guy who sported thick, muscular biceps and a graphing calculator in his back pocket instead of an iPhone. I recognized Brett, the square-jawed captain of the football team, by his jersey and signature loud voice, but wasn't sure if I knew the petite, lavender-haired girl, dressed head-to-toe in black.

And then there was Dylan.

I almost dropped my tray.

"Hi," I said, hoping he didn't notice the flush that was working its way from my chest to my face. "You guys sure it's okay if I sit with you? I mean, Molly is probably here somewhere."

Before I could scan the lunchroom again for someone else to hang out with, the lavender-haired girl jumped up. She gave me a long hug that I thought was never going to end, the scent of patchouli in her hair. "I *knew* you'd be coming back to school, Rachel. I just knew it!" she said. "We've been saving a seat for you all week long, haven't we, Dylan?"

My heart skipped a long beat when I looked at Dylan.

He gave me a sexy grin and patted the empty chair between him and the lavender-haired girl. At the same time, Lauren grabbed my arm and tried to lead me toward two empty chairs on the other side of the table, where we could sit together.

"Come over here, Rachel. We've got *so* much to talk about," she said.

I still didn't know for sure what my relationship with Dylan was—were we boyfriend and girlfriend, had we hooked up once or twice, were we friends with benefits? I wanted to find out.

I pulled away from Lauren. "I'd rather sit here."

Lauren's mouth dropped open, probably as surprised by my boldness as I was, but she recovered quickly. She sat across the table, eyes downcast, picking at her salad with a fork.

I slid into place, Dylan's arm around the back of my chair while everyone said things like, *we've been looking for you* and *we never gave up hope* and *it hasn't been the same without you.* Their eyes told me things their words didn't, that these emotions were real and that somehow I belonged with this bizarre, mismatched group. Like instant sunshine, warmth washed over me, flowing from my head to my feet. I may not have recognized all of these people, but I knew this was where I belonged.

This was my other family. These were the people I hung out with in the middle of the night, the ones I got drunk and high with. But there was more. A lot more.

I just couldn't remember it yet. But I knew I would.

Soon.

CHAPTER NINE

School was over. Cars pulled away, and tires ground over gravel, while the faint scent of spring hung in the air. I stood in the student parking lot, staring down at a memorial. A row of Japanese flowering cherry trees lined the sidewalk, all of them in bloom, all glowing in the sunlight and dropping petals that fell like snow. At the parking lot entrance, beneath the largest cherry tree, there lay bundles of dying flowers and a poster board covered with photos, surrounded by candles, crosses, and strings of rosary beads.

The photos were of me.

"What the heck?" I mumbled as I moved closer to the tree. Notes written to me hung from ribbons tied to the lower branches, tiny white slips of paper that dangled and twisted in the wind.

I turned the notes in my hand so I could read them. Most of them were comments from people who barely knew me.

I hope you're safe.

We're praying for you.

Others were long and sincere, almost too painful to read.

You were in my sophomore geometry class and we didn't really know each other. I wish we had, but now I'm afraid it's too late...

I miss the way you laugh and how you always used to blame me for using all the hot water when we were getting ready for school...

"Crap," I said, choking up when I read the last one, knowing it was from Kyle. I recognized his back-slanted, left-hand scrawl. I pulled the note down and slipped it in my pocket.

Most of the other papers were water-stained from the rain a few days ago. One was so blurry it was almost illegible. It must have been one of the first notes hung up. As I struggled to read it, I realized it was a poem and that it might have been written by Dylan. I tugged it loose and cradled it in my palm, wondering what we meant to each other. I had already missed our first kiss. What had that been like? Had it been rushed or long and sensuous? Had it been recent or nearly a year ago? Then I remembered those condoms in my drawer and I blushed, like my life was an R-rated movie that starred somebody else.

That was when I noticed the other notes, the ones that had been posted more recently. These weren't blurred by the rain and all the letters were large and sharp-edged.

Wish you had stayed dead!

Bitch, go back where you came from.

Hope those kidnappers come back and do the job right this time!

I stumbled backward, blinking as if it could make these cruel words disappear. My stomach ached, just like someone had punched me, and I curled over, gulping for air.

That's how I was when Kyle found me. Everyone at school had acted like they all missed me terribly. In every class, people had greeted me with hugs, showing me their pink wristbands. But according to those dangling pieces of paper, some of those people secretly hated me and wished I'd been found dead on the side of the freeway.

"You shouldn't have come here," Kyle said. He pushed me away from the tree and made me sit on the curb. Then I heard him yank down those last notes, felt the snow of petals fall around me as he pulled on one cherry branch after another. I was hyperventilating, my head in my hands. "Stupid, jealous twats!" he grumbled as he ripped up the notes and slivers of paper began to join the falling petals, white and white and searing black, snippets of words swirling over my shoulder.

bitch—

dead—

kidnappers—

Tears began to fall, too, but they couldn't wash away the pain. "I shouldn't have come back to school," I said, one hand still clutching Dylan's illegible poem.

Kyle put one hand on my shoulder and knelt beside me. "No. You did the right thing. It's what you wanted to do, even though you knew it would be tough. So the hard part's over. You found out there are some nasty bitches in high school. But we already knew that, didn't we? In case you're wondering, there are plenty of pricks here, too—"

He was on a rant and he may not have meant to, but he made me smile. Somehow this was all about him now.

"They pick on you in PE because you're not big enough or strong enough or fast enough. The big dicks shove you around in the showers and the little pricks stand there and laugh, glad it isn't them for a change. I know girls are just as bad, only in different ways. It's a zoo in there," he said, tossing his thumb back toward the school building, "and nobody cares enough to do anything about it."

Still wobbly after having my guts ripped out by the notes, I held my little brother's hand as he helped me back to my feet.

"Do they really pick on you that much?" I asked. "How long has that been going on?"

He didn't answer. He blinked fast, just like I had earlier, probably fighting emotions he was trying to hold inside. We headed toward the parking lot, side by side, until we had to weave our way through the rows of cars. Then he walked in front of me, as if he wanted to protect me from whatever might be up ahead. Even the set of his shoulders and the angle of his jawline—exposed every time he swung his head to the side, as he swept a gaze at passing students— told me he was concerned about me.

Part of me was worried about him, too.

I wouldn't have been able to stand it if that memorial had been set up for him, if my little brother had been the one who had gone missing, all those handwritten notes waving in the breeze as if they could magically take away the pain. There weren't enough words in the world to take away that kind of hurt.

I paused in front of my Volkswagen, keys in my hand.

There had been only three freshly written notes hanging from that tree, and all three slips of paper had contained harsh words. But if someone really hated me that much, wouldn't there have been more messages, ones that had been hanging there longer, blurred by the rain and the dew?

"Kyle, were there more notes like the ones you took down today?" I asked.

He almost looked at me, but averted his eyes at the last second. "Maybe."

A small thud of grief hit me in the chest. My little brother must have been going to that tree every day and taking down all the horrid notes, all those mean-spirited messages spiraling in the wind, as if casting an evil spell, as if by wishing it, they could put me in the ground and keep me there.

"Kyle?" I said.

"Huh?"

"Thanks for being a good brother."

I unlocked the doors and we climbed into my car, the engine purring and the sounds of the outside world fading away. We drove home in silence, my thoughts returning to the notes Kyle had ripped up and the fact that not everyone at Lincoln High was glad I was back.

"Hey," I said, not taking my eyes off the road as I drove past our house, toward the trails where he and I had gone hiking last week. "You still want me to teach you that move, the one where I throw you to the ground?"

"Seriously?"

"Yeah." I turned off my car and swung the door open. "Come on. Maybe it'll help you knock some of those school bullies on *their* asses for a change."

Chapter Ten

Dinner was already on the table when we got home, but Mom and Dad were waiting for us on the front porch. Mom had the night off and she sipped a glass of wine as she followed us inside the house. I could tell Dad wanted to say something. But the barrage of twenty questions didn't begin until Kyle and I started eating.

"Why didn't you answer my calls?" Mom asked. "We were one step away from calling the police. Your dad was out for an hour, driving around, looking for you."

Kyle did his best monosyllabic replies while Mom went on and on. "Fine. I dunno. Forgot." He added a shrug now and then, and usually answered with his mouth full.

Dad stared at me for a long time. "Is everything okay?"

"I just turned off my phone during class and forgot to turn it back on, is all," I said. "I can't seem to call anyone lately. I try, but I just can't." It was the truth and my voice wavered when I spoke, but at the same time I knew I was manipulating my parents. What I couldn't figure out was, why did it seem so easy? Had I done this before? "Besides,

I had to stay after to get homework from a couple of teachers."

Dad nodded. "Text us next time you're going to be late, okay?" His gaze went from me to Mom. "You can send us a text, can't you?"

"I guess so." My cheeks were burning, but there was a part of me that felt better knowing how much they cared.

An awkward buzz of chatter started then, and it was the first time since I'd been home that we felt like a family again. Mom talked about something that had happened at Methodist Hospital last night where she worked as a nurse. Dad mused about whether he should plant Lily-of-the-Nile or African Iris along the fence in the front yard. He'd turned into a novice gardener now that he wasn't a Navy SEAL anymore. Most of the time he puttered around, wearing gardening gloves, the knees of his jeans covered with dirt. Kyle tried to get permission to go to Comic-Con in San Diego in the summer. When that didn't work, he tried to get a Vespa. He finally settled for a Bose multimedia speaker system on his birthday.

He whispered, "Score," under his breath, so soft no one but me heard it.

I listened to the quiet spaces between their words as I moved the food around my plate, forcing myself to eat a bite of salmon with mango relish. After Grams had cancer, Mom had gone on an organic binge and, honestly, she was a great cook. Problem was, I hadn't had an appetite since I went missing. I broke out in a sweat whenever I stepped on the scale, terrified I'd gained weight. I'm sure my therapist would have a great time analyzing that.

Dad seemed to be the only one who noticed I wasn't really eating. He glanced at me from time to time, smiling if our eyes met.

We hadn't had The Talk yet. The you-were-kidnapped-

and-my-life-was-hell talk. Mom and I had discussed my disappearance almost as soon as I got home, and it had been devastating. Kyle and I had talked about it, too, sort of, when we were sparring in the forest after school. In between him being thrown to the ground and getting the crap beaten out of him, he'd said things like, *it's good to have you back* and *you know I can never get Mom and Dad to do what I want when you're gone.*

But Dad had been quietly watching—maybe waiting for the right time.

There was no right time to watch your father—who's been sent around the world to hunt down terrorists—start crying. So we'd been avoiding each other, knowing it was coming. It became an awkward dance, looking the other way when we passed each other in the hall, holding each other a bit too long when we hugged.

I needed to get my life back, before all this quiet mourning killed me.

As soon as dinner was over, I slipped up to my room. There, I spent half an hour going over the routines Ms. Petrova had given me, warming up my muscles with several grand pliés, then letting my body flow into one *rond de jambe* after another, until every move felt as natural as breathing.

Finally I paused, wanting to watch some dance videos online. There was one move—the *brisé*—which involved a small leap while your feet made quick, sharp scissor kicks. I couldn't seem to get it right and I knew if I just watched another ballerina perform it, I'd be able to catch on. But once I got my laptop powered up, I found myself doing something else. Something unexpected and slightly creepy.

I typed my name into Google's browser window, then waited as article after article popped up about the Santa Madre girl who went missing after school a few weeks ago. There were photos of me from tenth grade. I needed to give Mom and Dad a more recent picture of myself, I didn't even look like that anymore—my front teeth crooked because I still had braces, my hair down to my shoulders, my nose speckled with summer freckles, a smile that said, *nothing bad has ever happened to me and it never will.*

It was weird to look into my own eyes and wonder if I would ever be that person again. I used to be someone who never lied to Mom or Dad. I should have felt guilty for sneaking off to teach Kyle how to defend himself. Instead I felt proud at how quickly he picked everything up, like it had been second nature.

I forced myself to shut off the internet and started clicking through folders on my desktop instead, looking for a better picture of myself than that one from tenth grade. But I quickly found myself checking out random details from the past year. Folder after folder opened, revealing lists of my favorite songs and books, a collection of ballet screensaver images, and photos of Buster, our Golden Lab who passed away sometime in the past six months. Looking at his pictures made my chest ache. I missed him, how we used to go for runs together, and how he used to sleep at the foot of my bed.

I was just about to close that folder when I discovered another folder tucked inside, so far down you probably wouldn't even see it. It was titled, "More Buster," but it was locked.

I sat back in my chair, pins and needles prickling the back of my neck.

Why would I lock a folder of dog photos?

It took several minutes and about fifty different passwords before I was able to open it. There was only one document inside, something labeled "Buster's Vet Records". One click later and a Word document scrawled across my screen. All just normal stuff at first, until I scrolled down to the end of the page.

There was that familiar list of names again—Janie Deluca, Alexis Cartwright, Nicole Hernandez, Shelby Lee and Lacy Allen—except this time, it had their addresses, too. I could almost feel the wheels spinning inside my head, all the questions I wanted to ask these girls. But it had to be face-to-face. No way I could send each of them a letter and then wait for the replies.

I'd have to go see these girls tomorrow after school, after I dropped Kyle off. He'd already begged me, promising he'd do my chores for a week if I took him to his friend's house so they could check out Civilization V: Brave New World. Knowing those two, they probably had something else in mind besides video games. Like watching Khalessi walk naked through fire on *Game of Thrones* or surfing the internet for photos of topless supermodels.

The less I knew about Kyle's after-school activities, the better I slept at night.

So, I printed out that list of names, folded it, and tucked it into my jacket pocket. I had no idea what connection those girls might have with the box of rave gear in my closet, but I hoped I'd find out tomorrow.

Chapter Eleven

I woke up earlier than I expected, maybe because I actually had a full night's sleep. No nightmares, no memories pretending to be dreams. Nobody chasing me through a forest in the mountains. I yawned and stretched, noticed a timid sun peeking through a thin layer of clouds. Inside, the house was quiet, everyone else still asleep. So, of course, my closet door creaked open, all by itself like it usually did, making me think of Molly.

Why hadn't she been at school yesterday? Was she sick? And why hadn't she called me or stopped over?

She and I had a ritual, one we'd been practicing every year since we were ten years old. We'd watch at least one of the *LOTR* movies together. Last year, right about this time, the two of us skipped school to go see *The Fellowship of the Ring* at a local movie theater.

We went in cosplay attire, me dressed as Arwen and her as Galadriel, both of us in full-length gowns and wigs. Afterward, we tucked our costumes into oversize shopping bags and washed off our makeup in the theater restroom, laughing and making a mess in the sink. On the bus ride home, a sweet old lady thought we were homeless and gave us each a crisp dollar bill. We tried not to accept it, but she refused to take it back.

I still have that dollar bill pinned to my bulletin board.

I wanted to talk to Molly so much. She'd make me laugh. Or she'd convince me to go out for frozen yogurt. Or she'd drag out a DVD of *The Hobbit* and say, *We're watching this now, girl.* Any one of those options would be great.

I picked up my phone. Maybe I could send her a text. I mean, she probably didn't have my new cell number and that was why she hadn't called.

Right then, when I held my phone, it buzzed.

I'd gotten a text.

My rib cage tightened, like my skin was too small, and I could only take shallow breaths.

I'd only given my number to a handful of people. Mom, Dad, Kyle, my therapist, Agent Bennet, Lauren…

And Dylan—we'd exchanged numbers at lunch.

Hey, U awake?

It was him.

Yeah, I typed back hesitantly.

Couldn't sleep thinking about you, he wrote.

I didn't know what to say. Me either? You're so cute. Why do you even like me?

Still there?

Yeah. Of course. I'd be crazy to hang up now.

Good. So glad you're back.

I didn't know what to say. *That one guy at lunch yesterday, was he like totally stoned?*

Jim? Always! LOL.

Who was the girl with lavender hair?

Zoe. She's a sweetheart. You and her are …

There were dots like he was typing, but then nothing came through. *We're what?* I asked.

You used to hang out a lot. She painted a picture for you once. Maybe it's in your closet?

I got up and went to my closet, searching. It took a minute to move things around, but I finally found a small canvas hidden in the corner and gingerly pulled it out.

You there? he asked.

The painting was of Dylan and me. He wore a black suit, while I wore stage makeup, a white bodice and tutu, and a glittering crown with wings made of tiny feathers. Just behind us stood a glowing marquee that read *Swan Lake*. I was Odette and I cradled a large bouquet of red roses in my arms.

Did you go to my Swan Lake performance? I asked, smiling.

Yeah. You were incredible. I could almost see that slow, sexy smile on his face, hear the soft, velvety purr in his voice. *We did a lot of things together.*

I was really glad he couldn't see the blush spreading across my face. *Oh,* I said.

He sent me a smiley emoji and a bunch of roses.

I grinned.

Sit with me at lunch again? he asked.

Sure.

He sent more emojis and I laughed and the two of us continued to chat, as if we'd known each other for years.

• • •

It was only my second day back at school and I was one step away from being late. Dylan and I had texted too long this morning. Now my brother and I crammed lunches into our backpacks, made a last-minute scramble for our textbooks and tablets, snarfed down a few bites of veggie/egg-white omelets, and then headed out to the garage.

I patted my back pocket for reassurance, where my driver's license and the list of girls' names and addresses rested. My wallet, backpack, and cell phone had all gone missing during my kidnapping, but for some reason my driver's license had been in my pocket when I wandered out onto the freeway. I'd never been able to figure out why. Either those kidnappers had overlooked that piece of ID, or they had wanted me to keep something to prove who I was.

Neither one of those made any sense.

That was why I needed to find the girls on that list. I was hoping one of them might have a clue about what had happened to me when I was taken.

Kyle sat in the car, seat belt on, drumming his fingers on his leg. He'd reached his limit of patience, which was about a minute and a half. "Hey, we're gonna be late if you don't speed it up here." He craned his neck to peer out at me. "I don't wanna miss first period. Amber Griffin was actually nice to me yesterday and she hasn't been nice since fifth grade and she's smoking hot now—"

"Okay, okay." I climbed in and started the engine. Kyle continued to ramble on while I backed out onto the road.

"She was pretty goofy-looking all the way through middle school, with short, frizzy hair and braces, but then POW, one day she just, I don't know, turned into a real, live girl, with boobs and everything—"

"I don't need to hear your horny drool fest over some

girl who smiled at you in class—"

"She didn't just *smile* at me. We said, like, words, real words about important stuff." He gasped when he thought I drove too close to a parked car, but other than that he never shut up.

We ventured slowly through a few intersections, him messing with the radio and me trying to block out his non-stop chatter. Then somewhere between Grove and Adams, I noticed a dark gray sedan following us. It must have been parked somewhere in our neighborhood, maybe down the street from our house or around the corner. It didn't register at first—everybody drives a car like that nowadays, like they all want to look the same.

It wasn't until we were halfway to Lincoln High—when I was adjusting my rearview mirror and wondering which one of the five girls I should hunt down after school first— that I realized it was a Toyota Camry following us. Exactly like the car that had been sitting outside our house the other night.

An apprehensive shiver slid down my arms, making all the tiny hairs stand on end.

They weren't going to take me again. They couldn't. And no way in hell was I going to let them hurt my little brother.

I took another glance in the rearview mirror. Whoever was driving the Camry sat cloaked in shadow. I couldn't see his or her face.

My breathing slowed, my conscious thoughts melted away, and a cold instinct took over. I turned the steering wheel, taking us down an unexpected side street, a meandering detour that would take us at least six blocks out of the way.

I had to see if we were really being followed.

"Hey, you're going the wrong way!" Kyle yelled.

"Never hurts to try a different route."

He slumped in his seat, a scowl on his face.

"We'll get there on time," I told him.

"Taking the long, crazy way to school seems like the perfect way to be late to me," he grumbled.

I shot another glance in the rearview mirror. The other car stayed with us, no matter where I turned. My pulse ratcheted up a couple more notches. Whoever was following me was wearing a baseball cap pulled low, the visor shadowing his face, even when he drove through a patch of sunlight. My alternate route led us back to Highland Avenue, and Lincoln High sprawled up ahead, a campus of seven acres.

"I'm going to let you off here," I told Kyle, slamming the car to a stop in a no-parking zone, right in front of the main entrance. The gray sedan pulled over half a block behind us. Within a second, it was invisible, hidden behind the line of buses that had just pulled up. "Quick! Get out and run inside."

He gave me a puzzled look. "What the hell's going on? Why are you dropping me off here?"

"You don't want to be late, remember? Get going!"

He opened his door and swung his legs outside, muttering. At least here he'd be in plain sight of the school security guards, the bus drivers, and about a zillion students.

Kyle sauntered out of the car, fingers wrapped around his backpack, glancing back at me with a curious expression. He stood there for a long moment, as if he sensed something was up but couldn't figure out what. Finally, he headed toward the front door. I kept my eyes on him and only him until he was safely inside. Then I pulled away from the curb, heading toward the student parking lot on the other side of the building. Sure enough, as soon as I got clear of all the morning traffic, that gray Toyota sedan appeared in my rearview mirror again. Only this time, the driver had taken off his cap.

He wanted me to see his face.

I sucked a long, slow breath between my teeth when a beam of sunlight spilled into his car, lighting up his features, carving human flesh and bone from shadow. Chiseled cheekbones, short, sandy-brown hair slightly mussed from wearing a hat, dark brows shielding cool green eyes that looked like they could read all the secrets of my soul— even the ones I didn't know yet.

Agent Ryan Bennet.

WTF?

I'd been expecting to see my kidnapper and now I was…disappointed? I'd wanted to see that monster again. I wanted to run him over. I wanted him dead.

I'd had myself under control, but now my heart started a rapid *thu-thump-thu-thump* despite all my efforts to slow it down, and my palms started to sweat. What had I been thinking? It's like I *wanted* some jerk to follow me to school. Tires crunching over gravel, I swung around a corner and pulled into the school parking lot entrance, then rolled my car to an awkward stop.

I grabbed my cell phone and forced myself to punch in the speed-dial number for Dad, careful to keep my phone on my lap so Bennet couldn't see it. When my father finally answered, I kept my voice low.

"Dad? Agent Bennet followed me to school and—and I'm going to get out of my car—"

I swung my door open, slipping the phone in my jacket pocket as I continued to talk.

"I'm going to walk up to his car. Don't say anything, okay?"

I glanced back at Bennet's Toyota, which was also slowing to a stop. We were both just inside the student parking lot entrance, a steady stream of cars pulling in around us, plenty of people watching in case he tried something.

I shot a quick glance back at his car and then mumbled his license plate number, hoping Dad could hear it.

"Be careful," his voice said from my pocket.

"Walking over to his car now."

And then I was heading toward Bennet's sedan. His window was rolling down, and all around us students were laughing and joking, getting out of cars and heading in to another day of school. But all I could think was, this is the last place I was seen.

This was exactly where I was kidnapped. And I had a feeling it had happened almost exactly like this.

Chapter Twelve

It felt like a memory, but it was really more like intuition, or a sudden overwhelming sense of self-preservation. The wind was singing through the nearby Japanese cherry trees, a sweet fragrance was staining the air, and my blood was rushing through my veins, my pulse becoming the bass note in a song I didn't want to hear. Someone leaned out the window, a slow grin spreading over his face, warming his eyes.

This was how it had happened.

I'd gotten into somebody's car of my own free will, knowing the person who had taken me. An unwelcome shiver worked its way across my shoulders, making me shudder. I crossed my arms over my body, a defensive move that wouldn't help, not one bit, if I needed to fight my way out of this.

"Morning," Bennet said in a low, husky voice. "I was only following your daughter to make sure she was safe."

I frowned.

"Your father's listening, isn't he? Let me talk to him."

The cell phone was cold in my hand when I pulled it from my pocket and then held it to my ear. "Dad?" I said.

"It's okay," he said. "Give him your phone."

"I just need to talk to your daughter for a few minutes," Bennet said. "But it needs to be private. She already gave you my license plate number. You want my badge number, too?" There was a pause and I thought I heard Dad threatening to hang Bennet from his balls if anything happened to me. Bennet gave me a thin smile, then spoke into the phone again. "She'll be fine. I promise. We're just going to talk for a few minutes. I'll have her call you when we're done, how's that? Of course."

I glanced up at all the other kids in the parking lot, all of them with normal lives that they didn't even appreciate. Maybe they were worried they wouldn't get asked to the prom or that they wouldn't get a good score on their SATs. None of them were worried that one day their past was going to overwhelm them and they would remember the most horrific thing that had ever happened to them.

"Get in," Bennet said, unlocking his doors.

I shook my head, still staring at all those people getting out of their cars. "Nope. I went missing here once before. Not going to happen again."

"Okay. Just remember, you picked this place to stop. Not me."

"Give me my phone." I held my hand out, palm up, realizing that it was a vulnerable stance. He could grab me and force me into his car. He seemed to read my mind and nodded his head. A second passed before my cell rested in my palm, lightweight and fragile, just like I felt. I kept one finger on redial.

Bennet sighed. "Can we go for a walk?"

"I need to get to school."

"Just for a few minutes—we need to talk." He opened his door and got out, then stood beside me, so close I could feel the heat from his body. I took a step away from him, instantly aware of the muscles that bulged beneath his shirt and his strong hands and those cool green eyes, fixed on a distant point over my shoulder. His lips were parted as if ready to speak, but instead he gestured toward the street.

"You're going to start remembering things," he said, a minute later as we walked on the sidewalk that surrounded the parking lot. All the while, I kept one eye focused on the security guard patrolling this side of the building. "And when you do, I want you to tell me. Okay? Nobody else. Not your therapist or your parents or your best friend."

"Why should I trust you instead of them?" A frown settled on my brow, my muscles flexed and tensed, flexed and tensed. I imagined throwing him to the ground, the same way I had done with Kyle a few days ago. But I had a feeling Bennet wouldn't be as easy a target.

"Because I don't think you were kidnapped by a stranger, Rachel. You're too smart for that. I think you willingly went with someone you knew."

His words echoed my fears. But it didn't make me feel better. Instead, a knot formed in my stomach, a cluster of muscles that tightened until I felt nauseated. "You showed me pictures of other girls that went missing. Back when you were interrogating me."

"Yes."

I swallowed, thinking about Nicole, the one familiar name on my list, my throat raw as fear surged through me. I knew what I was going to ask next and, somehow, I already knew the answer. "Are any of them dead?"

A guarded expression filled his eyes. "I can't talk to you about that."

"This isn't going to be a one-way street. You have to tell me."

There was sadness in his eyes now, probably because he knew he had to tell me the truth and didn't want to. His voice was hoarse, cracking in the middle of the single syllable that came out. "Yes."

Even though that word had been spoken softly, it filled my ears. It rolled like thunder down the street, it drowned out every other sound in Santa Madre until it was all I could hear and all I could know. At least one girl was dead. Maybe more than one. Killed by whoever had taken me. And now that I'd lost my memory—now that I didn't remember who the kidnappers were—they could slip back into my life, ready to kill me, too.

"I want you to start wearing a tracking device," he said. "Something so small no one will notice. Just in case whoever took you comes back."

I stopped walking and he did, too.

"At some point your memory will return," he continued. "And when it does, you'll remember who kidnapped you. To them, you're a walking, talking liability."

We stared at each other. The noise of the students and the cars faded until all I could hear was a flock of sparrows singing from those cherry trees, their high notes interspersed with trills and warbles.

"It was you lurking outside my house the other night, wasn't it?" I asked.

"I was just doing my job."

"How is a tracking device supposed to help?"

"We'll know if you go anywhere unusual or if you don't go home for long periods of time. We—I—want to prevent you from ending up in another ditch." He paused, his eyes locked on mine. I remembered that expression on his face when he had looked down at the eight-by-ten glossies of the other kidnapped girls, as if those girls could have been his nieces or little sisters, girls he had taught how to play softball, girls he had teased at birthday parties and joked with while playing video games.

I got the feeling he had lost someone and wanted to make sure it never happened again.

"So far we've only found a few things that connect the missing girls." He flipped up a finger for each item he named. "They were all about the same age, sixteen or seventeen. They were involved in either sports or dance." He pulled something out of his pocket, an elastic kandi bracelet, similar to the ones that I'd found hidden in my closet. "And at least four of them were regularly going to raves. We found bracelets like this in two of the girls' homes. The other two girls had written about PLUR in their journals."

"You can make that five girls."

His eyebrows raised.

"I don't remember going, but there's a bunch of rave stuff in my closet."

He nodded slowly, then handed me the bracelet. "You think you could wear this without causing too much attention?"

A flush worked its way up my chest to my neck and settled on my cheeks. How much did he know about me? If he thought I could get away with wearing a bracelet like this, he already knew that I'd been going to raves. If his team had been going through those other girls' bedrooms, looking for clues, did that mean they had gone through mine, too?

I took it and slipped it on. "Is this the tracking device?"

"Yes. You can take it off for showers or swimming, but

it'd be best if you wore it or kept it with you as much as possible, even when you're sleeping. And here." He tugged a business card out of his wallet. While he was doing that, I saw his badge, but there was nothing personal inside. No photos, no Starbucks cards, no receipts. Completely different from Dad's wallet, which brimmed with pictures of Mom, Kyle, and me, discount movie tickets, Disneyland passes, and frozen yogurt coupons. "I want you to call me if you remember anything or if something happens—like you get into a situation where you need help. Okay?"

I took his card and held it between my thumb and forefinger, squinting because the sun was breaking through the morning cloud cover.

"I want my life back," I told him, even though I wasn't sure which life I wanted. The old one where I was a wannabe ballet dancer with a handful of friends and grades barely above C. Or the new one where I bleached my hair, dressed in black, had track marks, and a hot boyfriend. I toyed with that list of girls' names in my pocket. "And I want answers. Was one of the missing girls named Nicole Hernandez?"

"Did you remember something?"

"Not yet."

A heavy sigh lifted his chest and he stared over my head.

"Remember what I said about how this wasn't going to be a one-way street?" I asked. I snapped the bracelet, making the plastic beads spin and twist. "I can take this thing off as easily as I can put it on."

"Yes. Nicole Hernandez was one of the missing girls." A long pause followed before he spoke again. "I'm not sure what you're planning, but be careful. I can't tell you everything about this investigation, except right now I'm the only one in my department who thinks these are all kidnappings. Personally, I think there are more than six girls missing. A lot more."

I'm not sure if he meant to, but he had succeeded in scaring the crap out of me. Still, it wasn't going to stop me. I had to do what I had to do. I lifted my chin, squared my shoulders, then turned away from him, heading back toward Lincoln High.

Chapter Thirteen

I had to pass those damned cherry trees to get back to my car, that memorial still in place, notes swirling in the wind, white petals falling like snow, landing in my hair and on my shoulders. Agent Bennet sauntered a few steps behind me, stopping to make a phone call, but keeping his gaze focused on me all the time.

I wished I could research him as easily as he could me.

When had those other girls gone missing—within the past three months? The fact that the FBI was involved made me think the girls weren't all from the L.A. area. Some of them must have been from other states. Did that mean there was a serial killer on the loose, or was this some sort of human trafficking?

By the time I grabbed my backpack and books from my car and then texted Dad, I realized that I'd missed half of first period—the only class I had with Dylan. If I didn't hurry, I might not see him again until lunch. Grumbling, I headed toward the building, weaving through tangles of students who didn't seem to care if they were late, some of them smoking cigarettes, some of them smelling like they'd been smoking stuff a little bit stronger. The student parking lot was the last space we had to ourselves before we were devoured by the school. It was our goal, our free zone. It was where couples hooked up and where stoners passed each other suspicious-looking paper bags—as if it wasn't obvious what any of them were doing.

I passed a Mini-Coop, surprised when Lauren climbed out, her eyes glazed, her walk unsteady. The closer she got, the more apparent the pungent smell of weed was in her clothes and hair. I'd never seen her like this before. She'd always been a model student, the one everyone's parents used as an example when their kids were flunking a class or getting in trouble. *Look at Lauren Maxwell, head cheerleader—she gets straight As and never misses a game or practice. Why can't you be more like her?*

She spotted me. Long, blond hair tousled, she waved and called my name, her footsteps unsteady as she walked in my direction, giggling. "Stoner 101," she said with a conspiratorial grin, talking behind her hand. We were hiking side by side, past tall oleander hedges that blocked the parking lot from the football field and the rest of the school. "Weed really takes the edge off *you-know-what*." Then her eyes widened as if she'd made a huge mistake. "I shouldn't have said that. I forgot you don't remember anything."

"I'm not an idiot. You shouldn't act like I am," I said, my irritation level higher than it should have been so early in the morning.

"You feeling okay?" Lauren asked, a curious expression on her face. "I saw you talking to some hot guy outside school grounds for a long time. Does Dylan have competition?"

The last thing I needed right now was for anyone at school to find out that an FBI agent was tailing me everywhere I went. "No. And don't say anything to Dylan about it, either." It felt surprisingly like I'd just given her an order…and she just bobbed her head in agreement.

"Oh, I'd *never* say anything. Girlfriends always come first, right?"

"Maybe," I said, my irritation fading. Even though I was still getting to know her, there was something about Lauren that I really liked. Some part of her resonated with that dark, secret part of myself. It felt like the Goth version of myself was coming back, little by little, so slow I barely realized it. It was getting easier for me to make decisions based on my gut, even when I knew those decisions might lead toward danger. Like the way I'd let Agent Bennet follow me instead of driving straight to the police station, even before I knew who he was. And the fact that I'd gotten out of the car to confront him, even though I was afraid.

This new me was a risk-taker, unafraid of consequences.

"Hey, do you know any of these people?" I asked as I pulled out that folded sheet of paper I'd found in my closet, smoothing it flat between my fingers. Lauren acted like we were good friends, so maybe she knew who these girls were. Maybe they were cheerleaders from other schools or maybe we all had a mutual friend. There had to be a connection here somewhere.

Her lips moved as she read each name. She looked back up at me, shaking her head. "Sorry, Rach, I don't. They must go to a different school. Maybe Saint John's or Santa Madre High?"

"Do you know anything about a rave called Phase Two?"

She stopped walking, an astonished expression on her

face. "I thought you didn't remember anything."

"I don't. I found a pair of ticket stubs in my closet. Just tell me what you know about it."

She shook her head. "I can't."

"Lauren, if you know something you *have* to tell me."

Her demeanor changed, her skin turned pale, her eyes shifting left then right. She leaned so close the smell of weed was overwhelming and her words came out in a hoarse whisper. "You made me promise not to talk about it, not at school, not at home! Never means never, that's what you said—"

What I did next surprised both of us.

I grabbed her hand and twisted her thumb sideways. She let out a little cry and her knees buckled. If I hadn't grabbed her around the waist with my other hand, she would have fallen. I spoke in her ear, amazed at the cruel tone in my voice. "You're *going* to tell me."

"Is this a test?" she whimpered. "Because I don't want to get kicked out! I promised I'd never talk and I *won't*. Not to anyone, not our parents or the cops or the principal. I swear!" Her last words were barely comprehensible, more of a moan without syllables.

I let her go and she quickly moved away from me, a frightened look in her eyes.

"You've—you've never done anything like that to me before," she said. "We've always been on the same side. Us against the world, always and forever. Remember?" She pulled back her collar and lifted her hair to show me a script tattoo, exactly like the one I wore on my wrist. "I'm on your side, Rach. I've got your back, just like you asked. But *please*, don't get me kicked out! Your memory's going to come back, I know it will. It has to."

There was a bad taste in my mouth, like I'd swallowed

something bitter. The expression in her eyes was causing two conflicting emotions—guilt and excitement—and I didn't like either one.

"I'm sorry," I said, the words burning my lips because they weren't true. I was only sorry that she wouldn't tell me what I wanted to know. She gave me a hesitant grin, despite the fact that the fear in her eyes hadn't faded. Had fear been there all along and had I only noticed it now? If so, what kind of person scares one of her friends?

"It's okay," she said with an awkward shrug, her words coming out like an apology, like *she* was the one who had messed up. "I gotta go." She took a cautious step away from me, then another, her eyes on me the entire time. "I have a nurse's note to miss first period, but I can't miss second, too. Can't let everybody know Lincoln High's Sweetheart has been smoking dope." She grimaced as if she secretly hated being the poster girl for perfection, then paused to straighten her skirt and top. "Do I look okay? You know, not like I've been out smoking?"

"You look fine." But she didn't really. Her eyes were bloodshot and she had a sheepish grin on her face like a dog that had been kicked. Neither one of us was addressing the fact that she'd refused to tell me about Phase Two or that I'd turned Ninja Monster on her. What felt even worse was the fact that she'd accepted it when I turned into an alpha bitch.

"See you at lunch!" she said, a forced cheeriness in her voice.

Then the bell ending first period rang and she turned and dashed toward the school building, leaving me with a dark hole in my gut.

Who *was* I? And why was I acting like this?

...

I fumbled with that piece of paper as I walked through the halls, folding it, unfolding it, then folding it again, hand tucked inside my jacket pocket, head down. I knew now that the list of names was a catalyst, forcing me to move forward, ignoring the burning buildings and scorched bodies I would leave behind. People were going to get hurt along the way. I knew that, but still I couldn't stop.

Whoever was taking these girls was worse than me.

I toyed with that slip of paper until it felt like fabric between my fingers, soft and pliant, names stitched with razor-sharp needles and sinew for thread. This paper was my secret history, it was the map that was going to lead me into my own personal cave of secrets. I might go in and never come out; my search could cause me to get captured again; the next ditch could be stained with my own blood. Agent Bennet's fancy little tracking device might let him know where I was, but it wouldn't protect me if somebody came at me with a knife.

I could be on a collision course with my own death.

What secret could Lauren be hiding that was more important than me finding out who had kidnapped me?

Everybody else sat in U.S. History taking notes because we had a test next week. Twenty-four other students sat curved over spiral notebooks and laptops and tablets, listening to Mr. Garcia drone on, none of them lifting their heads. The sound of keyboards clacking and pens scratching against paper filled the room, occasionally accompanied by a harried whisper, *what did he say?* or a hand shooting up followed by, *will this be on the test?* Like me, three other girls were pretending to pay attention, but they were secretly texting each other, stifling giggles and rolling their eyes. All three of them sported purple dragon tattoos that snaked down their right arms, curving from their shoulders to their wrists.

I couldn't remember their names, but just looking at them put me on edge. Every now and then one of them would glance at me with a sly grin.

Tacky bitches.

I wasn't myself today. A dark cloud had drifted over me. Some switch had flipped on when Agent Bennet followed me—when I thought Kyle might be in danger—and I hadn't been able to turn it off. The back of my head ached and I was subconsciously rubbing my fingers over the track marks on my left arm when one of those tatted girls looked at me.

She laughed—a short *ha*, almost like an exclamation— then she quickly texted something to her friends. I soon heard muffled giggles and the other two girls turned around to look at me.

I gave them all the finger, then lifted my eyebrows and thumbed toward the hallway.

Wanna take this outside?

What the heck was I doing? Did I just challenge three girls to a fight?

Two of the girls instantly looked at their spiral notebooks, their shoulders hunched, their heads down. The third one gave me a wide grin, revealing silver grillwork on her upper teeth. Her eyes remained fixed upon mine, lids narrowing, until finally my expression forced her to shift in her seat, turning her focus back on the teacher.

Apparently I wasn't the only crazy alpha bitch in this school.

Feigning disinterest, I turned away from the Dragon

Tattoo Girls and stared out the window instead, looking down at the cars that drove past the school. At the trio of pine trees that lined the front walk. At the cherry blossoms that had drifted onto the lawn and now collected in fragile, white clusters.

Most of the class continued to transcribe every word the teacher said.

Not me.

I was counting the minutes until I got out of school. Until I could go looking for the girls on that list.

The bell rang and part of me—the part I didn't understand— wanted to follow those Dragon Tattoo Girls out the door, my fists clenched. Lunch was here. I knew I could easily corner one of those tramps, maybe lure her into the upstairs girls' bathroom—nobody went up on the third floor during lunch—and there I'd have a chance to teach her a thing or two about classroom etiquette. Number one being don't laugh at me. Number two, don't act so tough because you really aren't.

Number three evaporated, a morning mist driven away by the heat of the sun.

Dylan stood outside my classroom, waiting for me. Black leather jacket slung over one shoulder, a pair of broad gray wings spreading over his long-sleeved shirt, pensive gray eyes smudged with black liner. He looked like a dark angel, ready to take me somewhere I'd never been, and here I was, more than willing to go.

He gave a brief nod to the Dragon Tattoo Girls as they exited the room and they all nodded back. It was a clandestine greeting, almost a symbol of respect. But I could tell by the expression on Dylan's face that he hated them almost as much as I did.

One more thing to add to my ever-growing WTF list.

Fortunately, it wasn't enough to take away the excitement I felt now that he was here. Nothing could change that, not Agent Bennet, not the Dragon Girls, not Lauren. All the confusion in my life vanished whenever Dylan was around, although truthfully, he might have been the biggest mystery of all.

When, how, why had we become a couple?

He didn't seem to wonder about it, though, didn't seem to like me any less, even though I wasn't the same girl he had been hanging out with for the past year. His mouth curved in a smile as I approached, his lip ring catching the fluorescent light and holding it like a star, poised on the edge of his mouth. His fingers laced with mine, as if our hands belonged together and always would, the warmth from his body flowing into mine, giving me strength. We walked toward the cafeteria united, shoulder to shoulder, two black-clad warriors pushing our way through the crowds and the other students moving aside. I hadn't noticed until now how the other teens bowed away as we passed them, heads turned aside, eyes looking down.

I felt like I was Odette, the swan queen in *Swan Lake*, and Dylan was Prince Siegfried, my beloved, and the rest of the school was populated by people who had been turned into swans. It was a strange bit of fiction, but once I latched onto it, it settled in my mind and took root. I glanced at him from the corner of my eye—he was truly adorable, in a scary, breathless way, and I still couldn't get over the fact that he was interested in me. That was what I got out of lunch period. I don't remember what I ate or if I ate at all, I don't remember if we sat with that strange group of kids or if we sat alone. All I remember is how he looked at me, with those big, gray eyes, his black hair wet and tousled from a PE shower, and how he smiled, as if he was sending me a coded message...*wish we were alone, can't wait to kiss you again, it's been too long*.

I had to agree with his unspoken words. It had been way too long. Like my whole life. As far as I was concerned, we'd never kissed before.

With every word he spoke, I found myself wondering what his mouth tasted like. Were his kisses soft and tender, or were they firm and passionate? Were they short and did they come in breathless clusters, or were they so long that they stole my heart?

We sat beside each other, knees touching, him leaning closer with each word—I think he was talking about his art class or something his coach said to the wrestling team, though I'm not sure. Words seemed to blur and become incomprehensible whenever he was around, which was strange because words meant so much to him. They were his DNA, the tools he used to understand life. The first line of Edgar Allan Poe's *The Raven* flowed in a tattooed script, spiraling around his wrist, and he carried a leather-bound journal with him all the time, the tips of his fingers stained blue from jotting down snippets of text whenever he was alone.

At one point, I remembered that I had a question for him.

I fumbled awkwardly through my pockets, finding and retrieving that note I'd discovered attached to my memorial, the one I thought he might have written. I slid it on the table between us. "Did you write this?" I asked.

He glanced down at it, then nodded.

"I can't read what it says."

"I hung it up before the rains started." His hand found mine beneath the table and his fingers brushed my palm, sending tingles up my arm. "Then the rains came and the water washed away my words—but, even though no one could read it, the poem did what it was supposed to do. It brought you back."

I sighed, my heart melting.

"I have—uh—some stuff I need to do tonight," he said. "But I was wondering if you might want to hang out Friday night."

Friday was tomorrow. So close and yet so far away. I didn't know if this was a real date or if we were supposed to hook up with a gang of kids somewhere. I paused, speechless, not sure what to say.

"I can pick you up on my bike. I've got an extra helmet you can wear." He sounded a little nervous, like he just realized I might say no.

I flashed on the two of us riding a Harley through night streets, my arms wrapped around his waist, me leaning against him, his heat warming me, the world flying past, a blur of colors and shapes that didn't matter. It was a memory—one of my first—and I gasped, low and soft, air flowing over my lips like I'd just woken up from a long nap, like an enchantment was lifting.

"I've ridden on your bike before, haven't I?" I asked.

"Lots of times." He gave me a shy grin. "Is that a yes?"

I nodded, suddenly eager for Friday. I didn't care if we were going to be alone or in a crowd of a hundred. As long as we were together, that was all that mattered. As far as I was concerned, Friday couldn't come soon enough.

CHAPTER FOURTEEN

I didn't see Kyle again until after school. I kept expecting to find him lurking outside one of my classes, a worried expression in his eyes, his voice lowered as he asked why I'd been acting so strange on the way to school this morning. He didn't know Agent Bennet had been following us or that I was now wearing a tracking device. I hoped it would stay that way.

The less my brother had to worry about, the better.

I found Kyle waiting for me by the side exit, backpack draped over one arm, attention focused on his iPhone as he intermittently texted, then chuckled, then texted again. He stuck out his foot like he was going to trip me if I tried to walk past him.

"Hey," he said, never looking up from his cell, thumbs punching in yet another message. "What the holy effing crap was going on this morning?" He gave me a sidelong glance, eyes peering through hair that had fallen over his face. Then he slipped his phone into his jacket pocket and loped along by my side, his legs longer than mine, his steps carrying a lazy bounce. "Why'd you take that crazy route to school and then dump me off at the front door?"

We were threading our way through the horde of students leaving the building, half of them jogging down the steps, the other half ambling slowly, some talking, some turning around to gaze back at the open doors as if they'd forgotten something.

"Just felt like doing something different," I told him, ruffling his hair as I kept walking, never breaking my stride.

Kyle shook his head. "You're weird," he said. Then he gave me a mischievous grin and held up his right palm, revealing a phone number written in blue ink.

"Amber's digits. Total score, despite your attempts to ruin my social life earlier today," he said. He scampered away from me then, running and jumping and whooping.

"I wasn't trying to wreck your life," I grumbled, knowing he was too far away to hear me. "I was trying to save it."

We'd both made our way down the steps and onto the path that wended toward the parking lot. Other students milled around us, some heading to the football field for practice, wearing shoulder pads and carrying helmets. Brett was among them and he waved at me from the edge of the field—something I still couldn't get used to, having friends who were either captain of the football team or head of the cheerleading squad. He cupped his hands around his mouth and called out to me, "Hey, I hear you're coming to the *thing* on Friday." He gave me a thumbs-up.

I waved back, confused. I was going to a 'thing' on Friday? I thought Dylan and I were going on a date—I'd been looking forward to us spending time alone together. I sighed, trying not to feel disappointed. We were probably going to some party and hopefully we wouldn't stay too long.

Then I froze in place, staring down at that kandi bracelet, my fingers running over the brightly colored beads as I remembered all the stuff I'd found in that box yesterday morning—the ballet slippers, the list of names, the ticket stubs.

Maybe we were going to a rave. Maybe a Phase Two rave.

I was so caught up in my thoughts I barely heard Brett when he called out again.

"It's gonna be a blast!" he shouted, then he turned and jogged onto the field with his teammates.

I couldn't decide if I was excited or terrified. Tomorrow night I was quite possibly going back to my own personal Ground Zero, the place where my transformation had begun, the place where I may have met my kidnappers.

"Must be nice to be so popular," a familiar voice said behind me. "Hanging out with the head cheerleader and captain of the football team, dating one of the hottest guys in Lincoln High."

I spun around and saw Molly McFadden following in my footsteps. Thick, black glasses sliding down her nose, red hair pulled back in a ponytail that exploded in curls, pale blue eyes studying me, looking me up and down. She stooped to pull up one of her sagging white knee socks, but she didn't stop walking.

"Molly!" I said. I wanted to tell her that I'd been looking for her at school and I'd tried calling her a hundred times, but I'd never been able to finish dialing. Calling Dad today had been the first time I'd been able to make a phone call since I'd gone missing. But I didn't get a chance to say anything. In typical Molly style, she took over the conversation.

"I know we're not besties anymore, but that doesn't

mean I don't still care. I've been so worried about you and then I have to find out you were rescued by watching the news." She leaned toward me for effect. "*The frigging news*, and you've been home for what, a week? Two weeks? I don't even know how long you've been home and you *still* don't call or answer my texts. And now you're back at school, which I have to find out through the rotten Lincoln High grapevine. You could have at least posted a status update on Facebook—"

"We're not best friends anymore?" I asked, puzzled. It felt like she had punched me in the chest.

She shifted her weight, her expression softening just a bit as she cocked her head to the side, her red plaid skirt catching in the breeze. One of her Doc Marten boots tapped against the ground.

"Your little brother told my little sister that you don't remember what happened. Is that true?" she asked, her voice lowered.

I nodded.

Kyle came up to us, said hello to Molly, then pointed toward the parking lot. "Come on, let's go, okay, girls? Rach can give you a ride home, but we need to go. I've got things to do, *important* things."

Molly hesitated and her brow furrowed. "I don't think so. I've got to write a paper and I was just gonna hang out in the library."

"I could still give you a ride to the library," I offered.

She studied me for a moment, then shrugged. "Sure, whatever," she said, her tone cool.

Together, the three of us rounded the last curve of the walkway and the parking lot opened up before us, a cement backdrop custom-designed to display the wealth, or lack of wealth, of the students who attended Lincoln.

Sparkling Mercedes, Mini-Coops, and Miatas lined up next to Pontiacs with missing bumpers and Chevys with busted headlights. My Volkswagen gleamed like an iridescent green June beetle, parked between a Smart car and a Fiat, as far from that line of cherry trees as possible.

But the fragrance of the flowering trees still swirled around us as I unlocked the car. It was impossible to get away from that smell.

"The holy of holies," Molly remarked, a smirk on her face as she stepped inside my car. "Never thought I'd be invited in here again."

"I'm really sorry, Moll. I lost my phone when—when I went—" Someday I was going to be able to finish that sentence, but obviously not today. I clicked my seat belt in place and checked my rearview mirror. "When I got home, one of the first things I thought was, 'I can't wait to see Molly, she'll understand, she always does.'" I hesitated, staring down at my lap, speaking so soft I didn't know if anyone would hear me, "But I have this thing with phones lately."

She nodded and thankfully didn't give me one of her signature are-you-serious-looks. We were pulling out of the parking lot and I was watching the cars behind me, looking for a gray Toyota, hoping Agent Bennet wasn't following me. He wasn't. The three of us rode in an uncomfortable silence for a couple of miles until we reached Kyle's friend's house. At that point, my brother jolted to life, climbing out of the backseat and heading up the sidewalk.

"Tell Mom I'll be home later," he called over his shoulder. "I'll stay here for dinner, K?" But he didn't wait for an answer. The front door swung open and the two boys gave each other fist bumps. Loud music poured out of the house and I had a feeling there were no parents home.

Now it was just me and Molly and a year's worth of awkward silence in the car.

"I didn't really expect you to call me, Goth Girl," she said as we pulled away from the curb. "I'm not exactly in your pack anymore." She shifted in her seat, tugging on the satchel she wore over one shoulder 24/7, part fashion statement, part necessity, since she had to carry an asthma inhaler and thyroid pills with her all the time. "How much did you forget, anyway?"

"Like a whole year. Last thing I remember, I was studying for geometry—"

"With Miss Wallace? That witch. I hated her."

"Me, too. After that I fell asleep. In my room."

I slipped into a familiar route, one that passed school buses and kids on skateboards until we reached the historic district of Santa Madre. Here, the streets were lined with Craftsman bungalows and Victorian cottages, which then gave way to tiny boutiques and thrift stores and coffee shops. I snatched the first parking spot I saw, one that happened to be half a block from the library and across the street from a Starbucks, our old after-school hangout. I wondered if they still made caramel macchiatos.

Molly stared up at the sky, her lips moving, maybe calculating dates or classes or maybe just counting how many clouds were up there. "Was that before or after the spring dance?"

"Before, I think. I don't remember the dance."

We got out of the car, both of us temporarily forgetting about the library and Molly's paper as we navigated our way across the street, dodging traffic. The door to Starbucks breezed open and the fragrance of coffee and chocolate wafted out, stirring up old memories of all the afternoons Molly and I had come here, all our conversations about cute boys and tough teachers and the deeper meaning of *The Lord of the Rings*.

"As Ricky Ricardo says, That 'splains everything. Sort of," she said after ordering a mocha Frappuccino. "You started acting like a Prima Donna Bitch at that dance, which I guess I could have handled 'cause I'm a bitch sometimes, too. But you basically told me to get lost. In front of everyone."

Other customers started staring at us. That happened a lot when I was with Molly. I ordered a caramel macchiato and we found a table in the corner.

"I said that?" I asked, my voice so soft I could barely hear it myself.

"Oh, you said that and a whole lot more. You made it really clear you didn't want to be friends anymore. Meanwhile, you somehow became super popular. With all the wrong kids, of course." She was snapping her gum, sometimes stretching it out of her mouth with her thumb and forefinger. Once she actually dropped it on the table, then grabbed it up and stuffed it back in her mouth, lint and all.

"I'm sorry, Moll." I wanted to say more, but didn't know where to start. "I don't know why I said that. I don't even remember it. I don't remember anything except waking up in that ditch." My voice cracked. I blinked and looked away from her, staring out the window instead, at all the afternoon shoppers walking past, all clutching brightly colored bags. Clouds were filling the skies, casting an ominous tone on an otherwise normal scene. "After that, I spent two days in the hospital. I guess I've got some bizarre form of amnesia and PTSD similar to what a lot of people got after 9/11. Nobody knows if I'll ever get all of my memory back."

Molly's eyes darkened and she leaned closer, listening with her head tilted slightly.

"Then, after I was finally released from the hospital," I continued. "I was interrogated by the FBI and they held me for hours. I thought I would never go home—"

"The FBI? *Seriously?*" Her words came out in a dramatic rush, as she sat poised on the edge of her seat, her blue eyes looking twice as big as they usually did. "You're not making this crap up, are you? What did they want? I mean, how did the FBI get involved?"

I frowned. "I'm not sure—"

I paused, thinking about that list of girls I'd found in my closet, about my new group of friends at school, about Lauren smoking pot before class, about me dating a guy I'd been crushing on since middle school, about the FBI agent who followed me around in an unmarked car.

"You can tell me," she said in a low, conspiratorial tone. She'd always loved crime dramas. I think she secretly wanted to be Abby on *NCIS*, a forensics scientist, dissecting the world one DNA sample at a time. "Look, if I have to, I'll pinky swear. And, damn, girlfriend, you and me haven't pinky sworn on anything since sixth grade."

There was a long pause when she stared at me for effect. That's the only time Molly ever got quiet. Silence was her way of using more exclamation points. I needed to talk to someone about all this. Molly and I might not be best friends anymore, but it seemed like she wanted to help.

"There are other girls who have been kidnapped, just like I was. Except I guess I'm the only one who got away," I told her, guilt flashing through me and making my chest ache. "And I'm not the same anymore. I'm—different."

"Girl, you always *were* different."

We both smiled. Our order was up and she went to get

our drinks. That's the way Molly was, a bitch most of the time, but nice when you needed her to be. A moment later we were both sipping on drinks laced with caffeine, syrup, and whipped cream. Neither one of us talked for a few minutes.

"How are you different?" she asked at last. "I mean, is it because you can't remember anything? Or is it because you realize you'd been a different person last year and now you feel normal?"

"A little bit like that last one." I glanced around us to see if anyone was listening, then I lowered my voice. "I found a note I left for myself." I reached into my pocket, pulled out the slip of paper, and showed it to her. "I wrote that sometime before I was kidnapped."

She read one side, then the other. "Sounds like you turned into a rave rat. Who are these girls on the back?"

I shrugged. "I don't know. I was planning to go see a few of them after school today. Maybe one of them will know something." I didn't want to overwhelm her, so I didn't mention the fact that I had tackled my brother like a Ninja, using skills I didn't know I had. "And there's this," I told her while I rolled up my sleeve, revealing the needle marks on my arm.

"What the eff?" She ran a finger over the fading purple bruises, then stared up at me. "Are you an addict or something? Is that why your memory's gone?"

"I don't know." My bottom lip trembled when I spoke. "I don't even know if I was doing this to myself, or if it was something the kidnappers gave me."

She gave me a pensive glance, her eyes narrowed. "Maybe you've been taking something for a long time. Maybe that's why you've been such a bitch this past year."

"Maybe."

"Well, maybe if you quit taking it, whatever it is, I could stand hanging around you again."

I gave her a weak grin. That was one of the things I loved about Molly. She was tough on the surface, but deep down she was someone you could always depend on. I took a quick look around the coffee shop, then checked the time on my cell. "Hey, I need to get going. I need to connect with some of those girls on my list before I head home."

"You're gonna do this on your own?"

I nodded.

"You want some backup?" A loud slurp followed as she sucked the last of her drink up the straw.

"What about your paper?"

She gave me a sly grin. "I lied. I don't have any homework tonight."

I smiled, glad that Molly was with me. She might still be mad at me for the way I had acted this past year, but as far as I was concerned, she was still my best friend and I trusted her like nobody else.

Chapter Fifteen

The California sunshine had already begun to disappear, and dark clouds were gathering overhead, pale gray fading to thick black. Soft rain pattered down as we headed toward my car. If I hadn't known better, I'd have thought the universe was weeping over what was up ahead. But I shook that thought off, refusing to give in to the nervousness I felt, flicking on the windshield wipers and then running my fingers through my hair, brushing the bangs out of my eyes. We had a lot of options and needed to figure out which ones were best.

"These two girls, Alexis and Lacy, live too far away. One is down in Irvine. There's no way we'd make it there and back in rush hour, not if we want to get home by dinner," Molly said. "Same thing for Lacy in Compton. We should focus on the other three. Wait." She looked up at me. "Did you want to call these girls or see them face-to-face?"

"Face-to-face. It might help me remember."

"Why don't we head over to Janie's house, she's in Pasadena."

"Good idea," I said, glad we weren't heading to Nicole's house first. I had a feeling I'd find some key piece of information at Nicole's and, whatever it was, it wouldn't be good. It might be that Big Trigger my therapist kept talking about. Maybe meeting another girl first would help.

I'd already preprogramed all the addresses into my GPS, so we set off on our journey. My palms were sweating and I had to keep wiping them on my jeans while I drove. We avoided the freeway—rush hour combined with rain had turned the 210 into a tangled snarl—so we zipped down one side street and over another, instead. Twenty minutes passed with us listening to Katy Perry's *Teenage Dream* while the windshield wipers *thwacked* back and forth.

"There it is." Molly finally pointed a chubby finger toward a small cottage on the left. I slowed my car, pulled alongside the curb, and we both sat there, staring at the house.

"Do you want to come with me?" I asked.

"Does the Pope like Easter bunnies?"

I gave her a look. Decoding her bizarre phrases was sometimes more work than it was worth. I bolted from the car, one hand shielding my head from the rain that had gotten more serious in the past ten minutes, Molly following behind me. She tried and failed to miss the ankle-deep water that gushed down the gutter on the other side of the street.

"Eww!" she said, shaking one of her feet. Apparently water had gone down inside her boot. Now there was a squishy sound with every step she took.

We raced up the sidewalk, then huddled on the cottage porch beneath a short roof overhang, me knocking on the door, rain falling all around us. To our right, lacy curtains parted and I thought I saw someone peek out through a smudged window, but by the time I turned to look, they were gone. The curtains remained parted a few inches. All I could see inside was darkness.

A snap of thunder *kaboomed* overhead.

My heart felt like a fist, hammering against my chest, knuckles bruising my ribs, and my breath came in short puffs. This was exactly where I had wanted to be, standing on the doorstep of one of those girls on my list, but now that I was here, a new emotion wrapped itself around me like an anaconda. The closest thing I'd ever felt was when I'd grabbed Lauren and tried to force her to tell me more.

It was like the thrill of doing something illegal and getting away with it. It made my stomach queasy.

I was just about to knock again when the door flew open and a girl my age stood in front of us, her hair dyed blue, the same bright shade as her eyes. For an instant she reminded me of Katy Perry…if Katy was strung out on heroin. She held something behind her back and I couldn't stop glancing down at her right hand, wondering what she was hiding and why.

"Bitch, what you doing at my house?" she demanded.

I sputtered, taken off guard, fighting a dark part of me that struggled to rise to the surface. "I—did—are—" None of what I said made sense, so Molly jumped in.

"Are you Janie Deluca?" she asked.

"What if I am?" The girl took a step out the door, revealing a baseball bat in her hand. "You're breaking the rules and if you come any closer, I'll *kill* you. Both of you!"

I shoved Molly behind me. She missed the step and almost fell to the ground with a loud curse. Nobody was going to hurt Molly, not now, not ever. My gaze focused on that bat, on the fingers that held it tight.

"Get out of here 'fore I break your head open!" the girl yelled.

I tossed my car keys back toward Molly. "Get in the car and stay there," I told her. Then I focused on the blue-haired girl. "Put down the bat." My words came out like a warning, my voice surprisingly calm. "I only want to ask you a few questions. There's no reason to act like I'm here to start a fight—"

She lifted her chin. "You're gonna get kicked out for doin' this. I got the right to protect my own turf—"

Kicked out. The same cryptic phrase Lauren had used earlier. But I didn't have time to contemplate the similarities or to wonder why this girl was on guard. Janie had seen me hesitate. Hesitation got people killed.

Before she could say anything else and before I could make a more rational decision, I slammed a lightning-quick fist to her jaw, my knuckles connecting with her flesh and bone. She blinked, her eyes rolled up, and she staggered backward, her grip on that bat loosening. I kicked it out of her hand and sent it flying back into the darkness of her house.

It was like watching a bizarre video of myself—every part of me acted on raw instinct, like this was how I handled every difficult situation. Except it *wasn't*. The last time I remembered being in a fight had been in ninth grade and I'd failed miserably, spending the rest of the day in the school nurse's office.

"I only wanted to *talk* to you," I said, although the tone in my voice said something else. I was daring her to hit me, to take this one step further. Some part of me wanted her to lift her arms and step back out that door toward me.

The wind made the rain blow sideways, hitting the girl in the face, turning her hair into blue stripes that stuck to her cheeks. She looked young and vulnerable, her lip bleeding, a grinding fear in her eyes like a wounded animal.

An unexpected impulse caused her to rub her left arm, accidentally tugging up her sleeve, revealing a row of track marks that looked suspiciously like mine.

"What are you taking?" I asked, pointing to her bruises.

"You *know* I'm dry as a bone after what you did!" she said with a scowl, dark circles under her eyes like she couldn't sleep any better than I could. "Nobody's buyin' me nothin' anymore. You got questions, you should ask your *own* damn girls." She kicked the door shut with her right foot, the deadbolt latching with a dull *thunk* a split second later. But I could still hear her shuffling about on the other side.

She could have shouted at me, but she didn't. Instead she spoke in a voice so calm it was almost scary.

"This here is your only warning. Get off my property now. I'm goin' to get my gun, then I'll fill your skinny ass with more holes than you can count."

Her footsteps retreated into another room.

She was going to get a gun and, despite the terror that fingered its way through my gut, I wanted to wait for her to come back. I wanted to grab the gun from her hands as soon as the door opened and knock her in the face with it. I wanted to force her to tell me what drugs she was taking and who was giving them to her. I shifted my weight from one leg to another, my skin tingling, a thick coldness pouring over me, suddenly aware of everything around me. A bark of excited laughter rose from my chest, but I reminded myself that I hadn't come here to fight. I'd come looking for answers and had gotten more questions instead.

I forced myself to turn and jog back to the car, feet sloshing through puddles, head tilted down to shield my face from the rain. Molly was waiting inside, just like I'd told her to do. She was safe and that was all that really mattered. My hands and legs trembled when I climbed in the driver's seat. If I'd been alone, I would have gone for a run. A long run.

"Should I call the cops? Did she hit you? Are you okay?"

Molly's voice filled all the empty spaces in the car, her words like little teeth, gnawing at me. My right thumb worked the muscles in my left forearm, kneading those track marks as if it would jump-start some hidden reservoir lodged beneath my skin, releasing a floodgate of what—what was I craving right now? I leaned forward, head against the steering wheel, eyes closed.

Who am I and what kind of person have I turned into?

My stomach heaved, bile in my throat. At the same time, I felt stronger, bigger, taller than I ever had.

That girl had recognized me and, for some reason, she was afraid of me. There were track marks on her arms, just like mine. She knew the same secrets as Lauren, but neither of them would tell me what I needed to know.

I slammed my fist against the dashboard, unable to hold back that urge to fight that was making all my muscles tense, even the muscles in my gut, the sound of my hand hitting the dashboard almost masking the footsteps that were splashing toward my car, the sound of someone running through puddles, a chaotic rapid-fire rhythm—

"Holy shit, Rachel, she's got a gun!" Molly screamed.

I didn't bother to look. I knew I'd see hatred and terror in the blue-haired girl's eyes as she came to a stop just outside my door. Again, I reacted by instinct, something that was fast becoming second nature for me, no matter how weird it felt.

No, not weird—*right*.

I sensed her presence even before I heard her approach

or Molly's scream. My left hand grabbed the handle and I kicked my car door open, body slamming Janie Deluca and knocking her on her ass in the street. I was out of my car in an instant, rain streaming down on both of us. Janie struggled to gain control of that gun, holding it with trembling hands, trying to lift it and aim it at me. I kicked her in the side, in the arm, in the gut, each strike causing her to curl this way and that, and sending new moans from her chest.

It was almost like someone else was inside my body, calling the shots, someone both cold-blooded and vengeful. My fourth kick sent that gun tumbling away from her, skittering across the street into a storm drain where it disappeared from sight, a glittering bauble that dissolved in darkness.

Molly gasped, either before or after I started kicking the blue-haired girl, I'm not sure which.

Janie lay crumpled on the ground, hatred in her eyes giving way to complete fear, her weapon gone, her body bent at the waist, her arms and legs stretched out.

Even though Janie had tried to kill me, I wasn't afraid of her. I was angry. Strange, disconnected thoughts started buzzing through my head.

She deserves to die.

She's worse than a cockroach, she needs to be exterminated.

She's weak.

And she lay in the street in front of me, soaked to the bone, blood on her lip, staring up at me, blue hair flowing around her face like tears that wouldn't stop, that *couldn't* stop, and an expression in her eyes that I knew I'd seen before. We knew each other, Janie and I, of that much I was certain. We'd fought each other before and, just like tonight, I had won. I stood over her, triumphant, knowing that I held her life in my hands and that this wasn't the first time.

I pointed a finger at her and she winced as if I had just struck her.

"Never raise your fist to me again, do you hear me?" I said.

She nodded.

Then I left her there, bleeding and wounded. I got back in my car, wiped the rain from my face and drove away, Molly wordless beside me, my tires spinning over rain-washed streets, gears whining as I pushed the car faster and faster. I didn't have a destination this time. All I wanted was to get far, far away, as if that could erase what I had just done.

Even though she had been one of the girls on my secret list, I didn't want to remember Janie anymore.

I wasn't sure whether I wanted to know who I was, either.

CHAPTER SIXTEEN

Molly didn't say anything for a long time. A thick tension hung in the car between us and I worried that she was afraid of me now. Now that the adrenaline had faded, I tried to focus on driving, but I kept seeing Janie's face, that expression in her eyes when she was helpless, and it sickened me. I pulled over, right before the entrance to the 210, got out of the car, and curled over the side of the road, heaving.

There was something awful inside of me and I had to get it out. Every breath made my face tingle, a thousand tiny needles of fear that pricked and stabbed, and all the while, rain soaked my back and neck.

"Are you okay?" Molly asked. She'd gotten out of the car and stood beside me, one hand gently holding my arm. "Do you want me to drive?"

"No." I shook my head, wiped my mouth on my sleeve, then held my face up to the rain, wishing it could wash everything away. I wished I could go back to last year, to that night I fell asleep, when the only thing I was worried about was my geometry test. I wanted my life to be simple again, but somehow I knew that was never going to happen.

"Come on, give me your keys," she said, her hand outstretched, using a familiar tone that meant *do-it-now-or-else*.

I reluctantly gave her the keys, and a few minutes later we were driving away from Pasadena—not very fast because we were now stuck in the 210 rush hour traffic that I'd been trying to avoid. Rain separated us from all the other cars, turning everyone else into blue-gray phantoms. Without meaning to, I kept rubbing my left forearm.

"Did you—" she started to say, then paused. "How did you do that? You fought her like, like, I don't know, what *was* that—Kung Fu, Jujitsu, Tae Kwon Do? One minute she was in her house, then she was standing outside the car with a gun, *a mother-frigging gun*, and then she was on the ground. *Blam*. End of story!"

"I don't know how I did it," I said, glancing at her from the corner of my eye. Molly seemed proud of what I'd done tonight or maybe intrigued, completely different from how I felt.

"What? That skank had it coming." She gave me a look. "First, she threatened to beat our heads in with a baseball bat just for knocking on her door and then, and then, *shit*! Once I got back in the car, I had to grab my inhaler and take a hit before I could even watch what was going on. I was ready to dial 9-1-1 when you came running back to the car."

There was a long pause when we pulled off the freeway and parked in a nearby shopping center. The lights from Target and Dunkin' Donuts and Supercuts gleamed through the rain, people hurrying to and from their cars, struggling with umbrellas and shopping carts and cardboard boxes filled with pastries.

"You don't feel guilty for hitting that girl, do you?" she asked. "I mean, I have no clue *how* you did it, but what were your options? We could both be in the ER right now if you hadn't stopped her."

"I didn't mean to do *any* of it," I confessed, my thumb rubbing against my chin. Molly just stared at me. "I was scared and mad and all I wanted was for her to tell me something—anything—about who I am and why I am the way I am."

"I think we all want that."

"Maybe. But we don't all flatten a girl in the street like she's a bug."

Quiet, a blanket of silence, as far as the horizon, a long breath and another and still, quiet. And then, when the quiet got so loud that it began to whisper things that sounded like accusations, Molly spoke.

"But how *did* you do that? I mean, at first I thought you'd slipped a hallucinogenic in my Frappuccino. Then I thought you'd gone to some secret, elite Ninja warrior school."

I sighed, rubbing my right palm against my left forearm. "I told you. I'm different now," I said, not meeting her gaze. She was watching me. I could feel her eyes on me, even in the dark. "Ever since I came back from being kidnapped."

"I thought that meant you were having nightmares or taking antidepressants or struggling with some new phobia, like 'fear of black cars because the people who took me drove a black car.'"

A short laugh shuffled out of my chest.

"But what, now you can fight like Uma Thurman in *Kill Bill*?"

I shrugged. "I guess."

Her jaw dropped open and a frown settled on her brow. "*Who* taught you how to fight like this?" She shifted in her seat to face me. "It's just, where and when did you learn how to do all that crap?" She paused and looked around, then leaned in closer. "And can you teach *me* how to do some of it? There's a girl in my chem class who's been stealing stuff out of my satchel and I'd love to give her a knuckle sandwich—except these knuckles are so delicate." She gave her fist a little kiss for dramatic effect.

"Are you asking me to beat her up?"

"I never thought of that, but yeah, okay."

I grinned. Molly always had a way of seeing the practical, logical side of things. I, on the other hand, always went for the emotional side. Maybe if I was more like her, I'd have been better able to control my anger and wouldn't have left Janie so messed up back in Pasadena. Already that blue-haired Katy Perry look-alike was haunting me, her eyes black with fear, her hands shaking after I'd knocked her gun away. "Do you think Janie got hurt? Like maybe she needed to go to the hospital?"

Molly leaned back with a sigh. "One can only hope."

I punched her in the arm. Not hard, though. Not like I would have if it were Kyle. She pretended like it hurt and flexed her arm, wincing and moaning. Then, when I acted repentant, she punched me back.

"How long before you have to be home?" she asked.

I sent Dad a text when Molly and I were in Starbucks to make sure it was okay if I stayed out past dinnertime. "About forty-five minutes."

"You want to check out another girl on your list?"

"Should we? I mean, seriously, what kind of person attacks somebody who knocks on their door? What if all the other girls on my list are like this? Maybe this was a list of people I never wanted to see again—"

"If any of the remaining girls start a convo with 'Hey,

bitch,' then we should probably turn and run," Molly said. "Other than that, yeah, we should keep going. You want to find out what happened, don't you?" She didn't wait for my response. Instead, she flicked through those addresses on my GPS, picked one, and hit the go button. "Let's see if Nicole Hernandez is home."

I drummed my fingertips quietly on the armrest, fighting the hesitation that surged through me whenever I heard Nicole's name. I didn't know what had happened to her, but I knew she wouldn't be home when we got there. She was a Lost Girl. Somehow that knowledge made her seem even more frightening than Janie.

"Let's go," I said.

Nicole might be the Big Trigger that changed everything. She could push me over the edge. But I'd been living on the edge since I came home and I was tired of it.

I stared out the window as a computerized voice gave us directions. I pretended Molly and I were on a quest, looking for the missing Orc sword that had killed an Elfen queen, plunging the kingdom into darkness. I imagined we drove down a winding road that led through web-infested forests, that goblins watched us behind picket fences, and trolls lurked inside every doghouse. It was a strangely comforting fantasy, made from familiar memories of long nights Molly and I had spent together as pre-teens, planning our own excursion into Middle-earth.

But this was nothing like *The Hobbit*—it was more like *The Bourne Identity*, and I didn't want to be Jason Bourne, some guy with a secret past who suddenly knew how to kill people. I just wanted to be myself, the old me, the girl whose worst secrets were the fact that she might flunk geometry and that she probably wouldn't get the lead role in the upcoming ballet production.

•••

We reached Arcadia and rolled to a stop in front of a stucco ranch-style home. There were only two lights on here—the porch light, as if whoever was inside was waiting for someone to come home, and a flickering light downstairs, maybe a fireplace, where the owner sat, trying to keep warm despite the chill and the rain. Molly and I were just about to get out of the car, both of us with our fingers on the door handles when I spoke, saying what I couldn't hold in any longer.

"Janie had track marks on her arm. Just like mine," I said.

Molly blinked. Twice.

"She said nobody was buying her drugs anymore, but it sounded like it was somehow my fault. And she told me to ask my 'own girls' if I had questions. But *who* are my girls?" I thought about Lauren, sporting a tattoo on her neck that matched mine—but she had adamantly refused to tell me anything about Phase Two. I doubted she'd be much help with any of my other questions, either.

"I don't know," Molly said. Rain streaked my windows, casting eerie shadows on her face, making it look like her face was melting. "Maybe some of the other girls on your list?"

I wasn't convinced, but I nodded anyway. We got out of the car and walked up to Nicole Hernandez's house. I was still hoping to find answers. And quietly praying that this time I could have a conversation that didn't include me slamming my fist in someone's face.

•••

It was a nice house with short, clipped grass and orange daylilies and a fence covered with pink bougainvillea. Brown shutters hung on the windows, but they were ornamental, since no one needs shutters in California. A stone walk curved from the curb, past short, squat palm trees, and rain dripped from all the foliage. Everything about the house whispered something, soft and repetitive, something that should have been sweet but somehow put me on edge.

It was like it was saying, *come home, please, please, come home.*

I pressed my finger on the doorbell, wishing I could turn around and run, no longer wanting to know what was behind Door Number Two. Molly took my hand in hers, holding it, probably trying to give me courage. Or maybe she was trying to stop me from punching anyone.

The door opened and a tormented-looking woman stood before us. Dark circles colored the skin beneath her eyes and her cheekbones were sharply pronounced, as if she couldn't eat or sleep. Long, narrow fingers toyed restlessly with the sweater that hung crooked on her shoulders, the buttons fastened wrong. An ache emanated from her, a bone-sharp loneliness that made the night feel even colder than before.

I fidgeted, longing for something to replace the words I needed to say, wishing I was selling magazine subscriptions or candy bars or time-shares, that I was here for some other reason. Molly jostled my hand, looking at me expectantly, waiting for me to speak.

I opened my mouth and nothing came out. Then I tried again, disappointed when words rolled out of my mouth, vibrations making my vocal cords tremble. I longed for silence, because I didn't want to know what the woman was going to tell me.

The inside of the house continued to whisper while I spoke. *Where are you, why don't you come home, come home, come home...*

"Good evening, Mrs. Hernandez. Is Nicole home?" I asked, hating the sound of my own voice. I knew what her answer was going to be, Agent Bennet had already told me that Nicole had been kidnapped and I was the only girl who had made it back home. That ache rolled from Nicole's mother to me and back again, sucking the air from my chest and making it difficult to stay standing upright. I braced myself for a different kind of battle than the one I'd had back at Janie's.

I didn't think I was going to survive this one.

She stared at me, running a quick gaze over my features, maybe wondering who I was and what I wanted. "Did you go to school with my Nicole?"

Molly jumped in. "No. We met at a football game last year. We haven't seen her in a while."

The woman nodded. "Then you don't know." She pulled herself straight, staring off to the right, getting ready to tell us something she'd repeated so many times she probably had it memorized. "Nicole went off to a game with a group of her friends a few weeks ago, but she never made it there. She disappeared for a while, two whole days, before somebody found her on the side of the road—"

With every word she spoke, the night air around us got heavier and thicker and more ominous. I slid an apprehensive gaze toward Molly. Mrs. Hernandez didn't say anything else for a long time, as if there was no end to this story, as if she'd just gotten the call that told her where her daughter was and she was now heading off to get her. That was why her sweater was on crooked and why she seemed so distracted.

"Is she, is Nicole—" I didn't know what to say. At that point, words refused to come out.

"She's dead." Her voice was flat and a long sigh followed, her eyes closed now that the worst words of all had been spoken.

I stopped breathing.

In my mind, it was me who was dead, sprawled on the cement, broken and bloody.

I unconsciously took a step backward, not wanting to hear more. But Nicole's mother wasn't finished. Now that she had a live audience, she had more to say. A lot more.

"Somebody beat her to death," she said, every word striking me across the face and kicking me in the gut. "She was covered with so many bruises and had so many broken bones that I almost didn't recognize her at first. I didn't know my own little girl." Tears glistened in the corners of her eyes but they didn't fall. They stayed there reflecting the light, making her eyes look unearthly. Her chest heaved beneath the weight of her words, yet she didn't stop. "They just threw her out on the side of the freeway, her poor little body broken to bits. She might have been alive at first, but in too much pain to get up and cry for help."

I thought of myself and how I'd desperately climbed up the side of that gully, clawing my way up through mud and rain, how I'd poised, wavering and weary, on the side of a busy freeway. Had Nicole been kidnapped, like I had, or had something else happened to her?

"I'm so sorry, I didn't know—"

"The police say they're looking for whoever murdered her," she said. "But they don't have any leads."

"Did the FBI contact you?" I asked.

She nodded and the motion kicked those tears loose. They tumbled over bronzed skin, sliding down until they reached the corners of her mouth. "Do you know something?" She reached out and took hold of one of my hands. "Is there something they're not telling me?"

I wasn't sure what to say at first, but I knew that my mom would want to know everything if our situations had been reversed and I was the one found beaten to death.

"I was kidnapped, too," I confessed. "But I lost my memory, that's why I wanted to see Nicole. I found her name written on a piece of paper and I thought she might know something."

"Did they beat you, too?" Mrs. Hernandez asked, a concerned expression on her face.

"No, I wasn't beaten."

"But you think the same person took my Nicole?"

I paused, not sure if I should tell her the truth. Even if it was the same person, that still didn't mean we'd ever be able to find them. "I do," I answered at last. "I definitely think it was the same person."

Mrs. Hernandez made us come in for hot chocolate and cookies, which we ate sitting in cozy, overstuffed chairs in front of the fire. The mantle was covered with photos of Nicole. One showed her playing varsity basketball—she'd been hoping to get a scholarship to UCLA—while in another she wore soccer shorts and a T-shirt. There was a snapshot of her as a little girl standing before a Christmas tree—she was dressed as an angel with broad, white wings—and a large, silver-framed photo showed her in a floor-length, white *quinceañera* dress, a glittering tiara holding her long, dark, curly hair in place.

She was here and she was not here; she was a ghost who would never leave; she was a teenage girl who would never come home.

Still, the house where she grew up continued to call her to *come home, come home, please.*

Molly and I stayed longer than we planned. I couldn't leave. I quickly thumbed a message to Dad, when forty-five minutes turned into an hour and then two as Nicole's mother told us stories about her lost daughter. The woman needed to grieve and we needed to properly exchange phone numbers and email addresses. Just in case one of us found out anything. We finally parted with hugs and she gave us something, a bag of cookies, I think, and we all mumbled good-bye. It wasn't until I was hugging her that I realized she was crying and probably had been from that first moment when she told me Nicole was dead.

All the parents of the missing girls were weeping and their tears were creating a lake—just like the one in *Swan Lake*. The water was getting deeper and deeper, rising around my ankles, lapping against my thighs.

I had a feeling that if I didn't find answers soon, we were all going to drown.

Chapter Seventeen

Molly yawned and leaned back in the passenger seat, closing her eyes. One hand fiddled with her purse, pulling out her ever-present vial of thyroid medication. She thumbed the lid off and popped a pill into her mouth, swallowing it. I'd never gotten used to watching her take her meds without a glass of water, but that was the way she did it. She was crashing, we both were. Emotionally, physically. The rain was throwing shadows on us, our skin melting in rivulets. We were changing, both of us, turning into different people than we were before. I half-imagined we were going to start sprouting feathers and that we would spend the rest of our teenage years swimming across a lake that continued to grow.

The monsters were winning. Only now, I was afraid I might be one of them.

"That was crazy," Molly said.

"Yeah. Her name sounds so familiar. I thought I'd remember something, that maybe I'd gone to her house before. But it didn't look familiar and her mom didn't recognize me."

"We've still got three names left on the list. One of the girls lives pretty close to my house—"

"Janie wanted to bash my head in and Nicole is dead," I said. "We've already been out later than we should for a school night and I can't handle any more of this. Not tonight." On top of that, my head was pounding, a dull ache that began in the back of my skull and radiated out. I could barely keep my eyes focused and I kept rubbing my left arm. I was obviously craving some unknown drug that would make me feel better, and this pain was my penance.

We drove away from Nicole's house, heading north, back to our own side of the 210. Once I reached Molly's townhouse, I parked. She stayed in the passenger seat, her door open, no words to say, which was unusual. I think she wanted to say something light like, *see you at school tomorrow* or *try not to punch anyone between now and then*, but I could tell by her hesitation that she changed her mind.

I never expected her to say what she did.

"I think you should ask your dad to help with all this, Rach," she said, staring at the dashboard, one hand stuffed in her pocket, the other tugging up the hood on her jacket. "This is more than the two of us can handle. I mean, honestly, you might have killed that blue-haired witch earlier tonight. Not that she didn't kinda deserve it, but do you really want to spend the rest of your teenage years behind bars? I don't think so." She paused, glancing at me, red curls tumbling out from her hoodie, pale blue eyes searching mine, maybe hoping I'd agree with her. "Your dad's got lots of military contacts. Does he still hang with that group of ex-vets he toured with in the Middle East?"

"I don't know."

"This doesn't mean I'm giving up," she continued hurriedly. "I'll do whatever I can, but you need to remember your dad spent about half his life as a Navy SEAL, saving the world from terrorists. I have a feeling he'd like to catch whoever kidnapped you." She shuffled in her seat, shifting her book bag from her lap to her shoulder. "Anyway, I'll see you tomorrow, right?"

A door opened in her townhouse, a rectangle of blurry, yellow light. Her mom was waiting.

"Are we still friends?" I asked, before she climbed out. Somehow this was the most important question of all, more than who kidnapped me or who these other girls were.

"We're not friends, girl. We're *best* friends," she said with a half-grin. "Always and forever. Like you had to ask."

And then she was gone, the one person I could talk to about all of this. She walked inside her front door, and turned back to smile and wave, feigning a lightness neither one of us felt. Then her front door closed, the light shut off, and I stared into the darkness, my pulse slamming against the back of my skull.

I glanced down at that tattoo on my wrist, ran my fingers over the words "ALWAYS AND FOREVER." Until now, I'd forgotten that Molly and I used to say that to each other. It had been our little code, our way to prove we would be there for each other, no matter what. Sometime in the past year, I'd told her to get lost and, after that, I'd had these words engraved on my wrist. Maybe I regretted what I'd done, or maybe I'd been trying to remind myself who my real friends were.

I had a feeling it was a little bit of both.

CHAPTER EIGHTEEN

I narrowly missed Dad's SUV as I pulled into the garage, my hands shaking, my head throbbing. It felt like tiny fissures were blossoming beneath my fingers as I rubbed my neck, like my skull had suffered an 8.0 earthquake during the evening and now bits of bone were cracking open. The headache had started sometime between Janie falling to the ground and Nicole getting beaten to death.

All I wanted to do was take some Tylenol and go to bed.

Getting out of my car, I grabbed that bag Mrs. Hernandez had given me and a photo of Nicole tumbled out. I hadn't seen this one—it hadn't been on the mantle or on one of the living room tables. Nicole stood in a group of girls, all with their arms around each other, all grinning like they were at a party. They were wearing white tank tops with the words "Pink Candi" written in glitter. For the first time I noticed thick streaks of pink hair in Nicole's brown-black tresses and that all the other girls had similar stripes of color in their hair.

They looked like some sort of athletic team.

The more I looked at their shirts, the more they reminded me of the handful of tank tops I'd found tucked away inside that purple box in my closet. I hunted through my pockets until I found that note I'd written, folded and refolded so many times the creases had darkened and the edges were starting to rip. I'd shown it to Agent Bennet, to Lauren, and finally to Molly...

Peace. Love. Unity. Respect. LOL. And then party like there's no tomorrow.

Had I been at the same party as Nicole?

I stared down at that photo again, turning on the light inside my car to see better. There was a flash of blue behind Nicole, someone moving so fast their features were blurred, but it was pretty clear that whoever it was had blue hair. Could it have been Janie Deluca, the blue-haired girl I'd left lying in the street, blood seeping from her lip? And on the right side of the photo stood another girl, her body cropped so you couldn't see her face.

A purple dragon tattoo snaked up her arm.

I pushed my door open, sending a cold flood of air rushing in, icy fingertips that moved over me, running up my legs, over my hips, across my back, and finally thudding to a halt at the base of my skull. I grabbed the steering wheel and closed my eyes.

Nicole knew Janie and at least one of those Dragon Tattoo Girls from school.

A rich, coppery taste like blood filled my mouth as I thought about how I'd wanted to fight those Dragon Girls earlier today, and how I'd baited Janie by kicking her bat away. I'd wanted to kick in teeth, to break noses, to flip someone onto her stomach, and knock the wind from her chest...and now the air in my own chest was coming in halting, slow gulps.

No matter what I did, it somehow wasn't enough, it was *never* enough—none of it would bring Nicole back. My feelings for her were different from how I felt about Janie and the Dragon Girls. I wanted to lock elbows with Nicole and take down the mangy crowd behind and beside her. I wanted to protect her, even though I knew it was too late.

I held that photo in my hand and all I could see was the triumphant look in Nicole's eyes, like she was staring right at me. I was at that party, I was certain of it.

Because I was the one who took the photo.

Light poured into the garage. Someone was walking toward me, concern in his voice. I didn't notice him or hear him until he was beside me.

"Are you all right?" Dad was asking, his hand on my arm, helping me out of the car and leading me toward the house. "Where have you *been*? Your mother was worried and she waited for you to come home as long as she could. She finally went in to work a few minutes ago, although she should have been there hours earlier—"

I wanted to talk, but all I could do was stare at that picture in my hand, realizing that this girl had been a friend of mine. A friend who was now dead. I could almost hear myself saying things like, *bigger smiles, come on now, you won, let's celebrate!*

I was at that party. I took the photo.

Dad's irritation and anger melted when we started to walk up the two steps that led into the house and I couldn't walk any farther. A soft moan came from my lips and my knees buckled. My head hurt like someone had kicked me, and I ran my hand over the back of my neck, expecting my fingers to come away red and sticky.

"Rachel!"

Then he was catching me in his arms and carrying me

into the house, so swift it seemed like it had been planned, like it was part of a choreographed dance that we had been practicing for weeks. I would start remembering things, Agent Bennet said. Strangers' faces would look familiar, but it would all be too much for me to bear, shadows too dark.

I rested my head on Dad's shoulder.

The hallway lined with our family photos reminded me of the pictures on Nicole's mantle. The single light that glowed in the kitchen reminded me of that porch light that would stay on forever, calling a dead girl to come home. The living room wrapped in warm shadows reminded me of Nicole's mother, sitting all alone as she stared into the fireplace.

Meanwhile, our living room sofa loomed closer and closer. Someone was covering me with a blanket, and someone else was placing a cool cloth on my brow.

Was I hot? Was that why I had this horrid headache?

"You should have come home hours ago, Rachel," Dad chided me while he slid a thermometer between my lips. A long moment passed, then, "You've got a fever. What were you doing out there? It's almost nine o'clock and you're soaking wet. Kyle, run upstairs and get your sister some dry clothes, something comfortable."

I waved my hand, trying to push the covers off. "Where's Mom?" I asked. She was the one who was supposed to take care of me when I was sick.

"She's at work. Have you eaten anything today? You haven't been eating lately, not since you came back—"

"Cookies, I think." But I realized I'd forgotten to eat lunch, and now I had missed dinner, too.

"Here, put these on. Take it slow." Dad handed me some dry clothes, then he and Kyle went into the kitchen where they whispered about me, all their words slurring together. I took off my wet jeans and tugged on a pair of sweatpants. Shivering, I removed my jacket and shirt, then pulled a long-sleeved flannel top over my head. For an instant I saw my reflection in a mirror that hung on the wall across the room, but it didn't look like me. This was a strange, imposter me, a girl with dark circles beneath her eyes and short, dark brown hair that exposed her ears and her neck and her jaw.

"Who am I?" I whispered, thinking about that uncontrollable blood lust that would come over me when I least expected it, that desire to beat my fist against people I barely knew. And the way I had casually ordered Lauren around earlier today, how she had acted like it was completely natural.

The way Janie had fallen into the street when I slammed my car door open, how I had kicked her like I was a lethal weapon.

I moaned again. My hands were on my knees, my feet were bare and cold, and my head was down. It felt like I'd never be able to raise it up again.

Dad put his hand on my shoulder, Kyle sat beside me. One of them handed me a cup of hot soup and pressed it against my lips until I took one swallow and then another, warmth flooding my throat, my stomach. I looked up at Dad and pushed the cup away.

"I think I almost killed someone tonight," I whispered.

He nodded. Kyle sat really still, like he was afraid to move.

"Who?" Dad asked, kneeling before me.

With halting words, my voice never rising above a whisper—like I sat in a confessional and didn't want my words to carry—I told him everything. Janie's name, where she lived, what had happened, how she came at me with a gun when all I'd wanted was answers.

"I didn't want to hurt her," I said. "Not at first. But then, when I did, when she was on the ground—"

Kyle's eyes were big and his mouth hung open, and he didn't move for a really long time, like he was afraid I'd notice him there.

"When she was on the ground, I was glad."

Dad nodded again. He didn't write down her address or name. He didn't need to. He could remember things like that easily, like he had a whiteboard in his head and was secretly writing down everything with colored markers and arrows and exclamation points. "Don't worry," he said, a calm authority in his voice that chased away the chill that had crept into my bones. "I'll take care of it."

I glanced at Kyle from the corner of my eye and he was staring at Dad, with that same shell-shocked expression he'd had while I was talking. He didn't move. I couldn't even tell if he was breathing. My nightmarish past was taking over our house. It was going to swallow us whole.

"I'm sorry," I said to my brother.

His eyes met mine and for the first time I realized he wasn't afraid of me. Now that he'd recovered from his shock, his muscles were flexing and his jaw clenched, and his hands rolled into tight fists. "She's lucky I wasn't there with you," he said, his words hot. "I'd have grabbed that bat from her the minute she walked out the door."

I gave him a weak smile, looking at those eyes that sometimes reminded me of Mom and sometimes of Dad, but most of the time they just reminded me of all the years we had been together, him laughing and joking and playing pranks because that's what little brothers were supposed to do. Him hiding in my closet and listening while Molly and

I talked about boys, him drawing big smiley faces on my Barbies with black marker, him taking the last handful of cookies, even though I hadn't had any yet.

Him saving his allowance for half a year to buy me new Barbies on my birthday, to make up for the ones he had wrecked.

"There's more," I told them as I held out that photo, still clenched in my fist. I told them about Nicole, how I knew she'd been a friend of mine, and that she was dead now.

Dad stood and began to pace back and forth while I talked. He was quiet for a long time, gears shifting inside his head, the muscles tightening across his cheekbones, his eyes taking on a glassy, faraway look.

"As much as I hated the idea at first, I think Agent Bennet was right to follow you today," Dad said. "I know he wants you to start wearing a tracking device. He and I had a long talk about it when you were in school and we both agree—you need to wear it. I should also let you know I've activated a GPS chip in your phone. You need to keep it with you *all* the time. If there's ever a problem, you can just send me a text. Okay?"

I nodded. "Yes."

"I think you should take some Tylenol and go to bed," he said to me. Then he glanced at Kyle to make sure he was listening. "And I don't want either one of you to say anything about what happened tonight to anyone else— *especially* not your mother. She wouldn't be able to handle it if she found out one of Rachel's friends was dead." He gave me a thin smile. "Your mother deals with death and pain on a daily basis at work, but that never translates into how she reacts when something happens to one of you."

He looked down at his hands folded in his lap, his words ripping me apart because I knew he wasn't just talking about Mom. He was the same way, except he didn't get weak when one of us was hurt—he got tougher. That SEAL inside him came to the surface, his face turned impassive, and he went into some sort of autopilot mode. It had happened when I was in the hospital for two days, when the therapists and doctors were running tests on me, and I wanted to come home and Mom's eyes filled with tears every time they let her in to see me.

Dad had made two phone calls—I saw him through the window in my room. The blood vessels in his temples stood at attention, his eyes narrowed, and his lips barely moved, like the words he had to say were so threatening they could melt his cell phone. After the second call, he switched off his phone, slid it into his pocket, and not even ten minutes passed before a doctor hurried into my room, scribbled something on my chart, then stopped to talk to a nurse at the nearest station. If I hadn't been watching, I'd have missed the way the doctor gave my dad a quick nod when they passed each other in the hall, both of them with no expression on their faces, like two spies signaling each other in a foreign country.

When my father said *jump*, the other guy said, *how high*.

I was released from the hospital within half an hour. Not even Mom realized that Dad had somehow orchestrated it.

Sometimes I thought Kyle and I were the only people in the world stupid enough to disobey him. Maybe we were the only ones—besides Mom—who knew that he would still love us. Even if we messed up.

Chapter Nineteen

I wanted to go to sleep, but ever since I came back, nights have been the hardest time for me. The house would shut down, from basement to attic, everyone tucked in their beds and sleeping. Outside my window, all of Santa Madre softened until it became muted and still, like a painting. The only thing I could hear was the distant whoosh of cars speeding down the 210, a river of wind that never stopped flowing.

I used to fall asleep with my earbuds in, listening to music.

I couldn't do that anymore. I didn't dare.

I needed to stay alert. It was part of my new survival plan.

I stumbled upstairs, two tablets of Tylenol in my system, my fever starting to fade, that headache softening — although it was hard to say whether eating had taken it away, or whether it had been the drugs. Mom had called and it had taken a long time for me and Dad to convince her I was all right and she didn't need to come home. But

Dad, Kyle and I all agreed she didn't need to know that I might have seriously injured another girl tonight.

I wasn't sure how Dad was going to 'take care of it,' but Molly had been right. He was the right person to turn to during an emergency. Between him, with his quiet strength, and Mom being a nurse, I'd grown up completely sheltered from the world.

Until that day, sometime last year, when I'd stepped out of my safe, little bubble.

One of my arms now wrapped around a toy rabbit Dad bought me when I was ten, the pink fur stained and discolored, the stuffing flattened. I'd hunted through my closet for half an hour before I found it, cursing softly, worrying that the "new me" had decided she didn't need stuffed animals anymore. I almost burst into tears when my left hand touched soft, plushy fur behind a stack of shoeboxes. Then I sat on the floor, rocking quietly back and forth, clutching the bunny and hoping that no one would walk into my room.

Almost as if I'd summoned it, my phone buzzed beside me. That thing still gave me the creeps. Every time I touched it, I remembered that flashback and how I had tried and failed to call 9-1-1 when I went missing.

I swallowed hard, took a deep breath, then glanced down at the screen. I had a text from Dylan. I grinned and ran a quick hand through my hair, glad he couldn't see me sitting on the floor hugging an old, stuffed rabbit.

Hey. Can't sleep, he said.

Me either, I thumbed back.

Wanna see something funny?

Sure.

He sent a photo of him and me trying to ride a skateboard together, both of us laughing, me about to fall off. It made me crack up.

Where was this? I asked.

Skate Park @ The Block.

My hands were on his waist and he was looking back at me. That grin of his made me wish he was here. It didn't matter if my hair was messed up or I had on sweatpants. He never cared about stuff like that.

I sat up straight, my eyes widening, the phone almost slipping out of my hand.

I'd just had a flash about what Dylan was like, what he was *really* like. Not all the surface stuff, like how cute he was or how his eyes could almost hypnotize you. This was the Dylan inside. Somewhere between the poet and the wrestler was a guy who knew how to make me laugh and what to do if I was crying.

Do you remember this? he asked about the photo.

No. Wish I did. Looks like fun.

It's OK. We can go again. Just don't knock me off the board like last time.

I didn't knock you off!

JK. You fell off, he said.

Liar!

LOL. Sure you don't remember?

I paused for a long moment, then typed in, *I remember you.*

He didn't say anything for a beat, long enough for me to worry that I'd said the wrong thing.

I missed you, he wrote.

That one comment gave me a feeling like sunshine bursting from my chest.

Hi, I'm Rachel. It's nice to meet you.

Same. Except U know, name's Dylan.

Then my screen filled with about a thousand emojis, laughing, dancing, happy, exactly how I felt.

...

That night, I dreamt about my dad.

He was talking to someone, making plans. We walked along the Santa Monica Pier, somewhere between the Ferris wheel and the roller coaster, the sunset turning the waves orange. I was ten or eleven and clutched a large, pink, stuffed rabbit under one arm, a prize he had won for me earlier in the day. Mom was at work and Kyle was at Magic Mountain with his friends, so this was one of those rare times when Daddy and I went someplace alone together. We'd eaten lunch at the Harbor Grill, strolled along the beach, fed breadcrumbs to seagulls, and took our shoes off to let the Pacific Ocean lick our toes. After that we played games and rode carnival rides, until Daddy glanced at his watch with a determined look on his face.

He took my hand and together we headed toward that part of the pier where people stared down into the water, fishing poles draped over the edge. We approached a man with a scruffy beard and furtive eyes, his hair hidden beneath a Dodgers cap, his clothes rumpled and ill-fitting, as if these weren't really his clothes but someone else's. Something about him frightened me and I pulled at Daddy's hand, trying to convince him to go in a different direction.

"It's all right. Don't worry, baby girl," he said to me, his dark eyes smiling and confident. "You're safe with me, right?"

"Yes," I answered. Although I wasn't sure if *he* was going to be safe with that strange man.

We moved forward, one step at a time, Daddy nodding at the stranger as we approached. It was one of his barely there nods, the ones he gave people I didn't know, and it was so subtle I was never sure whether it had happened or not. The smell of fish turned my stomach. My fingers sweated inside Daddy's hand and I glanced over my shoulder at the carnival lights, wishing I was back there, on the wave jumper or the scrambler. Anywhere but here.

The other man looked down and gave me a smile, the only time he acknowledged I was there. Then he and Daddy stood side by side, talking about fishing and had he caught anything, and what kind of fish swam around here. But in between those casual comments that anyone could make, even one stranger to another, they said other things, their voices lowered, talking in a language I'd never heard before. Daddy nodded from time to time, as if memorizing what he heard, writing things down on that white board in his head, getting all the facts in their proper places.

They said one phrase three times, until I memorized it myself, even though I'd never spoken that language before.

Later, when he was tucking me in bed, Mom still at work, Kyle spending the night at a friend's house, I repeated those words back to him. I thought he'd be surprised or maybe glad that I'd been able to remember something that made no sense. He just smiled, nodded, and said, "You have a gift for foreign languages, baby girl."

"I won't tell anyone else," I promised him.

"I know."

We didn't talk it about it again. I knew that his meeting had been secret and even the words I'd learned were potentially dangerous. His missions were classified and top secret, but they were usually done in Middle Eastern countries, not on the Santa Monica Pier.

I wrote the phrase down, phonetically of course, and spent days trying to translate it. It was Czechoslovak and it said *Příští týden v Tel Avivu.*

Next week in Tel Aviv.

Daddy left on a mission two days after that meeting. I watched the news every day when he was gone, trying to figure out what his mission might be, but nothing happened. There were no bombings, no terrorist attacks, no kidnappings. It was a surprisingly calm week for that part of Israel.

That was when I figured out what my father really did.

He stopped bad things *before* they happened.

Chapter Twenty

Morning came like fire, too bright when it poured in my window, beams tracing lines across the carpet, reaching out as if looking for me. I blinked my eyes open and for a minute all was right. I was me. Rachel Evans. Sophomore at Lincoln High. Sure to fail Miss Wallace's geometry test, but also sure to hang with my best friend Molly McFadden at lunch, and then sure to watch an episode of *Vampire Diaries* when I got home. I smiled. I even sat up, stretching, ready to do some jazz splits and lunges before heading down to breakfast.

That was when I remembered what had happened yesterday, how Molly and I had gone looking for those girls on my list, how I just about killed one of them and then found out another one was dead. Talking to Dylan last night almost made it feel better. Almost.

Knowing I had a date with Dylan tonight should have taken away the sour feeling coiled in my gut, but it didn't. I stumbled to the bathroom where I weighed myself. One hundred and nineteen pounds. I took a few deep breaths, trying to calm myself. I needed to keep my weight down, that was the only way I'd fit in, I couldn't get over one hundred and twenty-five, *ever*—

Those were the thoughts that kept going through my mind, although every time one of them would appear, I'd try to shove it aside. I wasn't bulimic or anorexic. Still the memory of that headache and fever returned and I vowed that I would eat every meal from now on, or at least part of every meal. I wasn't sure my stomach could handle too much food yet.

Dad and Kyle watched me quietly when I walked into the kitchen and loaded my plate with scrambled egg whites and turkey bacon. Mom, who knew nothing and it needed to stay that way, just grinned and patted my hand when I sat beside her.

"Is your fever gone?" she asked, a cup of coffee poised at the edge of her lips. She wasn't going to take a drink until she knew I was okay.

"Yeah. It went away last night, before I went to bed."

"Good. You sure you feel okay to go to school?"

"Yes," I answered quickly, fighting the panicked sensation that my chest was filling with ice, my throat tightening. I couldn't stay home today, I just couldn't. I glanced up at Dad, hoping to get some support but he stood with his back to me, scrubbing out the pan. Kyle watched me as if trying to learn my methods of manipulation. "I have a test in physics," I said, which was true but not why I needed to be there. I needed to see Dylan. He hadn't answered my text this morning and I had to make sure we were still on for our date. I didn't even know the details of where we were going or when.

I might be going to a rave tonight.

My fork slipped from my fingers and clattered to the table.

"And I—um—I sort of, you know, have a date tonight," I told them, not looking up, not wanting to see the expressions on their faces while they talked to each other without words. Mom would be raising her eyebrows, Dad would be tightening his lips, one of them would be thinking, *no way* and the other, *well, maybe*. But in the end, they always came to some sort of silent agreement. They argued about other things—where to take vacations, what cars to buy, what movies to rent—but they never argued about Kyle or me. At least not in front of us.

"Have we met this boy?" Dad asked.

The fact that he was asking a question was better than hearing *no*. "I don't know. I've been dating him for a while, but I don't remember if he's been here or not."

"He needs to come inside for a few minutes," Mom said. "We have to talk to him."

I swallowed nervously, but nodded. "Sure."

"Be home by midnight."

"Eleven thirty is better."

I frowned. Seriously? Eleven thirty? I wanted to argue, but I knew this wasn't the time or place. Maybe they'd let me stay out later next time. Or maybe—

I glanced at Kyle, who was trying to keep a low profile. He'd said that I used to sneak out in the middle of the night to get high and drunk. So, obviously there was a way to get back out if I wanted. Maybe he knew how I used to do it.

"Okay," I said, forcing a smile. "I won't stay out late."

The rest of the day was a blur. One class flowed into another, faces passed me in the hallway, assignments were given and forgotten almost immediately. Only a few things stood out: Molly meeting me at my locker in the morning, giving me a hug, and then blending in with the crowd, like she didn't want to blow my cover; Dylan not being in first period, which might have meant that he was sick and we weren't going on a date after all; Sammy, that head Dragon Girl with the grillwork, trying to get a reaction out of me by 'accidentally' slamming into me on the way out of class and knocking my books out of my hand.

Yesterday I would have flattened her, we both would have gotten suspended, and I'd have gotten grounded. But it wasn't the threat of suspension or being grounded that stopped me. It was the memory of Janie sprawled in the street, me standing over her, alien emotions warring inside me.

I'd been tempted to kill her.

If that was the new me, I hated her. I wasn't going to let her rule my life.

"Watch it!" I'd said to Sammy, elbowing her out of my way.

She'd glared at me, defiant, chin thrust out, disappointment in her eyes because I didn't hit her. She'd been expecting a fight. I could feel her girls watching us from the other side of the room, and when I turned to look at them, their gazes shifted from Sammy to me and back again.

I wasn't sure how or why, but it was obvious that she'd just lost their respect.

Dylan still hadn't shown up by lunch and, despite all my earlier promises to myself, I wasn't able to eat. I toyed with the pizza on my plate, stabbing it with a fork, moving it around, cutting off a bite but not lifting it to my mouth. Lauren sat beside me, chattering away, asking me if I liked her skirt, her shoes, her new Burberry purse, her eyes glittering as she sought my approval, her laugh nervous and high-pitched. Molly watched me from the edge of the crowd, a thin smile given whenever I glanced in her direction, as if our friendship was supposed to remain secret. Everyone who sat at my lunch table was acting different today, almost as if they were all taking drugs, something that amplified their personalities about a thousand times. The girls laughed, the boys pushed and argued with each other; they all slugged down cans of Red Bull and Coke and ate foods high in sugar and carbs. They seemed excited about something, something they didn't talk about but it thrummed beneath every look and every word.

It seemed as if they all had something amazing going on later.

I thought I did, too, but since Dylan wasn't here and I hadn't heard from him, it looked like I was just going to be staying home. Playing video games with Kyle and his friends. Or worse, watching some RomCom flick with my parents.

"Why so blue?" Lauren finally asked when she'd run out of ways to try to impress me, after she'd bought me a chocolate milk—because I always got one at lunch, every day except today—and after she'd tried to get me to wear her earrings, the brand-new platinum diamond studs that she got for her birthday.

I shrugged. I didn't feel like talking about it.

"It isn't Dylan, is it?"

I winced. Was it that obvious?

She grinned. "You don't think he's going to stand you up tonight, do you?"

"He must be sick today," I said, wishing she would shut

up. The other girls at the table were starting to look at us and the last thing I needed was for my Big Date Fail to become the topic of school gossip.

"If he asked you out, he *totally* meant it," Lauren continued. "Brett's having a party tonight—his parents are in Aspen for the weekend—and he's Dylan's best friend, so that's probably why he's not here."

I frowned. She wasn't making any sense. I picked up my tray and stood up, ready to leave the cafeteria. There had to be someplace better than this to spend the rest of my lunch hour, someplace where a pack of girls weren't watching my every move. Lauren grabbed my wrist and started talking even faster.

"He's gotta be setting up the music for the party. He always does that. We pitch in and pay for it, even though he'd do it for free. But it's like a part-time job. You knew that, didn't you?"

"Maybe I knew it. Before."

She grabbed my phone and started thumbing something, her fingers moving fast.

"What're you doing?"

"I'm sending him a text—"

"You're *what*?"

"No worries, girl. He just needs to know you're concerned."

"I already texted him this morning and he didn't answer," I said as I grabbed the phone away from her. "I don't want him to think I'm one of *those* girls." I fumbled for words. "You know, the kind who are insecure and weird and sit around, waiting for some boy to call."

She gave me a look somewhere between pure innocence and admiration. And yeah, she was kind of giving me the creeps. Like this was some new form of idol worship, but I'd never done anything to deserve it. All I'd done was treat her like crap for ten minutes yesterday and ever since then, she'd been trying to make herself invaluable.

"He'd never think you were like that. Not in a million years. Not ever." She leaned closer so none of the guys would hear. "But if he did, there are a *lot* of other guys out there who are dying to get with you."

I was beginning to wonder if Lauren was really stupid, if maybe she'd been fooling all of us for years. I was trying to figure out how she got straight As, since her reasoning abilities had been seriously impaired, when my phone buzzed.

I had a text.

My upper lip prickled and the back of my neck turned hot.

"Might want to read that," Lauren said, a grin spreading across her too pretty face.

I stood up and walked away from the others, my right hand holding my cell phone. Back turned, I glanced down at the tiny screen, at the backlit letters that appeared.

We're still on for tonight, aren't we?

It was from Dylan and it had that same slightly panicked tone as when he first asked me out, when I had paused and fear had flickered in his eyes as if I might say no.

Of course, I thumbed back, pretending like there had never been any doubt, although until now, doubt was all I had.

Pick you up at seven?

Sure. But, be prepared to come in and say hi to my parents.

There was a long silence, maybe him whispering, *shit,* and looking for a way to back out. But my parents had made it crystal clear this morning—if I was going out, they were meeting the boy. End of my teenage dating story.

Can't wait. Should I bring white or red wine?

I laughed, then replied. *Both?*

K. C U. Gotta go.

I flipped my phone off. When I glanced back at the table, all the girls—Lauren, Stephanie and Zoe—were staring at me, as if something really important had just happened. I lifted my hands, palms up. "What?" I asked.

Lauren grinned. "Told you," she said. Then she and the other girls got into a long discussion about what to wear to Brett's party, all of them making tentative suggestions from time to time about what I should wear, too. Even though, as far as I was concerned, it wasn't certain that I was even going to the party.

"That black and white T-shirt with the sequins and glitter," Zoe said.

"Your jean jacket. Definitely." Stephanie nodded, flipping her long, glossy brown hair over her shoulder.

"Black leggings and a miniskirt," Lauren added.

"And those silver ballet slippers—"

Everything they were talking about sounded like stuff to wear to a rave, not a party. I just quietly nodded, wondering about the jacket and planning my own outfit while they continued to chatter away like a flock of birds fighting over breadcrumbs.

CHAPTER TWENTY-ONE

My mouth dry, I paced back and forth, rummaging through my closet and throwing clothes on the bed. Seven o'clock drew nearer and nearer. I'd already weighed myself three times—one hundred and twenty-one pounds. Crap, somehow I'd gained two pounds today! Dad had watched me while I ate dinner like he was my commanding officer and I was a lowly private, so I didn't have a choice. I *had* to eat.

Once dinner was finished and the family room had filled with a handful of Kyle's video game buddies, I'd gone upstairs to get ready for my date. So far, I'd changed my clothes four times, buttoning and unbuttoning shirts, zipping and unzipping skirts and jeans until a pile of clothes spread across my bed. Shoes littered the floor and my room looked like a messy Goth boutique. The only thing I had on was a pair of black leggings and my makeup. Unfortunately, the leggings were the only thing I was certain about. I tugged a white minidress over my head, something Mom had bought me this week. It was really cute, but was it right for riding a motorcycle? Everything needed to be perfect, although my version of perfect seemed to change depending on my memories.

Blood shows on white, a voice whispered in my head.

I didn't question it, didn't even wonder why I'd had that random thought. The dress came off in a flash.

Find something black, the voice said and I obeyed.

That black miniskirt, the one the girls had suggested, slipped on, suddenly looking like it was made for tonight. I'd be able to ride Dylan's motorcycle, I'd be able to dance, I'd look hot...

And I'd be able to kick.

I practiced in front of the mirror, my right leg swinging up, high over my head, the skirt shifting and stretching while the leggings kept everything covered. If I hadn't needed a shirt, I would have been ready to go.

Just then a knock sounded on the front door and I started to hyperventilate. Voices came from the foyer downstairs, Dad's baritone blending with another deep voice, one that I'd recognize anywhere.

Dylan was here.

Crap and double crap.

I didn't have time for this dressing game, I wanted—no, I *needed*—to get downstairs before my parents sabotaged my date with their hundred and one questions. I threw on a shirt and jacket, fixed my hair, touched up my makeup, not even realizing that I'd chosen the exact same outfit the girls at school had suggested. I jogged down the stairs and almost ran into Dylan when I rounded the corner from the hallway. Kyle and two of his friends slouched on the family room sectional, faces aimed at the big-screen TV where they played Halo 4, my little brother simultaneously carrying on a convo with Dylan, who was giving Kyle tips.

Dylan stood behind my brother, while Dad and Mom were in the kitchen cleaning up the dinner dishes. Apparently Dylan had survived their interrogation. Unless Kyle had secretly been put in charge.

"Hey," Dylan said when I slammed to a halt, two inches away from him. "You look really nice."

I wanted to say the same thing; every inch of him looked better than it ever had when we were in school. His dark hair hung in choppy layers, some of it shading his forehead, his pale gray eyes making time stand still when he gazed at me. He wore a black leather jacket, a ripped black shirt, and jeans with a long, studded belt that coiled twice around his hips. Black shadow rimmed his eyes, almost making him look like a rock star.

And a bruise colored his cheekbone.

It wasn't a black eye, not yet. But it probably would be by tomorrow. Somehow it made him look even hotter.

"What happened?" I asked as we moved away from the sofa.

"Wrestling practice last night. Hudson gave me an elbow in the eye."

"Ouch."

"Ask him what the other guy looks like," Kyle said, glancing back at us and missing a score.

Dylan gave me a half-shrug, and looked away as if he didn't want to brag. But apparently Kyle had already heard the story—this was what guys did, they shared gruesome tales and laughed, while the girls listening usually winced.

Kyle drew a line across his forehead. "Sixteen stitches."

"Really," I said. My blood flowed hot through my veins and I was a little surprised what a turn-on it was to hear that my boyfriend had sent someone to the ER. His eyes met mine and he studied my expression carefully, silently.

"He's fine," he told me a moment later, and I knew that this had been part of the original story. My little brother just didn't think it was the important part. "This kind of stuff happens all the time."

"Yeah," I said, not completely convinced. "Boys will be boys, right?"

He grinned and we headed toward the front door. Away from my family and my home and everything familiar, out into the night where darkness waited.

His Harley was parked at the curb, in a pocket of shadow, blocked from the streetlight and behind one of the flowering trees Dad had planted earlier this year. Dylan started to hand me a helmet, but stopped, as if there was something else more important.

"There's something I have to do," he said.

I thought maybe he needed to give me a few pointers on how to ride a motorcycle, that I should lean into the curves, that I should hold on to him, that I shouldn't be afraid because he was a great driver.

I was wrong.

He slipped one arm around my waist and pulled me close, so close that I couldn't have gotten away if I wanted to, while his other hand cupped my jaw, thumb just below my mouth, long fingers brushing against my ear. "I've wanted to do this since you got back," he said, his voice a low, hoarse whisper.

I wanted to say, *me, too*, but I didn't get a chance.

His lips found mine in the darkness where we could barely see each other, where the heat of his body melted into mine. There were two short, gentle kisses as if he didn't believe I would be here very long, that I might disappear at any moment, and then after that came the third kiss—

The third kiss stole my heart.

And my soul.

I didn't remember our first date or what we had in common or who was his favorite band, but I remembered this. I remembered a thousand kisses, a hundred nights, a million stars glittering overhead. We leaned into each other, as if we were each drawing an electric charge from the other, as if we'd been unplugged and powerless but now we were stronger, invincible, immortal. The world stopped spinning and we were all that existed; there were no other people, no cities, no countries; there was only this.

His lips pressed against mine, his scent filling the air, his hands touching me.

And then at last, the kiss ended and we stared into each other's eyes, me remembering, him knowing, both of us breathless.

"I almost lost you," he said, his words soft as if he couldn't say them very loud because it would show how strong the emotion was.

"I'm here, I'm safe."

He shook his head. "I'm not going to let anything happen to you," he said. "I haven't always been"—he hesitated—"a very good person. But I'm going to do everything I can to make sure no one ever hurts you again."

He had a way of enchanting me with his words, maybe it was the poet in him, maybe this was easy for him, but it didn't matter. I knew he was telling the truth.

I just didn't know if I wanted to be safe.

...

We drove around for a few hours, going places we used to hang out together, and at first I was a little disappointed since I'd expected something almost violently exciting. But when we ended up on a turnout in the San Gabriel Mountains, staring down at L.A., all lit up, streams of traffic glittering like strands of rubies, his hand found mine and I finally remembered—how he had first asked me out and we had gone to a skateboarding park, how we had sat for hours in a local Starbucks, drinking lattes and talking, just talking about everything.

Neither one of us were the dark creatures we were now. Back then we were just two awkward sixteen-year-old kids, me a wannabe ballet dancer, him a poet/wrestler that no one seemed to understand. We both had rough edges hidden beneath our sweet and innocent veneers. We had gone Goth together. We'd lost our virginity together.

And there were other things, secret things that I still couldn't remember, that we had done together, too. They followed us like revenants wearing ghostly shrouds, huddling together amidst the trees and the rocks, just far enough away that I couldn't see them clearly.

Whatever the secrets were, he didn't want to talk about them. From time to time, I'd see a flicker of guilt in his eyes, like he thought he was to blame for every bad thing that had ever happened.

And then finally, when it was about nine thirty and I only had two hours left before I turned into a suburban pumpkin, I asked about the party.

"I heard Brett's parents are out of town," I said. We sat side by side, feet hanging over the edge of the mountain.

Nothing below us but five thousand feet of yawning black canyon.

He didn't say anything.

"Lauren said he's having a party tonight."

"Yeah."

A long pause followed before I asked, "Did you want to go?"

He picked up a rock, cupped it in his hand, then tossed it out into the unfathomable darkness. There was no sound. It was almost as if the rock had never existed. I imagined it tumbling through space, falling ever downward, never stopping, always sailing through a dark universe.

"If you want," he said, although it sounded more like a question than a statement.

"Everyone we know is supposed to be there."

"Sure. Let's go. Come on."

He stood and took me by the hand, lifting me up, a move that felt almost like part of a dance. His hands were around my waist and he pulled me close for another long, amazingly beautiful kiss. Then we climbed on his bike, helmets on, my arms around his waist, my head on his shoulder.

And we flew down the mountain, two birds with wings spread wide.

CHAPTER TWENTY-TWO

Wind rushed past, a tunnel of cold air that pushed me closer to Dylan, his warmth flowing through me like a sigh. Mountain roads gave way to city streets, which then changed into five-lane freeways, lights flickering around us as we headed back toward Santa Madre. We followed a familiar road that led us through the historic district and then up into the hills. Here, the houses cost ten times as much as the ones in the valley, every curve in the road revealing views that made my part of town look cheap.

I wondered if I had been up here before, if there had been other parties. I still felt like an outsider with this crowd and wished that Molly and all the other kids I hung around with last year would be here.

But I'd given them all up. They didn't fit in with these people any more than I did.

Brett's house appeared when we rounded a corner. Not that I recognized it. I knew because the motorcycle slowed down, growling in a deeper pitch as we headed toward the curved driveway. Jammed with cars, it would have been hard to park if we hadn't been on a bike. As it was, Dylan slipped easily into a spot between a Jaguar and a Kia Soul.

Loud music thumped from the open front door. A balcony stretched out over a ravine and people were out there dancing, talking, drinking, all of them poised over a hungry cliff.

Dylan took my helmet and hung it from the handlebars, next to his.

"You sure you want to go inside?" he asked, maybe responding to the look on my face.

"Yeah," I said.

He took my hand and together we ambled up the steps that led to a gorgeous, split-level home, part glass, part concrete, part stone. Even from the outside, I could see the floor-to-ceiling canvases that decorated the living room, the brightly colored splashes of color a stark contrast to the gray and taupe furniture. Every inch of this house was exquisite.

And inside, it looked like a frat party.

The dining room table had been turned into a beer pong table, with teams of girls and guys competing, taking turns tossing ping-pong balls, then downing plastic cups filled with beer. Stephanie chugged down a drink when we walked in the door, beer slipping down the sides of her mouth while the rest of the kids chanted something I couldn't understand. Girls and boys filled the living room, some dancing, some joking around, while others sat in awkward silence on sofas, looking out of place.

That's where I should have been. Sitting with the geeks who didn't really belong.

Instead, there was a welcoming cry as soon as we walked through the door. Brett shouted and came over to slap Dylan a high five and Lauren let out an excited whoop, nearly stumbling in her three-inch stilettos when she tried to get to me before anyone else. Before I knew it, we were both surrounded. We stood at the core of a widening circle with all the kids we hung out with at lunch. On the outer edges were other teens who seemed to stare at Dylan and me with admiration, as if they wished they could be part of the inner circle. Brett handed us both a beer and Dylan glanced down at me, maybe wondering if my dad would have a fit if I came home drunk.

"Just one. I promise," I said with a grin, then I took a long sip.

He smiled back hesitantly, then set his cup aside. "Not tonight. Not for me anyway."

I was surprised. I'd always imagined him to be the life of the party. He must have been holding back. Meanwhile, Lauren and the other girls hugged me and squealed, and pointed out a group of older guys who had crashed the party.

"They go to UCLA. I think the blond guy is friends with Brett's older brother. Isn't the tall one hot?" Lauren said. She flashed him a grin and licked her lips when she got his attention.

Stephanie rolled her eyes. "She's got a thing for older guys lately. Nobody from high school is good enough for her anymore."

"Did you guys see the Skittles bowl in the living room?" Zoe asked. "The college crowd just dropped a handful of Ecstasy and Forget-Me-Pills in it."

"Ecstasy? Where?" Lauren asked, turning to look back toward the living room.

Dylan overheard what we were saying and he grabbed Brett by the arm. "You said you weren't having a pharm party. Don't you remember what happened last time?"

Brett laughed, a deep, booming sound that always made you want to join in—except now. Right now it gave me the chills. "Hey, dude. Drink a beer and relax."

"I'm not gonna relax. Last time two guys ODed and ended up in the ER. I told you no more drug parties—"

"We got a new rule this time. One pill per person."

"And who's enforcing that? You?"

Brett pointed toward the cluster of outcasts, who perched nervously on the sofas that lined the room. "The Misfits. I told 'em it was the entrance fee to the gig."

Dylan shook his head, obviously mad. He picked up the beer he had refused a minute ago and slugged it down, all of it.

"That's my boy!" Brett said, clapping him on the back.

Dylan shrugged his hand off. "Remember who you're talking to. I'm *not* your boy."

Brett looked away, a sheepish expression on his face. "Sorry," he mumbled in a low voice.

"Ooooh! Way to put the captain of the football team in his place," Lauren said with a laugh. Both Dylan and Brett shot her dark looks, then the two of them wandered off, their voices raising and lowering, then raising again.

"Are they going to fight?" I asked, an unexpected shiver of fear snaking into my chest. Up until now, I'd thought the dark side of Dylan was exciting. But as he walked off with Brett, both of them evenly matched in size and strength and athletic abilities, it didn't feel right. A thick tension filled the room, mixing with cigarette smoke, the stench of spilled beer and sweat from people dancing. I started to push my way through the crowd, wanting to follow Dylan. I had some crazy idea that I could somehow give him backup—if he needed it. Not that I could take Brett down, not in a zillion years. That guy was ripped and then some. I began to wonder if he was on steroids. I'd seen how he dominated the football team, how he led our school to state finals, and knew that he had a scholarship to Notre Dame waiting for him.

But I didn't get far because Lauren and Stephanie and Zoe grabbed me by the arms, dragging me back into the living room.

"Let them go," Stephanie warned.

"Yeah, you don't wanna get between the two of them when they're mad," Zoe said, her hazel eyes wide.

"There's a lot of stuff you don't remember, Rach. Maybe you'll never remember it," Lauren said, her tone condescending. Almost like she enjoyed me being in the dark because it gave her more power. "The guys, they've got their own way of dealing with things. They're not like us."

I could still see the two of them, silhouettes out on the balcony, arms gesturing as they talked. Things must have gotten even more heated since they got outside, because Brett pushed Dylan, hands against his chest, shoving him several feet away until he collided with the guard rail. I gasped, unable to move because the girls still hung onto me. I started to twist away from them, tempted to land a few kicks and jabs of my own to break free.

"Stop it," Lauren whispered in my ear. "Dylan wouldn't like it if you went out there now. Trust me."

I didn't want to trust her, though. Not if Dylan could get hurt.

Just then, Dylan grabbed Brett and took him down, flipping him on his back and pinning him to the ground. I stood on my tiptoes, trying to see over the crowd that had formed around them, irritated that everyone had started chanting, *fight, fight, fight*, their voices raising, louder and louder.

"I won't do anything, but I *have* to make sure he's okay," I said as I wrenched my way free, hoping I hadn't hurt one of the girls in the process. One of them yelped, but I couldn't tell if it was Stephanie or Zoe. I ran then, shoving people out of my way, elbows jamming into ribs and making kids wince and cry out as I passed, my mouth open, sweat streaming down between my shoulder blades. I was ready to leap on top of Brett and kick him in the face if I had to—it didn't matter that he was my friend. Not now. Not if Dylan was in trouble—

That was all I could think about.

Dylan. Hurt.

I wasn't going to lose another person I cared about.

The crowd opened up, most of them boys, the air testosterone-charged, as if lightning flowed from one pair of biceps to another, all the guys flexing their muscles as if they were the ones fighting.

I saw the two of them then, best friends in a thickly muscled heap on the balcony floor, Dylan on top, arms and legs wrapped around Brett, pinning him down, Brett with a bloody nose and unable to break free.

"Okay," Brett muttered, each syllable coming out with difficulty, as if he really needed to breathe more than he needed to speak. "I *give*."

"You'll get rid of the drugs?" Dylan demanded, his voice loud enough to carry through the party and beyond, words echoing down toward that black canyon below, the abyss that would have loved to claim every single one of us, that would have wanted all of us to disappear. Just like I had.

"Yeah."

"You know what'll happen if you don't?" Dylan asked, his voice ominous.

"Yeah, I *said* I'd do it. Let me up, okay?"

Dylan released him slowly. All the while, I watched, astonished. I'd never thought Dylan could take Brett down. I didn't think anyone could take that guy down. But it was obvious Brett had been beaten; there was a difference in his countenance when he pulled himself up and began to move through the throng of party-goers. There was an unspoken hierarchy here. Brett had challenged it and Dylan had put him back in his place.

Dylan was the alpha.

The party temporarily took a somber turn, the dancing stopped, the music sounded muted and far away, no one drank or laughed. Brett marched like an errant schoolchild throughout the house, moving from one room to the next, gathering up three different Skittles bowls, each filled with a variety of colored prescription drugs, some with names stamped on the side. Xanax, Valium, Vicodin, Percocet, Viagra. Mixed in with familiar drugs that populated our medicine cabinets were candy-colored mysteries that could have been tabs of acid, Ecstasy, GHB, Special K or Meth. I shivered as I thought about the highs and lows that could come from mixing handfuls of that stuff.

But while Brett disposed of the drugs and Dylan watched over him with arms crossed, I noticed how kids—especially boys—from other schools stared at me. I guess I'd been pretty low-key until I forced my way through the crowd, knocking several boys to their knees, boys who were still having trouble getting up.

They were whispering to each other.

Lauren, Stephanie, and Zoe stood at my side, scowls on their faces.

The boys were saying things like—

She's the one who went missing—

I've heard about her—

She's even hotter in person—

I frowned. What was hot about a girl who'd been kidnapped? Heat gathered in my chest as I glared at the nearest boy, the one who had just let a loud whisper escape, not realizing that I would hear it.

"You think it's hot to go missing?" I asked, stepping nearer, my gaze focused on him like he was prey. Beneath my skin, the need to *do something* burned, but this guy wasn't worth it. Still, I grabbed his collar and twisted, pinching his throat.

The silence around us grew even louder. I realized that no one was watching Dylan or Brett anymore. I'd stolen the show.

It was like they were all waiting for me to do something.

I just wasn't sure what.

"Jerks," I said, dropping the guy's shirt like it was on fire. Then I joined the girls, all of us gathering on the far side of the living room. Dylan had paused, just long enough to make sure everything was okay, his pale gray eyes studying me, then flicking briefly to the guy. Dylan gave a small nod as his gaze moved through the room, focusing on each and every guy.

He was telling everyone that he had my back.

That strange, bizarre thrill flowed through me again when our eyes met, just like it had when I'd first seen him with the bruise on his cheek. It was hot and steamy, and I found myself smoldering as I watched him leave the room, continuing his hunt for drugs spread throughout the house.

Once he was out of the room, Lauren lifted her chin toward the guys who still shot admiring glances in my direction. "Didn't I tell you there were lots of boys who'd give just about anything to be with you? Take a look at your fan club, girl."

Puzzled, I swept another gaze across the room. She was right. I hadn't deterred these guys, not one bit. If anything, I'd made them more interested.

"What the heck? What's wrong with this crowd tonight?" I asked.

"All in good time, Rach, all in good time," Lauren said, again acting like she enjoyed her role as Keeper of the Secrets. "Meanwhile, since the 'overlords' are busy, what do you say us girls rev up our engines?" She gestured toward one of the sofas, chasing a small cluster of Misfits away with a grimace. The four of us sat in a row, the other girls with gleaming eyes, me a confused onlooker. She opened her Kate Spade purse, pulled out a small, black leather case, then held a finger to her lips. "Don't tell anyone I brought this, K? It's just, what're we supposed do now that the boys have taken away all the fun stuff?"

She flicked the black case open, revealing four pristine syringes filled with a pale pink liquid. She rolled up her sleeve, exposing a row of track marks, and before I could react, she plunged the first needle into her arm, her head sinking back, her eyes closing, a slow grin spreading over her face.

"That's what I'm talking about," she said when she pulled the syringe out, a deep sigh filling her lungs. "Which one of you wants a hit of Pink Lightning?"

Stephanie grabbed a syringe and pumped the needle into her flesh, looking like she did this on a regular basis. Zoe shook her head. "I had some before I left home. Still buzzing."

"How about you, Rach?" Lauren asked, a gleaming syringe rolling in her palm. "It'll put you right back in the game, where you belong."

"What is this stuff?" I asked. But we'd all been so engrossed in what we were doing that none of us noticed Dylan and Brett had returned to the living room. A shadow fell over us and I glanced up, surprised to see Dylan glaring down.

"Are you effing kidding me?" he asked, grabbing the syringe and leather box from Lauren.

"Don't tell me what to do, Poe!" she yelled, jumping to her feet and trying to get her drugs back. "Give it back—"

"Don't call me that!" he said as he handed the stuff to Brett. He leaned closer, grabbing her by the wrists and talking just loud enough for our group to hear. "You've just broken two rules and I could get you kicked out. Right now. No one would even ask any questions. You've been walking a fine line these past few weeks and I understand why, but this—" He pointed back toward the black box in Brett's hand. "This is the kind of trouble even *I* can't protect you from."

"You should leave," Brett said. "Now."

"Like your party is *so* much fun! Oh, boohoo, you're breaking my heart. Come on, girls, let's go someplace where we're wanted," she said. Stephanie and Zoe stood up hesitantly, watching me as if wondering whether they were making the right decision.

"Why do they have to go?" I asked. "Other people were taking stuff. You took her drugs. So let her stay—"

Lauren stuck her face dangerously close to Dylan's. "See, she doesn't even remember everything yet and she's already on my side. Just *wait* until she remembers. It's gonna hit the fan then." She poked him in the chest with her finger.

"You better not get her back on that shit," he said.

"Hey, both of you." I stepped between them, pushing them apart. Everyone watched me with stunned expressions, as if I'd just put my hand inside a pit bull's mouth. "Neither one of you is going to make decisions for me. I don't even know what that stuff is, but I was obviously taking something."

I rolled up my left sleeve, showing them and the world the track marks that had faded so much you could barely see them. Dylan and Lauren looked away.

"Fine," I said. "I'm no angel. None of us are. But if you guys would tell me something—anything—about what's been going on, I might be able to figure out what happened to me." I put my finger on Dylan's chest, surprised by the anger flooding my veins. "And you. Get the hell out of her face." I lowered my voice until it came out in a threatening rumble. "Nobody touches one of these girls, *ever*."

He blinked. I'd hurt him more than if I'd hit him.

"I wasn't going to hurt her. I'd never do anything like that," he said, shock and betrayal in his eyes. He took a step away from us, dropping his hold on Lauren's wrists. "I thought you knew me better than that." Bitterness crept into his voice then and I realized he could use his gift of words to cut, just as easily as he could use them to seduce. "I thought you remembered me, that tonight you had remembered who we were to each other. But I guess I was just fooling myself. The girl who knew me is gone. Forever."

CHAPTER TWENTY-THREE

The party changed then, all the colors turned gray and black, all the music downbeat and hollow. I knew that the girls and I should have left, but I couldn't. Dylan sulked away from us, joining the beer pong game in the kitchen and slugging down one beer after another. Before long, all the girls out there started flirting with him, casting an occasional nervous glance back in my direction. My mood changed, sinking lower, deeper, darker.

I'd just had my first date with Dylan—at least the only one I really remembered all the way from beginning to end—and now we'd had a huge fight.

Had we just broken up?

I watched him from the shadows, how his face lit up as he joked with everyone, how he gave a sultry grin to some blond in heels and tight jeans, how Brett joined him and they now competed on opposite teams, laughing, shouting, cheering.

It felt like my mouth was full of dust. His words turned things to gold, mine destroyed them.

"Hey, girl, enough with the sad face." Lauren took me

by the hand and pulled me to my feet. "Don't you hear the music? This is your song."

Taylor Swift was singing, something about heartbreak and getting revenge. It felt like her song poured out of my soul. Stephanie and Zoe were already dancing, arms wrapped around boys I didn't know, and I had a feeling they didn't know these guys, either. Lauren cocked her head to the side, closed her eyes and started singing the words to the song, pretending she was strumming a banjo. I couldn't help myself. I laughed.

And I joined the party.

One of the girls handed me another beer and I chugged it down, my dance turning into something more like ballet. I spun on my toes, my movements sensuous and graceful, despite the fast tempo of the music. I flowed from one song to the next—not paying attention to the rest of the crowd. I imagined I was playing the part of the Black Swan, dancing an adagio—slow, lyrical and seductive—waiting for my partner to join me, my steps including *plié*, *arabesque* and *fouetté en tournant*.

That was when I realized I was the only one dancing and everyone else was standing around, watching. The old me would have stopped or gotten embarrassed. But I didn't. I flashed a big grin and kept going, doing a slow turn that ended when I faced the kitchen.

Dylan had stopped playing his game and now stood in the doorway, staring at me, his mouth slightly open. That blond chick stood at his side, trying to get his attention, but it wasn't working.

I lifted an eyebrow, then stretched out an arm suggestively. *Wanna dance?*

If he didn't, I knew half the guys at the party would say yes.

I didn't wait for his answer, instead I swirled back around, my eyes closed, still moving to the music, changing my style to something with more jazz in it, swaying my hips.

A moment passed before an arm slid around my waist. I leaned back, my head nestled in the hollow of his shoulder, knowing it was Dylan. He kissed my neck, his lips trailing up toward my ear. Then he whispered, "I'm sorry. I didn't mean what I said."

"I know," I told him, although I wasn't sure. I wondered if the girl I used to be—the one he had fallen for—would ever come back. I had a feeling she might be lost forever.

Lauren, Stephanie, and Zoe pouted when I climbed on the back of Dylan's bike, getting ready to head home. Behind us, a glass or a beer bottle shattered inside the house, the sound of tinkling glass followed by a boom of laughter. Somebody cranked up the music and bodies jumped and people cheered in response.

"The party's just getting started," Stephanie said, a whine in her voice. She stood on the front steps, one of her arms draped around the waist of a black-haired boy wearing big, silver gauge earrings.

"Yeah, nobody goes home at eleven thirty. No. Body." Zoe crossed her arms, her short hair changing from lavender to pink to blue when Brett switched on a set of colored strobe lights.

Lauren watched me silently, a determined expression that I couldn't quite figure out. She'd already tried to talk me out of leaving, claiming that Dylan was too drunk to drive. Surprisingly, he wasn't. He didn't act like he'd been drinking at all. I guess it was one of those mysteries about how boys and girls were different.

Dylan flashed her a look when he thought I wasn't paying attention. It was as if he was saying, *don't even think about it.*

There was something strange going on between the two of them, some power play I couldn't figure out. I'd gotten so caught up in the emotion of the evening, the wild electricity of being with Dylan again, that I had ignored some of the puzzling things that had arisen. It wasn't until he and I were flying back down the mountain, leaning into the curves that made me feel like we could go plummeting into midnight skies at any moment, that those questions came back.

Why had Lauren called him Poe and what was Pink Lightning and why had he gotten so mad at her, threatening to get her kicked out?

Why was everyone I met always talking about getting kicked out? Kicked out of what?

Those questions chewed away at me, leaving me unsettled. And *no one* would give me answers. Not Lauren. Not Dylan. Not any of the spiraling notes on that blasted cherry tree.

I fought against the useless questions, wanting only to feel Dylan's warmth. We'd argued and made up. Shouldn't that have been enough? Maybe I should just leave all the puzzles alone, at least for one night.

We breezed over city streets, back in the valley again, the mountain a hulking shadow behind us, the party a memory. Dylan was the only thing that was real, his scent, his touch, his taste. He was my visceral reality, he was the one thing that connected my mysterious past with my unknown future.

I trusted him. Somehow even when he'd been angry, I'd

had a feeling it was because he was trying to protect me. But why would I need to be protected from Lauren?

The familiar houses of my neighborhood surrounded us now, slipping away behind us like running dogs, eager to keep up. We passed Mrs. Daniel's house and then the place where the Reyes triplets lived and, after that, a house that had been in foreclosure for more than a year, a weathered sign posted in the yard. There was the vacant lot—surprisingly still vacant—where Kyle, Dad, and I had played Ultimate Frisbee when I was thirteen, and there were the townhouses where Molly had lived when we were both younger, back before her father left. My childhood surrounded us, memories that made sense, a life I understood.

And there was my house up ahead, porch light on, just like at Nicole Hernandez's house, a soft voice calling me to *come home, come home*, even though I wanted nothing more than to keep on going, to drive right past and stay out all night long.

Dylan's resolve was stronger than mine. Maybe it was a guy thing. Maybe my dad had proven he was the alpha dog when he'd been alone with Dylan earlier, while I was still upstairs, figuring out what to wear.

I fought a grin.

Dad was definitely a take-charge kind of guy. As tough as Dylan and Brett and all the other guys at the party were, I knew they were no match for my father. I'd never been afraid of him, but I'd seen how other men reacted to him, when we were at the mall or a car show or a Dodgers game. They always took a step back and let Dad pass. It was an unspoken rule.

Nobody messed with my dad, not if they had any sense.

Dylan's bike slowed to a stop in the driveway and a quick glance at my cell told me it was eleven forty-five. Not bad. I climbed off the bike and Dylan grabbed my hand, pulling me toward him. His lips found mine and his arms wrapped around my waist.

"Why don't you like Lauren?" I asked, when we both finally came up for air.

He stared down at my lips, maybe wishing we were still kissing instead of talking about some other girl. "She's a bad influence." He ran his thumb over my chin, tempting me to lean back into him. "Just like me."

I let out a short laugh. "So I should just walk away from both of you."

"Basically." But the expression in his eyes said the opposite. It was if he was begging me to give him a second chance. "I tried to stay away from you," he confessed. "That's why I didn't come see you. I wanted to visit you in the hospital, even if all I could do was look at you through a window. I needed to know you had survived—" A pause followed while he searched for the right words. "I drove past the hospital every day and then when you were released, I drove past your house, hoping I'd see you standing in the yard or in front of one of the windows."

A sigh flowed from him to me, his chest emptying of air.

"I tried to stay away," he said, "but I couldn't."

"Why?" I wanted to know why he tried to stay away—instead he told me why he hadn't been able to.

"Because I'm so in love with you."

I blinked and took a half step away. I hadn't expected to hear this. I'm not sure what I imagined our relationship was, but I'd never guessed it was this serious.

He took my hand again, maybe afraid I was going to run away.

"I shouldn't have said that." He wouldn't look me in the eye.

My heart thundered, as if it wanted me to remember how much I cared about him, but I wasn't ready to leap from middle-school crush to full-on love. Not yet. Still, I couldn't ignore the fact that there was a lightness in my chest, like every breath I took came easier now, like that one thing I'd been needing was finally here—the crash cart to jump-start my heart, the miracle drug to cure my cancer.

I stepped closer, a wild fawn moving toward a hunter with outstretched hand. "That's a lot to take in on a first date," I whispered with a half-grin.

"Yeah."

"I don't know how I feel. Not yet. Except I don't want you to stay away. No matter what you think about being bad for me—"

"You don't know why I said that, you don't remember all the things I've done, things I regret," he interrupted.

I put my finger to his lips, stopping his words, those magical words that might be able to charm me into changing my mind. "Maybe this is a chance for *both* of us to start over," I said.

"I hope so." He kissed me again, a soft, gentle, tentative kiss. "And I hope you still feel that way when your memory comes back."

Chapter Twenty-Four

I stumbled when I walked through the front door, when Dylan's bike thrummed away, my body not connecting with my feet. The floor of the foyer felt non-existent, the hallway like I was walking on air. I was vaguely aware of Kyle and his buddies still playing video games in the family room, explosions mingling with bursts of laughter. Mom and Dad were sipping wine and playing cards in the kitchen when I walked past, heading toward my room. I think they asked me things like, *how was your date?* and *did you have a nice time?*

But all I could hear was Dylan's voice, his words shy and raw.

I'm so in love with you.

The party had faded away, the tension between him and Lauren, the drugs she'd tried to get me to take—all of it erased by that one confession. Now his words rang in my ears.

My feet barely touched the stairs, all of my weight on the balls of my feet. When I reached the second floor, I did a *grand jeté*, arms over my head, legs spread so far it felt like I was doing the splits while flying, glad that no one was watching me. Once I reached my bedroom, I turned on my iPod, clipping it to my shirt, earbuds in my ears.

Then I danced for about an hour, until I finally collapsed on the bed, still not tired. So I grabbed my phone and texted Molly, hoping she was still awake. She was. It was like she'd been waiting up for me.

Just got home and guess what?? Dylan said HE LOVES ME! I thumbed.

Duh.

And he kissed me!

When's the wedding?

Smart ass.

LOL. Srsly. Like I already knew all that. Everybody in the solar system knew.

Everyone but ME. Also, Lauren was kinda weird tonight. I said.

She's a jerk. Wake up and ditch that crowd. I'm way better.

ROTFL. Yeah. We need 2 do some LOTR cosplay.

When, where, I'm there. Bring the flash mob.

We chatted for about fifteen minutes. It was great to be talking to her again. My new friends were fun, I guess, especially Dylan. I just never knew what to say or how to act around them. Being with Molly was easy.

This was one of those nights when I wouldn't be able to sleep, no matter how hard I tried. I jumped in the shower, ran a towel through my hair, then decided it was time to dig out my summer clothes. My wardrobe needed serious attention. No way I wanted another Can't Figure Out What To Wear episode like tonight. I started pulling storage bags out from under my bed, until one bag hit a snag. It had tangled on something and wouldn't come out.

On my back, I crawled under the bed, flashlight in one hand, trying to figure out what the bag had caught on. All the while Kyle's video game music vibrated the floor beneath me, stirring something, some memory of dancing in a large crowd, all of us laughing, strobe lights and black lights and stage lights flashing, girls wearing skimpy outfits, guys dressed in cargo pants and mesh tank tops—

It was a rave. I knew it. I almost bumped my head on the bed, trying to sit up. Something crackled above me, shifting, something taped to the bottom of my bed.

I readjusted the flashlight beam, aiming it toward whatever was up there.

The light focused on a slender black box, carefully fastened with tape and thick cords, hidden in a place where no one but me would have ever found it. Lips dry, anxiety flickering through my chest, I stared at that box, recognizing it because it looked exactly like the one Lauren had.

I didn't want it, didn't want to be a girl addicted to some strange new drug.

But my hand refused to listen to me, it reached out and yanked the box free, my fingers fastening around it protectively, as if I didn't want to drop it, didn't want to break or damage the contents. With a shudder, I clutched it to my chest as I slid out from beneath my bed.

I set the box on the dresser, then stepped as far away from it as I could, ignoring it, putting all the storage containers away. After that I sat on my bed, staring at the box. I still didn't want it. I knew I never would have been able to sleep—not tonight, not ever—knowing that thing was resting beneath me, like a knife lodged between my shoulder blades.

The longer I stared at it, the more I wanted to run away from it.

A thick panic settled in the room. I kept remembering Lauren shoving a needle into the flesh of her forearm, the ecstatic expression on her face, how her mood had brightened afterward. I didn't want to face the fact that I had a black box, too. I wished I could turn back the clock and that I was still at the party, music surrounding me like warm, familiar arms, my friends beside me as we all danced.

I curled up on the bed, knees pulled to my chest, eyes closed, my teeth grinding, my gaze still fixed upon that box. I wanted to open it and look inside, but I didn't dare.

I couldn't stay here. I had to get out.

Just then—when some primal instinct forced me to my feet and I started rooting through the closet looking for something to wear, my hair still wet and tousled from my shower, the muscles in my stomach clenching—my cell phone buzzed. I paused, wondering if I should answer it. Was it Dylan with another confession I wasn't ready to hear, or was it Molly with ideas about our next *LOTR* movie marathon?

I grabbed the phone, quickly read the text, the tightness in my muscles releasing and a welcome smile replacing my clenched jaw.

It was from Lauren.

Wanna come out and play?

I texted back. *Where R U?*

Outside. Waiting.

I peered through my curtains toward the curb. Down the street, half a block away sat a Mini-Coop. The headlights flashed on for a second when I appeared at the window.

Come on, girl! Party's waitin'.

Gimme 5 seconds.

I didn't wonder where we were going at one thirty in the morning or whose party we were going to. All I cared about was the fact that I was getting away from that box and my own dangerous past. I tossed on some clothes and shoes, only knowing that I wanted to be comfortable, ran my fingers through my hair, and then hesitated when I saw the kandi bracelet. I'd taken it off when I took a shower and it now rested beside my cell phone. I was sneaking out. Did I want everyone knowing what I was doing? Wouldn't that only get me in trouble? I held my breath, thinking.

In the end, I didn't care if my dad or Agent Bennet found out what I did, as long as it was after the fact. I needed to get out of here and I needed to find out what had happened to me.

So, I tucked that black box deep inside one of my dresser drawers, then crept down the hallway, leaving both my cell phone and that kandi bracelet behind.

PART TWO
Tell NO one.

Chapter Twenty-Five

Lauren's car was filled with smoke, and all the girls were giggling and acting a little bit stupid when I got in, saying stuff like, *it's about time* and *let's go dominate that place* and *we rule, we totally rule.* Zoe tried to pass me a joint, but I shook my head and rolled down my window, catching a breath of fresh air. Lauren laughed, her long hair braided and clipped up, her shirt unbuttoned to show the white bikini top she wore underneath. She looked at me with a puzzled expression.

"You sure you wanna wear that?" she asked.

I glanced down, noticing I had put on one of my black ballet unitards, a jean jacket and my silver ballet slippers. I shrugged. I had no idea where we were going, but I didn't care about my clothes.

"She looks great," Stephanie said, puffs of smoke coming out between her words.

"Do you guys have to smoke weed in here? It smells disgusting," I said.

Zoe didn't bother to ask the others what they thought.

She just tossed the half-smoked joint out the window.

Lauren frowned as her Mini-Coop pulled away from the curb. "Don't be a buzzkill, Rach. You don't remember how bad the headaches are sometimes, or that pot's about the only thing that helps," she said. "Tonight's about having fun. So lighten up, K?"

I sat across from her in the front seat. Smoking dope was the key to the headaches I'd been having? Sounded like the cure was about as bad as the symptoms. I shrugged and gave her a look that said, *WTF*. Meanwhile, we headed toward the 210, Stephanie and Zoe chattering about the boys they'd met at Brett's party, rating them on some imaginary kissing chart they'd invented.

"I'd give him a 6," Stephanie said. "Cute, but not much going on in the hot and steamy department."

Zoe giggled. "Mine gets an 8, mostly for effort."

Both she and Stephanie cracked up. They kept laughing and analyzing all the boys they knew for the rest of the ride. We passed Pasadena, Eagle Rock, and Glendale, then swung onto the 5, and somewhere around Burbank we took an exit, heading down one side street after another, through seedy neighborhoods that got worse and worse the farther we drove. Tenement buildings with graffiti loomed over cracked and pock-marked streets; gang members sold drugs on street corners next to houses with boarded-up windows and crumbling roofs; a dilapidated building with signs that read SUPER MARKET and CHECKS CASHED HERE and BEER AND WINE stood abandoned, the windows painted white and the doors hanging open. I tensed up, biting my lip, glancing at Lauren from time to time.

"Do you know where you're going, 'cause it sure looks like we're lost," I said.

Right about then, that little black box on my dresser

seemed pretty innocent. It would have left me alone—as long as I ignored it. Not so with the streetwalkers and pimps who tried to get our attention, or the homeless guys who wheeled natty shopping carts filled with stereo speakers and DVD players and other electronic equipment that had obviously been stolen.

"No worries," Lauren said. "We'll be out of this area in a minute."

I regretted leaving that kandi bracelet and my cell phone behind. Even having Dad mad at me and getting grounded was better than what could happen if Lauren's car broke down here.

She was right, though. A few minutes later, the streets began to empty of all the dangerous street thugs. Houses and liquor stores gave way to weedy parking lots and long, flat-roofed warehouses. Lights gleamed up ahead, casting long shadows, and the cars parked on the streets started to look nicer. Mustangs, Hondas, a Scion here and there, no cracked windows or red plastic tape covering broken taillights. A steady stream of people drifted in the same direction as us—girls in platform shoes and shorts, guys wearing ripped jeans and strange costumes. Music thumped in the distance, not loud yet, but I knew it would get louder soon.

"Almost there," Stephanie said from the backseat. "Wish we had time for another joint."

"You've had plenty," Lauren admonished. Apparently one freebie was all the others were going to get, although that was fine with me. I'd rather have us all level-headed when we got there—wherever that was.

"Are we going to a rave?" I asked, feeling like a kid going to her first girl/boy party, unsure what to expect.

"Most definitely," Lauren said.

"A Phase Two rave?" I asked. She'd never answered that question before.

"Oh, yeah."

The other girls started giggling again.

The building appeared then, lit up by moving spotlights. From the outside, it looked like we were going to a circus. A pack of girls wearing pink wigs, black swimsuits and fishnet stockings wandered around, handing out kandi bracelets and glow sticks and pacifiers on beaded necklaces. Guys wore devil horns, red face paint and pants wrapped with bright green glowing bands; they had long hair or short hair, were clean-shaven or sported gross, waist-long beards; they wore skintight shirts or no shirts, most of them exposing muscles that looked like they'd been carved by a Renaissance sculptor.

"Oooh, baby," Lauren said, after we slid into a parking spot and climbed out of the car. "This place is epic tonight. Come on, let's get inside." Stephanie and Zoe took off their jackets and tossed them in the backseat. I started to do the same, knowing it would be hot inside. Lauren stopped me. "Leave your jacket on," she said with a grin. "I've got a surprise for you."

Zoe grinned. "That's right! Rachel doesn't know—"

"Shhh! Don't wreck it," Stephanie said.

"What kind of lame-ass surprise involves me wearing a *jacket*?" I asked, but I had to jog to catch up with them, because they were already running toward the door. I was a bit amazed that Lauren could move so fast in those stilettos and still make it look elegant. It was like she was some kind of gazelle, loping across the Serengeti, finally in her natural habitat.

Meanwhile, two girls, wearing rainbow tutus and purple tank tops, dashed toward us.

"You guys want some E? We got some. Real cheap."

They lowered their neon-colored sunglasses to look me in the eye, as if that would convince me. Lauren paused, looking tempted. No way was I letting her get higher than she already was.

"Beat it!" I shook a fist at one of the girls.

"Whoa!" She backed away, hands palms up. "What about the peace and love, girlfriend? Remember where you are."

"And *you* remember *me* and stay the eff away. Got it?"

They scampered off, looking more like fairies than real girls. Lauren grinned and pointed a finger at me. "Once we get inside, the real you is coming out. I promise." She latched onto my hand. "Let's go, we gotta get inside quick. We're late."

I wanted to ask late for what, but I knew she had some sort of surprise going on here. Maybe we were going to meet up with some of our friends and do some street dancing—if so, that would be *way* fun. My heart began to match the steady, pounding beat that thrummed from the warehouse's open doors. Clusters of brightly colored beams of light—blue, red, green—illuminated the crowds that danced inside, bodies jumping and swaying to the music. The closer we got, the more the music consumed me until, once we were inside, it took over, pulsing through the soles of my feet, vibrating up my spine and across my ribs. I pulled away from Lauren, tossing my hands up toward the vast ceiling, laughing and dancing, instantly at one with the ocean of teenagers who were doing the same thing. Glow sticks flashing like magic wands, we were all washed in blue-green light, stars spinning overhead in time to the music. I closed my eyes.

This was where I belonged. In a land where music and

dance merged and became one.

I wasn't a geek here, I wasn't that student who got all Bs and Cs or the ballet-wannabe who watched everyone else get all the starring roles. Here, I was somebody. I could feel it.

I never wanted to stop dancing, never wanted to leave, but Lauren took my hand and pulled me away from the crowds.

"Look!" she said.

A black strobe light flashed where we now stood, changing her lipstick white and her eye shadow silver. She stretched her right arm out in front of me, an arm that had been completely normal before.

Now her arm was covered, from wrist to shoulder, with an elaborate, gorgeous tattoo. I gasped, enchanted, holding her wrist still so I could examine it.

"Oh. My. Wow," I exclaimed.

Glowing white scrollwork turned into feathers, which then turned into swans with curving necks. It was more beautiful than anything I'd ever seen. It was a black-light tattoo, invisible until exposed to the right spectrum of light.

"You like?" she asked, her grin widening.

I nodded.

Stephanie lifted her right arm, revealing an identical tattoo. Zoe did the same. They grinned at me, their teeth glowing.

"Now. For the grand finale," Lauren said. "Take off your jacket."

My eyes widened. "No way. You're shitting me."

"Off, off, off!" all three girls chanted until several boys stopped to see what I was going to take off.

I slipped off my jean jacket, both nervous and excited. My tattoo appeared in reverse, from shoulder to wrist. First, a delicate swan head appeared, resting on my right shoulder as if she had been waiting for me to see her, as if she'd been watching over me all this time. Her head curved gently to one side, her long neck twining with that of another swan and another, their wings spread wide across my biceps, each feather perfect, drawn with glowing white light, as if this lamentation of swans was immortal.

It was Odette and the other girls from *Swan Lake*, young girls who had been enchanted by a sorcerer, turned into swans and condemned to swim forever on a lake made from the tears of their parents.

Tears formed in the corners of my eyes.

"We're sisters," Lauren said, taking my hand, our glowing tattoos forming an arch that bridged us together. "Always and forever."

"Always and forever," Stephanie and Zoe repeated with one voice.

I nodded. I wasn't sure why or when we had made this commitment to one another, but it felt right. Just as right as that black box had felt wrong.

"Always and forever," I said.

At that moment, I could feel the new me pushing her way to the surface, starting to reveal herself, just like that black-light tattoo. Dangerous, seductive, beautiful.

I couldn't ignore her anymore.

She was me.

We were moving away from the central dance floor, although I didn't want to leave. I kept dancing as I walked, twirling and spinning, inhaling the perfume of a thousand sweaty dancers, my attention wandering from one visual experience to the next. Girls waved their arms as they rode atop their boyfriends' shoulders and faces blurred beneath the colored lights, while a huge screen displayed an ever-changing psychedelic light show. I knew there were other things going on below the surface here, dark and dangerous things. Kids were taking drugs and some of them would possibly overdose, girls might go home with boys who had bad intentions, people were selling drugs that weren't what they were supposed to be, and guys would get robbed on the way back to their cars.

It was horrible and wonderful, evil and perfection combined.

But the dancing and the music were heavenly.

The girls and I walked down a long hallway, past the bathrooms, the music sounding muffled now. I wiped the sweat from my forehead with the back of my hand, wishing I had a bottle of water. Stephanie had one arm draped over Lauren's shoulder and they were whispering.

"Where are we going? We're not leaving already, are we?" I asked.

Zoe giggled and gave me a hug. "The party's only getting started."

Lauren continued to lead the way, looking different tonight, her hair pinned and braided, the set of her shoulders even more confident than usual. Something was coming. Something I needed to be ready for. A heightened awareness kicked in, stirred by a sixth sense I'd forgotten I had.

"Do you trust me, Rach?" she asked, spinning around to face me, stopping all four of us.

"Of course," I answered, although my pulse quickened in the hollow of my throat.

"Good. 'Cause we're just about to enter Phase Two." She held up four tickets that looked almost exactly like the stubs I found in my closet. "I'm sorry I couldn't tell you about this the other day at school, but *you* were the one who brought me here and you made me promise to *never* tell. None of us can tell, can we?"

For the first time tonight, Zoe and Stephanie looked at me with serious expressions. Zoe drew an *X* over her heart and shook her head.

"We'll never tell," they both vowed.

"Okay," I said, starting to feel a bit spooked. "You'll never tell *what*?"

"What happens on the other side of those doors." Lauren pointed toward a pair of steel doors at the far end of the hallway. We were about twenty feet away. We still had time to turn around.

"You guys aren't talking about some kind of sex club, are you?" I asked, remembering those condoms in my drawer. "Because if you are, I'm *not* going!"

"It's definitely not a sex club. It's *better* than sex." Lauren watched me, excitement in her voice. "Just one thing, before you go in, you have to choose a fake name. Nobody uses their real names once they get inside. Okay?"

I frowned. "What name did I use before?"

She shook her head. "This is like a new beginning. You get to choose one. Anything."

I didn't have to think long. I chose the girl I imagined myself to be. "Odette," I said, knowing she was the Swan Queen.

Zoe laughed, holding out her palm. Stephanie groaned and handed over a five-dollar bill.

"What?" I asked.

"You picked the same name as before," Zoe said, linking arms with me. "I *knew* you would."

Then the four of us linked arms, an act that gave me a

little more courage than I would have had if I were alone. Lauren knocked on the doors, producing the tickets when a burly six-foot-six guy appeared, looking like he spent his days at the gym and his nights guarding the River Styx. He ran a quick gaze over the four of us, tickets in his palm.

"Team?" he asked, his lips barely moving, a cigarette hanging from one corner of his mouth.

"The Swan Girls," Lauren answered, her chin held high.

"Good. Haven't seen the whole team here in a while. Thought you broke up." He kicked a low, silver platform toward us—a scale. "Weight, one at a time."

I gave him and the girls a weird look, but we all did what he asked, each of us getting a necklace with a letter dangling from one end after we'd been weighed. I glanced down, saw that Lauren and I both had *Fs*, Stephanie had a *B*, Zoe had an *S*.

Then he held up a plastic Ziploc bag. "Phones."

"What?" Lauren asked.

"New rule. Upper management says you gotta leave your cell phones and cameras with me. Look, I'll mark your bag." He took a black permanent marker and drew a large, sloppy *S* on the bag. "You'll get 'em back when you go home."

The girls grumbled as they dug out their phones, but a flash of warning thudded in the back of my head. I narrowed my eyes. "When did this new rule start?" I asked.

"'Bout ten days ago."

A shot of panic fanned across my chest. They changed the rule after I was kidnapped. That horrid memory returned—that time I'd tried to call 9-1-1 and someone had knocked my phone out of my hand, then tied a gag around my mouth.

Had that happened here?

"Come on, give me your phone." He held his hand outstretched toward me.

"Don't have one with me," I answered, glad that I'd made a last-minute decision to leave mine behind.

I probably should have been afraid, but I wasn't. Another emotion was taking over, something stronger than fear. I was determined. It was finally time to find out the answers to the questions that kept me awake at night. I pushed my way past him and the other girls who were still digging through pockets and purses. Lauren lifted her head for a brief moment, as if she had wanted to be the one to go inside first, me on her arm. I merely nodded at her, knowing she would be at my side soon. But I didn't wait for her or the others.

Something was calling to me, something I could no longer ignore.

Destiny.

I walked through the door and into the unknown. Alone.

CHAPTER TWENTY-SIX

A brilliant chaos waited for me on the other side. A crowd of teenagers cheered, all facing the center of the room, bright lights shining down on a stage, raised a few feet off the floor. Two guys were up on the platform, skin glistening with sweat, both of them naked to the waist, their muscles straining, the sounds they made being amplified by a loudspeaker system. They were fighting, a style that mixed boxing and wrestling and some form of martial arts, every punch spraying sweat that spun away like diamonds in the bright light. The sounds of *oof* and *uh* and *thud* echoed louder than the cries of the people who faced the stage, fists clenched.

The energy from the crowd was infectious.

The room was huge, about half the size of our high school gym, and it was packed with kids my age, most of them standing in clusters like mini-gangs, dressed in ways that distinguished them from the rest of the crowd. Six boys to my left wore long-sleeved green shirts with the word "Orcs" printed on the front and the back. Three girls

wore rainbow wigs, hot pink shorts and matching sport
bra tops; five boys had shaved heads and the word "Skulls"
tattooed across their backs in big, violet Gothic letters.

I flashed on that photo of Nicole Hernandez, her
hair streaked with pink, standing with a group of girls all
wearing shirts that said "Pink Candi" in glitter.

Had that been her team? Had I met her here?

I spun around slowly, taking it all in, the feeling like
I was at a big party, the smells of sweat and cologne thick
in the air, smoke bombs bursting at the edges of the room,
black in one corner, violet blue in another, everyone
chanting words that I couldn't distinguish, not at first.

Then I recognized one of the words being chanted.

Poe—Poe—Poe.

Despite the steamy heat from the crowd, a chill washed
over me. *Poe.* That was what Lauren had called Dylan
earlier and he had gotten angry, telling her she could get
kicked out.

He was here. Dylan was here.

The thunder of music beat against my feet and my
chest—I hadn't even realized music was playing until now,
a wild techno mix—and I started pushing my way through
the crowd, through the boys and girls who chanted *Poe, Poe,
Poe!* I had to get to the front of the stage. I didn't wait for
Lauren or the girls. All three of them were *my* girls, I knew
that now, the Swan Girls were my team and I was their
leader. But I didn't care about them. I bounced as I walked,
shoving myself up on my toes with each step, trying to see
above the shoulders and heads of tall guys who shouted
and growled and cheered.

Was my boyfriend up on the stage? Was he fighting?

I could see two guys up there, one with his back to me,
a large, intricate tattoo spreading across his shoulders, a

black bird with wings spread wide as if captured in mid-flight. A raven. Even though I didn't remember ever seeing Dylan with a tattoo like that, I knew it had to be him. I thought about the poem that circled his wrist, the first line from *The Raven*. Dylan was up there and he was fighting one of the Skulls; his opponent's head was shaved, a red iron cross painted on his forehead that stretched down over his nose. It made him look inhuman and a shudder raced through me.

This place was both exciting and scary, the rush much stronger than anything I'd ever felt when attending other sporting events. It was more like white-water rafting, wild and untamed.

I made it to the front, although even here I continually had to fight to claim my position, shoving elbows into ribs and knees in crotches. Twice I had to turn around and slam my fist into somebody's gut to make them back up and stop pushing me against the edge of the platform.

My blood thrilled through my veins, hot and fast.

I watched Dylan's every move, instinctively under-standing his game. Standing and delivering kicks wasn't how he would win. He needed to take this Skull to the ground and pin him down in a wrestling hold.

"Grab him by the waist and take him *down*!" I yelled.

I didn't think about the fact that he would hear me or that my voice might be a distraction. Dylan twisted his head, searching the crowd and finding me, an astonished look in his eyes.

"Get him on the mat!" I screamed.

The other guy took advantage of the situation and punched Dylan in the stomach; Dylan curled over, then took another punch, this time in the side of his head.

I winced when blood flowed down his face.

Poe—Poe—Poe—

It seemed like everyone in the crowd was yelling his name, although some of them had to be cheering for the Skull. The crowd parted behind me, a soft cool breeze wafted forward and I looked over my shoulder. Lauren, Stephanie, and Zoe had made it to the front and they joined me, all four of us linking arms to keep the others back, as if our presence alone could make him win.

He *had* to win.

He stumbled, blood dripping from his nose and we all thought he would fall, that he would end up on the ground—but not the way he was supposed to, not in a dominant position. We were wrong. Dylan used his forward motion to propel himself into his opponent, to knock the other guy off-balance, a wicked grin on his face as he wrapped his arms around the Skull's waist, then slammed him down.

Wham.

The Skull's head hit the floor.

A moment of silence swept the room. We all sucked in a breath and held it, waiting. For the first time I saw the video cameras that were positioned around the room, high up on the walls, some of them scanning the crowd, most of them focused on the fight, all of them pointing in different angles.

Closed circuit TV.

I remembered that somewhere, safe and anonymous in their homes, adults were watching this on big-screen TVs. They were placing bets. Money was flowing, changing hands. We were the event, we were the fighting dogs, and we didn't even care that we never got paid. Adrenaline was why we did it. I could feel it and taste it, like I was soaring high above the earth, invincible, impervious to pain.

This was better than any drug.

I felt electric, more alive than I had in weeks, blood rushing, my heart a machine effortlessly thumping, thumping, thumping—damn, how I'd missed this. Up until now my life had been boring, everything black and white, instead of color, instead of this brilliant blood red—

The real me had been hiding until now, just like my tattoo.

Meanwhile, an ominous silence continued—the only sounds were the air flowing into my lungs and the high-pitched whine of cameras as they panned from right to left, as their lenses refocused for close-ups. Even the music got put on pause.

Then—as if I was the only person who could step outside of time, outside of this unending moment where the Skull lay on the ground helpless, the wind knocked out of him—I lifted my clenched fist high and I screamed.

"Poe—Poe—Poe!"

Time started again, other people shouted and cheered. A deafening rush of noise bounced off the walls, reverberating, sounding like the cry of an army going into battle. Dylan punched the guy in the gut and the side and the face. He wrapped his legs around the guy's waist, pinning him in place. The Skull tried to open his eyes, blinking several times, but finally his head thudded back to the floor. Unconscious.

CHAPTER TWENTY-SEVEN

The crowd cheered even louder, something I didn't think was possible. Then someone pushed his way through the mob, someone taller and broader than the rest of us. It was a man wearing a dark gray business suit and a red and black *lucha libre* mask, his identity concealed. He made his way onto the platform and his voice proclaimed over the loudspeakers, "We have a winner!" He took one of Dylan's arms and lifted it high. I didn't recognize the man, but his Brooklyn accent sounded familiar. I'd probably heard it here many times.

Dylan stood, bowing his head slightly to the frenetic crowd. A girl came onto the platform and wiped away his blood, then handed him an ice pack. All the while, his gaze remained fixed upon me and heat flowed from my shoulders down my back, all the way to my feet. He pointed at me, maybe telling me to stay where I was, then he turned to descend.

The crowd came alive to me then, for the first time since I had walked into the room and realized that Dylan was onstage and in the midst of a fight. Faces came into focus. I saw several other guys surrounding the stage, all without shirts, large black ravens tattooed on their backs. When they turned, I recognized them—Brett, Jim, and Mike, all the crowd we hung out with at lunch. I was temporarily stunned.

The boys from school were the Ravens, the girls were the Swans.

I glanced down at the *F* that dangled from my neck, my fingers running over the letter, trying to remember what it stood for. Lauren leaned nearer and shouted in my ear.

"You're a flyweight, just like me," she said. Then she held up her letter, an *F*. "Stephanie's a bantamweight and Zoe's a strawweight."

I still wasn't sure what it all meant, but I nodded. Acting like I was in charge was crucial here. I knew there was no room for confusion—it could be interpreted as weakness. I grinned at Brett when his eyes met mine, giving him a thumbs-up sign. He hadn't expected to see me—that much was clear in his eyes—but he also knew that we both had to feign strength. He returned the gesture with enthusiasm, adding a loud whoop along with it. The other Ravens turned and saw me, a slightly surprised look on their faces that quickly turned to joy.

One of them bowed toward me. The other gave me a salute.

Their actions caught the attention of the crowd and soon many of the teens surrounding the stage were looking at me. I recognized many, some from Brett's party, the boys who had been watching me throughout the evening, whispering about me, saying I was hot. A few feet away stood the boy I had kneed in the crotch. He gave me a wry grin and a nod. I returned the gesture.

Unfortunately, not all of the crowd was friendly.

To the left, I caught a glimpse of blue hair, five girls clustered together, one of them staring at me with her jaw clenched.

Janie Deluca. The girl I'd left lying in the street last night.

I lifted my chin and she lowered her gaze, bowing her head, a public act of submission. When she finally raised her head, I gave her a smile. She stared at me, puzzled at first. Maybe I'd never been kind to someone I'd beaten before, maybe it wasn't proper etiquette, but I didn't care. I'd beaten her and won. There was no need for bad blood between us. Her smile came back, hesitant at first, then with more confidence, the steely look in her eyes softening.

I turned back toward the stage, an unsettling feeling in my gut as I realized I had been a real bitch this past year— just like Molly said yesterday. A Prima Donna Bitch.

A huddle of people worked up on the stage, all overseen by another disguised man, this one wearing a gold and blue *lucha libre* mask. He directed the rest of the Skull team as they tended to the loser's wounds and then carried him offstage. A couple of creepy old guys were mopping up blood and sweat from the floor, getting the stage ready for another match. Excitement buzzed through me as I wondered who was going to compete next. I had just started to examine the chattering huddles around me, trying to figure out which of them would be going up on the stage when Dylan pushed his way toward me.

"Look out," Lauren said, rolling her eyes. "It's gonna hit the fan now!"

Zoe took a step back, a startled expression on her face. I held her by the arm, preventing her from retreating any further. "There's nothing to worry to about," I told her.

"You don't know," she said.

Stephanie stood beside me, silent, not moving, as if she would be there for me if I needed her. Dylan's eyes narrowed and he pointed a finger at Lauren, his voice raised as he approached.

"What the hell are you doing, bringing Rachel here?" he demanded.

Lauren shrugged, trying to look tough, but it wasn't working.

"What kind of friend *are* you?" He was in her face now, his muscles gleaming from sweat, his chest and arms still naked. His brow furrowed when he glanced at me and for a second I could see how glad he was that I was here and that I had watched him fight. Then that expression faded when he turned on Lauren again. "You've always been jealous of her, haven't you? And you know it's Open Floor Night—"

"She can handle it. She's *never* lost a fight!"

"She's not ready for it—"

I pushed my way between them. "What are you two arguing about?" I demanded.

But before either one of them could answer, the announcer started talking from the stage, his voice booming throughout the room. "It's Open Floor Night and our next contestant is coming up right now. Give up a cheer for Komodo!"

The crowd roared and I turned back toward the stage, cheering along with them, eager to see another battle. The first fight had just gotten my engine started. I was hoping that the next contestants would fight standing—I wanted to see kicks and spins.

"You have to get out of here, *now*!" Dylan said, grabbing my arm and trying to drag me away from the stage area. "Before anyone sees you."

"A lot of people have already seen me," I said, pulling away from him. "By the way, it's good to see you, too." My tone was snarky and I kept my attention fixed on the stage, wanting to find out who was up next. A girl rose to the platform, wearing purple shorts and a matching tank top, her hair braided in tight cornrows. Something about her looked familiar, but I didn't recognize her until she turned around and pointed a finger at me. A purple dragon tattoo covered her right arm. It was Sammy, that bitch from my history class. She glowered at me and I gave her the same look back.

She leaned toward the announcer's microphone and said, "I choose Odette, leader of the Swan Team, as my opponent." She took off the necklace that proclaimed she was a flyweight, the same as me, and for the first time I understood—we were in the same weight class and she wanted to fight me.

Fear zipped through me, stirring other emotions along the way, primal feelings that couldn't be expressed in words.

"No, you can't!" Dylan yelled, trying to stand in my way, but I walked around him, the crowds parting easily, just like they did when he and I walked through the halls at school. Behind me, my team started the chant, *Odette—Odette—Odette*, until it echoed through the room, so loud it became a drum that said *da-dum, da-dum, da-dum*. Not many people were cheering for Komodo, though, and anger flickered in her eyes, as if she knew I'd made a huge mistake by coming here tonight. The expression on her face said she hoped I would be weak, that she would have an easy win and an opportunity to destroy my unbroken title.

Fear stuttered through me as I stepped onto the stage.

Every inch of me was praying she was wrong.

CHAPTER TWENTY-EIGHT

Everything changed the moment I stepped onto the stage.

The cheering crowds faded away. Everything beyond the edge of the platform blurred and became meaningless. I was only vaguely aware of the smoke bombs that proclaimed our rival team colors, billows of white for the Swan Team to my left, clouds of purple for the Dragon Girls to the right. For a brief sliver of time, Komodo and I leaned toward each other, our bare knuckles touching in a short fist bump before the fight actually began. I narrowed my eyes and lowered my chin, hoping that was a defensive stance, but I wasn't sure. She gave me a threatening look, and maybe to the rest of the world it looked scary, but I could tell a small part of her was worried.

I needed to bring the worried part of her to the surface. I had to shake her confidence.

But I had no idea how to do that.

We started circling each other. She feigned a punch with her left fist; when I dodged it, she gut-punched me with her right. She leaned in for another double jab, a heavy-hitting right-left duo, and I somehow managed to block the first punch, but took the second one square in the chest. I stumbled backward, sucking air through my teeth, knowing I had to keep her away from my ribs.

She was out for more than blood. I could feel it.

She wanted me on the ground, her foot on my throat.

The crowd roared as I staggered away from her, trying to get my balance. Trying to remember what I was supposed to do. Dylan and Lauren were down there yelling fight tactics at me. I wanted to tell them to shut up, to tell them that they were giving away any advantage they might've been giving me, but I didn't.

Because I *didn't* have an advantage. Not without my memory.

I tried to analyze the scene. I had to beat her standing or this was going to be over too soon and I would end up flat on the mat. Her shoulders were broader than mine, she was shorter and her weight was centered low, all things even I knew would make her better at fighting on the mat. I ducked her next sloppy swing and managed to land a blow to her gut at the same time. She stumbled, then righted herself quickly.

Komodo moved in for a quick grab and jab, her left arm pinning my right fist against her shoulder, leaving her right hand free to slam me in the side and the back. One punch was all she got, though, before the same instinct that took out Janie roared back to life. I kneed Komodo over and over—groin, abdomen, groin. She crumpled away, tried to catch her breath.

I leaped at her, surprised when my first kick struck her neat in the jaw, knocking her head sideways and putting a glazed look in her eyes.

Puffs of white smoke drifted onto the stage, an anthem

of my name along with it.

Odette—Odette—Odette—

It distracted me and Komodo looped an ankle around my knee, pulling me forward, trying to make me fall. I grabbed her around the waist—imitating a move I saw Dylan make—and when we tumbled to the ground I kept my momentum going, flipping her over me until she was the one who thudded to the floor. Meanwhile, I continued to roll until I was back on my feet. Two swift kicks pushed her far enough away that she couldn't pull me down again. Then when she finally stood up, I jabbed, punched, and kicked until she wavered, her knees weak, a sick expression on her face.

My skin tingled, my blood scorched my veins, and I became more than human, I became a Swan Girl, able to fly high above the earth, wings catching the wind and the sun.

I was back in the game and my opponent was seconds away from kissing the mat good night.

I did a roundhouse kick, mainly for show, feeling the cheers from the crowd more than I heard them. My heel caught the side of her head and she fell back to the ground, her arms shaking and trembling, her eyes blinking. She wasn't unconscious, though, and she didn't say, *I give*, the words that could end our fight. Still, I knew she could be seriously injured if we continued. Seeing her on the mat bothered me more than I expected; it sounded an alarm inside my skull and the muscles in my arms started to tremble, almost as much as hers. I couldn't hit her again. I just couldn't.

For an instant, I saw Nicole Hernandez on the mat, those pink streaks in her hair drenched in sweat, that Pink Candi logo on her shirt stained red with blood, someone relentlessly pummeling her face. *No, this isn't real, it's not happening now. I can't handle a Big Trigger, not here.* I shook my head, hard, until Nicole disappeared and I saw Komodo on the ground instead.

I shot a nervous glance at the announcer—silently asking if I should stop, hoping he would say yes because I couldn't land another punch or kick, I just couldn't—and he nodded, quickly ascending back onto the platform, his voice bellowing as he moved.

"We have another winner! Odette from the Swan Team!"

Komodo jerked awake on the floor, startled by the announcement. She struggled to get up, arms pressing against the floor, legs moving, but he pushed her back to the mat with his foot. "Stay down," he warned, his microphone switched off. She grimaced, not ready to stop despite the blood dripping from her mouth, the bruises on her jaw, and the fact that one of her eyes was swelling up. Both of her fists were clenched, although the right one wouldn't tighten all the way. It looked more like a claw than a weapon. Still, she didn't want to give up.

"I wasn't finished," she growled, her words slurring.

"Another word and you're *definitely* finished. For good," the announcer said, still with the microphone off. Then he gestured toward her team members and another masked man. "Get her off the stage before I kick her out of the club."

The stage quickly filled with Dragon Tattoo Girls, all of them sporting matching purple tattoos and outfits, their hair in cornrows. I recognized two of them from history class and I think some part of me expected them to act like we were still in school—to look away nervously, eyes darting left and right, shoulders hunched as they turned aside. Instead, they both glared at me as they gently lifted their teammate, icing her wounds, wiping away her blood, then helping her off the platform.

It hit me then, although I should have figured it out sooner, and it hurt more than any of the punches or kicks I'd gotten tonight.

These were the girls who had left the cruel notes on my memorial. *Wish you had stayed dead, go back where you came from, hope those kidnappers come back and do the job right this time!*

One of my knees loosened beneath me and I wavered, not even realizing that the announcer had my right arm lifted high or that Lauren had come up onstage and wrapped her arm around my waist. When I started to stumble, she held me up, her expression never changing, never letting the crowd know for a split second that she was keeping me on my feet. Another man joined us, his arms spread wide in a victory stance, his *lucha libre* mask silver and black.

He slipped an arm around my waist, and together he and Lauren led me down from the stage, making it look like they were celebrating my triumph, rather than holding me steady. It wasn't until I cleared the steps that the strength in my legs returned and I pulled away from both of them, my arms raised to the crowds who cheered again. Lauren followed the two of us, until the masked man turned and gestured for her to stop.

"I need to talk to Odette alone," he said.

Lauren started to protest, but I stopped her. "It's okay, we won't be long," I said, then I turned to give the man a look that told him I didn't remember or trust him.

"Good to see you back and safe," he said as we moved away from the stage. We headed toward the corner, away from the crowds. If he tried to take me into another room or outside, I was going to give him the fight of his life. Already the muscles in my legs and arms were tensing and he must have sensed it. "It's okay, I'm not going to hurt you."

I kept my gaze fixed on Dylan who had come around to this side of the stage and now watched the two of us, his arms crossed, his head lowered, looking like he would take this strange masked man down if necessary. Brett and Jim and Mike were with him, too. Just knowing they were there comforted me.

It wasn't until we were away from the others, in a corner where our words didn't carry, that things began to fall into place—although, at that point, I was even more confused.

"What the hell are you doing here?" the man wearing the mask demanded. "You could have been seriously injured. Are your memories coming back?"

I stared at him, at his mask, at the unfamiliar eyes that burned inside. After a long moment, I thought I recognized his voice and those eyes, but I wasn't sure.

"Who are you and why do you act like I belong to you?" I asked.

"You don't even remember how the system works," he said with a condescending snarl. "I'm your patron. You and I have worked together for about eight months. I'm the one who paid for all your training, but you could have ended both of our careers tonight."

"I don't understand." I looked around, at my team, at the other fighters. "Everyone here has a patron?"

"Everyone that fights in Gold Level, yes."

"Why are you wearing that mask?"

"The same reason you have a stage name. This isn't exactly legal. The system was set up to provide anonymity.

Look, you need to stay home until your memories come back. At this point, I'd rather have you quit than get injured in a fight you're not prepared for."

He paused, as if trying to keep emotion out of his voice, but his words had already wavered. I couldn't tell if he cared about me because I made him money or if he just cared about all the people he supported. "You don't deserve this, not after taking a risk like that, but here." He handed me a black box that looked a lot like the one I'd left back on top of my dresser. My hands shook when I held it.

"I don't want—I'm not taking any drugs, I don't care if everyone else is or if you think I should or—"

He chuckled, a humorless sound. "It's obvious you're not taking your Pink Lightning. Just open it, okay? People are watching us. Make sure you act like you love it."

It rested on my palm, so light it almost felt empty. I slid a glance toward Dylan. He stood with his back against the wall, about twenty feet away, his attention focused on the current fight. Is this what patrons did? Give black boxes filled with drugs to the teams they supported, sharing in the victory when we won, reprimanding us when we lost? And if so, what were the reprimands like?

I thought about Janie Deluca, here tonight despite the fact that I'd beaten her pretty badly yesterday. Was she trying to get back in her patron's good graces, hoping he'd supply her with Pink Lightning again? Was her addiction that bad?

My thumb flipped the catch on the box and the lid opened slowly, the contents glittering beneath the moving spotlights. It caught my breath, it was so lovely. My eyes widened and my lips froze in a silent *O*. A delicate chain held a white gold swan, her body crusted with tiny diamonds. She was perfect.

"Holy wow," I whispered.

"Here, let me put it on you. You won't be fighting anymore tonight and everyone needs to see that you've done a good job." He took the chain and fastened it around my neck, his fingers warm against my skin for a moment, his breath close to my ear. "Be careful," he warned in a low whisper. "Don't get separated from your team tonight. Okay? Last thing I need is for you to go missing again."

I nodded, a chill running over me. Was this what he had really wanted to tell me? That I was still in danger? I swept a cautious glance over the crowds, pretending that his words hadn't put me on edge. "Thank you," I said.

He bowed his head, then he silently led me back to Dylan. Once my hand was in Dylan's, my patron took a position against the wall, watching the crowd, his gaze returning to me from time to time. He stayed there for the rest of the evening, quiet and stoic, like a sentry on a high wall, watching the horizon for an approaching army.

Dylan's hand was in mine, his lips brushing my cheek and neck, his breath hot against my skin. The fingers of his left hand toyed with my new necklace, causing it to cast tiny rainbows when the lights flickered overhead. Another fight, the fourth since I'd walked through the door, raged in the center of the steamy room, blow after blow feeding the hungry crowd, all of us getting a surge of excitement from the chanting. I had the surreal feeling we were warriors, ready for battle.

"You shouldn't be here tonight," he murmured in my ear.

"I know." I sighed. I couldn't tell him that I'd just gotten the same lecture from my patron or that I'd had some sort of meltdown on the stage, seeing Komodo turn into Nicole Hernandez. A sick feeling wormed through my gut. I'd never fought against Nicole, I was certain of it. She was taller than I was and she had to be in a different weight class. But I must have seen her fight before—that had to be where that memory came from.

"You've never lost a fight. Did you know that?" Dylan asked.

"Lauren told me." My gaze kept drifting back to the stage and the unending battles that both repulsed and attracted me.

"Your opponents would love to get you when you're weak, so promise me you won't come back here if you're injured or not feeling well."

"I promise," I said. I thought that once I came to a Phase Two rave, I'd know what I'd been doing this past year and that I'd be able to walk away from it. I'd be able to close that chapter and move on. But I could tell by the way Dylan was talking that we both knew I wasn't going to be able to do that.

Unless my memory of the kidnapping came back.

Then I probably wouldn't want to leave the house.

"Do you think the people who kidnapped me might be here?" I asked, keeping my voice low.

"I don't know." He turned to face me, wrapping his arms around my waist. "I've been trying to figure that out. You don't remember who it was, do you?"

I shook my head.

"Well, it's no secret you lost your memory," he said. "Whoever took you probably doesn't want to take a chance on you seeing them again. You might recognize them."

"That's true," I said. Already some of my memories had

been triggered by meeting Janie and seeing Nicole's photo. And then there was that creepy vision I had of Nicole getting the crap beaten out of her. I fought the shudder that crept over my shoulders, making my arms shake.

"So, they might be laying low," Dylan said. "Or maybe they never planned on coming back."

I remembered those photos Bennet had placed on the table in front of me, the other girls who had gone missing. Nicole had been left in a ditch, just like me. "They're not finished," I confessed. "There are other girls missing and there will probably be more. Unless—" I paused, thinking.

"Unless what?" he asked, his gray eyes searching mine.

"Unless we can find a way to stop them."

His skin turned pale and his eyes widened. "No. Definitely not. You are *not* going after the scumbags who kidnapped you. Promise me you'll forget about that idea—"

I bit my lip and gave him a half-nod, then fixed my attention back on the stage. I couldn't talk to him about this. He wasn't going to change his mind and neither was I. I didn't really like the idea, but it looked like I might have to go after my kidnappers by myself.

"What an epic adventure!"

"Every night should be like this!"

The four of us girls headed across the broad parking lot that surrounded the warehouse, spotlights searching the skies, while Dylan and Brett and the other Ravens stopped a few steps behind us to discuss something. When I glanced back, I noticed they were all staring at a cluster of gleaming cars lined up on the road, almost like a private valet service.

A group of seedy men had descended upon the cars, discreetly thumbing out thick wads of cash, then snatching up keys and climbing behind the wheels of Mercedes and BMWs. I couldn't help but wonder if there was another side business going on here that involved stolen cars.

I froze in place, trying to remember something that kept slipping away, something that tightened my throat.

Dylan met my gaze and seemed to understand what I was thinking. He elbowed Brett and then all the boys jogged to catch up with us.

Meanwhile, the rave still thumped and glittered, thousands of people dancing at an unending party, the perfect cover-up for the Phase Two event that had just taken place inside a well-guarded room. Even after Dylan was right behind us again, I continued to nervously finger the diamond-studded swan that nestled in the hollow of my throat, wondering how dangerous it was to be walking through this neighborhood.

"Gold Level is *so* much better than silver!" Zoe said, enthusiasm in her voice.

"What do you mean? I still don't understand what Gold Level is," I said.

She came alongside me, looped her arm through mine, leaning her head on my shoulder for a moment, her lavender hair looking like the color of blood under night skies. She was more petite than I was, weighing only a hundred and ten pounds and standing five foot one. The weight classes were becoming more familiar to me now and she definitely fit in with the strawweights.

"We all started at Silver Level, fighting as individuals. Then, once we got accepted into teams, we each got a patron, and we moved on to gold. Now we have each other—all of us Swan Girls—to back each other up. It's safer and more fun," she said.

"You got that right," Stephanie chimed in.

"But there are rumors of another level," Lauren said in a low, dramatic tone. "Some people say it's platinum, others say it's titanium. And you need a special invitation to get inside—"

"Those are just rumors," Dylan said. "Gold is as high as it goes. Everybody just wants a greater thrill and a bigger high, that's all, so they make up stories. But Gold is the place to be. Especially when you're with the right team." He and Brett gave each other loud high fives and the Raven team said things like, *right on*, and *amen*, and *what he said*.

But I wondered. A needle pricked me in the gut, making me uncomfortable, as if I'd just learned a dangerous secret. Something about those cars changing hands behind us and what Lauren had said chipped away at the high I'd been feeling ever since my fight. My feet connected with the ground with solid slaps, no more toe-heel bouncy steps, and the pit of my stomach felt hollow.

There were illegal things going on here, more than just dancing and drugs. And there might be another level above Phase Two, another venue where the promoters of this event lured fighters away from their teams and their friends, where they'd meet in secret.

If that was true, it sounded deadly.

The crowds thinned as people drifted away from the rave and toward their cars. The sleazy nature of the neighborhood became more evident than it had been when we first drove through. Vagrants and homeless guys staggered about, weaving down cracked sidewalks, clothes rumpled and stained, some wheeling shopping carts, some struggling to carry all their earthly possessions in their arms. I winced as we approached Lauren's Mini-Cooper and saw one of the homeless wretches leaning against it. The stench of urine and liquor wafted from him, and he lifted his head from his chest to gaze at us with world-weary eyes.

"Ewww," Lauren said. She stopped and refused to walk any closer.

The other girls stayed at her side. Dylan was still behind us, so I wasn't afraid. That is, until the homeless guy started ambling away from the car, shuffling toward us. The closer he got, the more I noticed the ropes of muscles that bulged beneath his clothes and the way a dark intelligence flickered in his eyes when he glanced up at me. It looked like he was going to pass us, his eyelids thudding closed as if he was barely awake, like he was going to swerve around us toward a nearby alley and then pass out.

But just when he was a few steps away from me he lost his balance and had to shuffle to the side quickly to keep from falling.

His shoulder brushed against mine, pushing me a step backward.

"Careful there, mister," Dylan called out a warning.

"Sorry," he mumbled loud enough for everyone to hear. Then his head dipped closer and I thought I recognized him, that unusual accent, those piercing eyes. When he spoke again, it was just a rough whisper that only I could hear.

"Make sure you keep this with you in the future."

His hand touched mine, just a brushing of flesh against flesh, and then he clumsily regained his balance. He coughed, spit on the ground, causing the other girls to turn away, saying things like *gross* and *yuck*.

A second later he was gone, a shadow blending in with midnight, slipping into the hidden recesses of the alley. The *thunk* of metal as his foot kicked a can and then nothing.

Nothing except my iPhone resting in the palm of my hand.

I shivered, pulled my arms closer, tucking the phone into my pocket, hoping that no one else had noticed it. All the while, I struggled to catch my breath, and my mind fought against what had just happened.

My father had found a way to return my cell phone to me. He knew I snuck out. And I had a feeling that homeless creep was the same guy I'd seen on the Santa Monica Pier seven years ago.

Chapter Twenty-Nine

There weren't any lights on in my house when I got home, but I knew Dad was in there, awake and waiting for me. The other girls were still running in high gear, all chattering and laughing and passing a joint around the car. At first, I thought about protesting. Then I realized that if I walked in the front door smelling like marijuana it wasn't going to make this any worse.

I pulled down the visor and stared in the passenger side mirror, grimacing at what I saw. My right cheek was swollen and red, my lip was cut, and blood had dripped down my chin. Fortunately my other injuries were hidden beneath my clothes, bruises on my arms and my rib cage where Komodo/Sammy had pummeled me repeatedly.

"Holy shit," I murmured.

"What's up?" Lauren asked, her eyes narrowing as she sucked down another hit from that dwindling joint. The girls had all relaxed a bit since they started smoking. This must have been what Lauren meant earlier, when I saw her in the school parking lot. Weed took the edge off

Pink Lightning and got rid of the headaches. I wondered if Lauren, Zoe, and Stephanie struggled with night terrors and tremors like I did, or if that only happened during withdrawal. I still didn't know what that drug did, but I guessed it improved performance when we were fighting. Maybe it improved mental clarity or memory, too. If so, that might be the reason why my grades had gotten better in the past year.

"My face," I said. "I can't go in the house looking like this."

"Nobody's awake," Zoe said, sitting up to lean against my seat. "Just slip into bed and put on some makeup in the morning. You should have some stage makeup in your kit, the one you keep in the closet."

I frowned. Is that what that box was? Even so, I wouldn't make it to my room before running into someone. "My dad's already up."

"Here." Stephanie had been digging through her purse ever since I pulled down the mirror. I thought she was looking for another joint. "Turn around and face me." She had a makeup kit unrolled on her lap, slender brushes and jars of powder and tubes of concealer and pots of blush. "Lean closer. You're a four, no, wait, a three." She pulled out a numbered tube and squeezed a dab of flesh-colored paste into her palm. Alternating between her finger and a brush, she smoothed makeup over my cheek and lips, dusted them with powder, then added some color. After that, she combed my hair, teasing it a bit and following it with a spritz of spray. "Check it out. Look in the mirror again."

I studied my reflection, turning my face from side to side. I looked pretty good, completely different than before. My cheek was still swollen, but my hair and the makeup covered it up. My lips looked completely natural. I grinned.

"Blame it on ballet practice," she said as she began to pack away her kit. "We all say we were injured during sports."

But as soon as that statement slipped from her lips, I knew I wasn't interested in ballet—not like I was before. With every punch I'd delivered back in the ring, blood had rushed through my veins like dark music and my muscles had been singing. It felt like I'd been singing this song all my life, but only understood what the words meant tonight. Part of it reminded me of ballet, how all my muscles needed to work together, how I needed to be limber and flexible and strong, how I had to push through the pain and when I did, it was as beautiful as any dance. Except this was a dance that could deliver broken bones and cracked teeth, it could make my opponent bleed and wince and cry. Something about that last part, the bleeding and the pleading, frightened me. Not because I didn't like it.

Because I did. Maybe too much.

I thought about the bruise on Dylan's cheek. He said he'd been wrestling, but had he really been injured in a Phase Two event?

Stephanie seemed to be the only one telling me what I wanted to know, so I decided to ask a question or two. "Do the boys take Pink Lightning, too?" I asked, wondering if Dylan and Brett were taking the same stuff we were.

She shook her head. Lauren and Zoe had lost interest in our conversation and were passing the last of the joint between themselves.

"They take Blue Thunder. It makes them stronger, but it also makes them more aggressive. Probably why Dylan and Brett got into a fight at the party. Sometimes they can't control it. Side effect, I guess," Stephanie said. She was slipping her kit into her purse, then applying a fresh coat of pink gloss on her lips.

"What is it? Amphetamines, steroids, muscle memory drugs?"

She shrugged and yawned, stretching her arms in front of her. "I don't know. Maybe a combination of all three?"

"Is there really such a thing as muscle memory drugs?" Zoe asked with a tilt of the head.

"I don't know. It just seems like that's what this stuff does—oh, holy freaking crap." The light over my front door just flicked on and it blinked three times. "I'm being summoned. To my death."

Lauren laughed. "Like your dad's gonna punish you. He's never done anything. Not in the whole year you've been going to raves and Phase Two."

I gave her a dirty look. It wasn't like I wanted to get grounded, but nobody disses my dad. Nobody. "Shut up."

She raised her hands, palms up, but there was still a smirk on her face. "Blame it on the drugs, girlfriend, but this all seems funny to me right now. You just about got creamed by Komodo, then managed to wipe the stage with her sorry ass, and now you're pissed because your dad hasn't been beating you, too? You need to know what it's been like in some of *our* homes. We've all got a reason for fighting, some more than others. For us, fighting isn't just a game. It's a way to survive."

There was something in her eyes, something like a combination of pain and defiance. Her chin was lifted, but there was a slight tremble to her lips. She averted her gaze from mine to stare out the window.

"Does your dad, does he—" I said.

She waved her hand, dismissing the subject. "Not tonight, *Odette*. Not unless you've got about three hours and two boxes of Kleenex. Just go inside, okay?"

The other girls got so quiet I could barely tell if they were still breathing. The presence of unspoken pain hung between us and it made my chest ache that I couldn't remember my closest friend's secrets, all the things we had confided with each other between whispers and hugs.

"I'm sorry," I said and I slid my hand across the seat to take hers. She gave me a half-smile, but didn't pull her hand away. "I don't remember everything, but it doesn't mean I don't care." I swept my gaze to include Stephanie and Zoe in the backseat. "I care about all of you."

Only Zoe acknowledged me with a nod, her eyes shining with tears that hadn't fully formed yet. For an instant, I thought I saw her face covered with bruises, barely hidden beneath thick makeup and, when the image faded, I realized it was a memory.

We'd been standing in the girl's bathroom at school when Zoe confided that she'd been raped by her older brother's best friend when he spent the night. I held her, listening while she cried and told me details. I wanted to go kick his ass, but I knew she needed more than that. She needed healing and strength. She needed a *friend*. I tried to get her to talk to the school counselor, but when she refused, I convinced her to skip school instead.

Together we went to that same spot in the woods where I now take Kyle, and I taught her how to fight and defend herself. She picked up my moves really fast, developing her own style that was both beautiful and lethal. With her spins and kicks and her lithe, delicate build, she looked like a woodland fairy come to life—except she was a magical creature ready to defend her kingdom to the death.

A couple of weeks later, the two of us cornered the prick who had raped her. He was alone, smoking a cigarette back behind the school bleachers during fifth period. I let her do most of the work—I was just there for backup and to give her the confidence she needed. He was surprised to see us, and a lecherous grin spread across his face when he first saw Zoe, as if she'd come back for more of what he had to offer. Then his head cracked back with her first spinning kick, his grin disappeared, and after a few well-placed punches, he was on the ground, sobbing, begging her to stop.

Just like she'd begged him.

We heard later that he pissed blood for a week.

Zoe was the first one that I invited into the Silver Level of Phase Two. I wanted to make sure she always knew how to defend herself—whether I was with her or not—and that she knew she'd never have to feel helpless again. She'd gone on to become one of the best fighters in her weight class, a girl who looked as innocent as Bambi but had the ability to take down her opponents in a matter of seconds.

motion caught in my throat. On the surface, it may have looked like we joined this club for the thrill it gave us and that may have been partly true. But there were other reasons, good reasons, powerful Stay Alive To Fight Another Day reasons, none of them more important than the others.

These girls were more than a team of athletes or sparring partners. They'd been there for me, every day, throughout the past year. I'd do anything to protect them.

They were my emotional backup system. Just like Molly had been before I mysteriously ditched her.

And I'd do anything to protect them.

Chapter Thirty

The minute I walked through the front door, I got grounded, my cell phone confiscated. Dad made sure I knew there would be no phone calls, no texts, and no visitors for the entire weekend. That meant I couldn't tell Molly about the rave or the teen fight club hidden inside, and I couldn't talk to Dylan or Lauren about what had happened.

On top of that, Dad already had a cruel and unusual punishment planned that would run through both Saturday and Sunday, one that would ensure I'd be too tired to sneak out again. Early Saturday morning, he corralled both Kyle and me when we were barely awake and he shuffled us into the SUV and started driving. Kyle slumped in the backseat, looking as guilty as I felt.

"I get why you're punishing me, but what's up with Kyle?" I asked, a sullen tone in my voice. I chewed on a cinnamon bagel as we drove, wondering if he was taking us up into the mountains for another round of survival training. I didn't know what to expect until we ended up in the parking lot of a private gym. A frown settled on my brow and I swung around to face Kyle. Had he told Dad that I taught him a couple of martial art moves?

"Did you tell Dad?" I asked.

"I was worried about you, okay?" Kyle confessed, his chin jutting out and his gaze flicking away from me to stare out the window. "You've been acting all spooky lately, like the other night when you almost passed out in the garage."

"Remind me to never help when you complain about guys picking on you at school."

"Whatever."

"That's enough, both of you," Dad said. "Get out, we've got work to do."

We both slunk out of the car, avoiding each other, standing on opposite sides of Dad as we headed toward the gym. Once we were inside, he made us do half an hour of stretching and warming up. Then the real punishment began—eight brutal hours of martial arts training mixed with bare-knuckle boxing. He knew techniques I'd never even seen before and, time after time, I ended up flat on my back, the wind knocked out of me.

I think part of him felt bad, or maybe conflicted, about what he was doing, although I understood his motives. He wanted Kyle and me to be able to fight.

It didn't take long for him to realize I had injuries from my fight last night, even though I never told him any details. He wrapped my ribs with a thick bandage and warned Kyle not to hit me there, telling him that if he cracked or broke one of my ribs it could puncture my lungs.

Kyle stared at me with his mouth open, his face flushed, something like fear or concern in his eyes.

After that we focused on kicks and jabs, careful not to touch each other. Even so, it was still a merciless workout that left me aching and moaning by the time we left. Once we got home, Kyle continued to avoid me, squirreling himself away in his room, glued to his video controller, the volume on his Xbox turned way down. He was probably trying to fly low, under Dad's radar.

TV and video games were off-limits for me, however. Instead I got plenty of time to catch up on my homework. Dad hired some college-age nerd that lived down the street to come over both nights and work as my tutor, both of us sitting in the dining room with a virtual library of textbooks and spiral notebooks fanned out across the table.

It sucked—not just because I was exhausted or because I'd gotten in trouble—but because my memories were starting to come back, one by one, snippets that floated in here and there, leaving me disoriented.

I'd be trying to spar with Dad and I'd suddenly remember that Lauren's dad hit her when she got bad grades—that's why she was such an A-plus superstar. I'd seen the bruises that covered her torso one day when we were changing for PE. She tried to keep them covered up, but her spandex tank top accidentally came off when she pulled her shirt over her head. A couple of days later, I started training her. After a few weeks, Lauren was able to stand up to her father. He cornered her in the living room one night, fist raised and his lips curled in a snarl. Two kicks and one knee to the groin later and he smashed to the floor, knocking over a chair and breaking the coffee table. He needed five stitches on his forehead, and his right arm was in a splint for six weeks.

He never punched her again.

Then, when Kyle was lunging at me, spinning kicks and feigning jabs, I remembered how Stephanie had approached me, how she had confided that being big and strong didn't mean people never picked on you. Even though she stood six feet tall, her older siblings always teased her, doing things like locking her out of the house when her parents went out of town, or writing curse words on her face with a marker if she fell asleep on the sofa. It was hard to teach her, since we weren't matched in size, and it took longer than I expected, but after a few months she was able to stand up to the ringleader—her oldest brother, who was six-foot-five and weighed 220 pounds. Once she put him in his place, none of the others ever bothered her again.

At that point, I had enough trainees to start my own team. Within a few weeks, we became the Swan Girls, all of us with chips on our shoulders and something to prove. We were each either assigned a patron or chosen by one, and then were invited into the Gold Level. From the beginning, we had something none of the other teams had—grace, strength, and speed—and between us, we had a variety of weights, so we could challenge any of the other girl teams. It wasn't long before we rose to the top, becoming a crowd favorite. Everybody knew our stage names and as soon as one of us stepped onstage, the chanting would start.

It was amazing and addictive.

But I didn't remember how or why I got involved in fighting until we got back from the gym on Saturday night and Dad closed his study door, retreating from all of us, even from Mom.

His absence triggered something deep inside me.

I remembered one of the last times he left on a short-term mission and how empty the house felt when he walked out the door. Mom had her typical night shift at Methodist and Kyle was spending the night at a friend's house. Then Dylan texted me, asking if I wanted to go to one of the local skate parks, and I said yes. I didn't notice how sketchy the crowd was that night. All I saw was Dylan, how he crouched on his board, then dropped down the ramp and sped past me.

So I was caught off guard when a group of five girls wearing gang colors followed me into the bathroom. Maybe it was initiation night. Or maybe it was just time to pick on The Girl Wearing Pink in a world that dressed in black. I don't remember exactly what happened, their punches and kicks came so fast. I think I may have screamed. Not that it stopped them.

But it did bring Dylan into the bathroom.

There was a stand-off for a fraction of a second. Testosterone snapped through the small space, my blood dripped on the tile floor, and my reflection watched from the stainless steel mirror.

"Leave her alone," he said, his voice a low growl.

"Or what?" one of the girls asked. She flicked out a switchblade. Her friends laughed.

"Or your parents will be getting phone calls from the hospital. They'll be needing someone to identify you."

A shiver ran through me.

Dylan looked bigger, stronger than ever before.

The other girls noticed it, too. The girl who had been holding me down let go.

"My boyfriend'll slice you up," the girl with the blade threatened.

Dylan took a step closer. "Then *he'll* be in the hospital, too."

She tackled him then, the idiot. With two lightning moves, he knocked the switchblade out of her hand and pinned her to the ground, his foot on her back. Another girl jumped him and he grabbed her, twisting her arm behind her so she couldn't move. He didn't hurt any of them, maybe because they were girls and there are some rules you're not supposed to break.

But I knew he could have put every one of them in the emergency room.

They knew it, too.

One by one they all backed out of the bathroom, wary. I worried that when we came out, they'd be waiting with a gang of boys at their side.

The park was empty, lights out, only a few cars left in the parking lot. They'd all run away.

Dylan stayed with me that night, making sure I was okay and that I didn't have any serious injuries. I fell asleep curled next to him on the sofa and woke up with his arm around me.

I'd never felt that safe with anyone before. Except my dad. But he wasn't around when this happened and I resented him for it. Too much.

On top of the resentment, there was fear inside me that kept surfacing when I didn't expect it. Just walking into a public restroom gave me a panic attack. I couldn't tell my mom, and I wasn't about to tell Kyle. They'd both freak out. Mom would've made me go see a counselor, but what good would that do? Counseling wouldn't protect me if I was jumped again.

Dylan noticed the change in me. "I can teach you how to defend yourself," he'd said.

"But there were *five* of them," I argued.

"Part of defending yourself is always being aware of what's going on around you." He paused. "But I can teach you what to do if you ever have to protect yourself again. In a way, it's a lot like ballet. You'd pick it up quick."

Once Dylan began teaching me how to fight, my fears started to melt away.

And, no matter what, I still liked, no, I *loved*, fighting.

But the feeling that I was invincible was gone.

It had disappeared on that night I went missing.

CHAPTER THIRTY-ONE

Monday came, a horizon of beautiful, blue sky and warm spring breezes. Today, some kids from school would be getting up early to dash off to the ocean where they'd walk on water via surfboards. Others would be writing last-minute term papers while their parents drove them to school. Still others would be smiling at family members and upperclassmen who had been regularly tormenting them, making them feel like they weren't good enough, like they would never measure up.

I wasn't sure which category I fit into anymore.

Was I the leader of the Swan Team or was I a Lost Girl, desperately trying to remember my past?

I downed a glass of juice, clutched a slice of toast between my teeth and headed out of the kitchen, walking toward the garage and my car and freedom. But I didn't get far before Dad stopped me in the hallway. I didn't lift my head to look at him. I just stared at the floor while he handed me my phone.

"Keep this with you, got it?" he asked, his tone deep

and serious. It was the voice he used that meant *Do This Or Else*. In other words, it was a voice he rarely used with me and it brought a flush of red to my cheeks.

"Yes, sir," I answered, still not brave enough to look him in the eyes.

"Come on, we're gonna be late!" Kyle called from the garage.

I resented my little brother right now. He lived in a free zone, untouched by our punishment this weekend because it hadn't been his fault. Just like a typical teenage boy, he was more concerned about his latest Spartan Op score than whether I was still mad at him.

I walked past Dad, that slice of toast still hanging from the corner of my mouth, my backpack slung over one shoulder. It was a long walk down the hallway, knowing he was watching me. The muscles in my back tensed up and they didn't relax until long after Kyle and I pulled into the student parking lot. I drove past those flowering cherry trees, fighting the urge to slam my car into one of them, taking it down, shaking those petals off the limbs until the tree was barren and dead.

Which was about how I felt right now.

Kyle and I hadn't said much to each other during the ride, not until he got out and reached into the backseat for his knapsack. "See ya," he grumbled, left hand grabbing for the straps, while his right hand cradled an open can of Red Bull.

Then everything happened at once.

His backpack flew open—as usual, there was way too much junk crammed inside—and stuff started spilling out all over my car. Spiral notebooks, Milky Way wrappers, a pack of Orbit gum, a pocketknife, three textbooks. He cursed and started grabbing everything as fast as possible. I swung around to help him, picking up papers and pens from the floor, but at the same time his half-full can of Red Bull spilled on my shirt.

"Shit!" I said, all my anger seething to the surface as I glanced down at the spreading stain. "Thanks a lot, jerk!"

"I don't know why you're making such a big deal out of it—"

"You can find your own way home after school today, smart-ass."

"Whatever."

"And I can't believe you told Dad I was teaching you how to fight—"

"You know what? You *suck*!" He got out of the car and stood up, glaring at me through narrowed eyes. Then he huffed his chest out and left his school books scattered all over my car and headed toward the school building, his whole body angry, shoulders hunched in, torso leaning into a jog-run, fists clenched.

I cursed, loud and long, and then slammed my fist against my steering wheel, inadvertently making the horn blast. Almost like it had been synchronized, a pack of sophomores all turned at the same time and gave me a weird look. "Get out of here," I growled at them through the open door. They started to run away, right as a gust of warm air blew a handful of cherry blossoms into the car.

I blinked. No longer able to fight their haunting fragrance. Or the spinning white petals.

"Hey, girl," a voice from the past called to me. "Over here."

I blinked again.

The gorgeous spring day faded away as a memory came over me. Stronger than any I'd had so far, it consumed me, it was so real—

•••

I was walking to my car, head down, still mad because the past few days had sucked, royally, totally. So much I could barely breathe. I'd lost my team, my friends, and my boyfriend, almost within a matter of hours. Even going to school had become a major effort. There should have been somebody standing outside the school doors today, handing out awards to all of us who wanted to be anywhere but here. I'd have a gold star tattooed on my forehead right now.

   She called to me again.

"Come on," she said, leaning toward me. She sat in a white Mazda hatchback, her long, dark hair catching in the breeze, those bright pink strands fading because she hadn't dyed her hair recently. I left my car behind and walked in her direction, toward where she parked at the curb, her car rumbling beneath those Japanese cherry trees.

   It looked like a postcard, one of those perfect shots that could lure vacationers to come visit Southern California. A pretty girl sitting in a white car beneath blossoming trees, mountains in the background.

"What's up, Nicole?" I called. She wasn't part of my problem. If anything, she was the solution. Nicole Hernandez and I had met back when we were both in Silver Level. At that point, neither one of us had a team yet and we used to spar together—back before I became Odette of the Swan Girls and she became Taffy of Pink Candi. Once we both got our own teams we vowed to never, ever compete against each other, so we rarely attended raves on the same nights.

   None of my other friends knew about her—not Lauren or Dylan or Zoe. Nicole was my secret friend, the person I talked to about everything. I even told her how bad I'd felt about ditching Molly. I cared way too much about my best friend to drag her into my dark, dangerous world of raves and drugs and fighting.

"You'll never guess what I got," Nicole said with a devilish gleam in her dark eyes.

I hoped she wouldn't say E or weed, because I wasn't in the mood to get high.

Long fingers snapped a pair of tickets against her steering wheel. So fast I couldn't even tell what they were. I leaned in her window and grabbed them away from her. Heavy black cardstock and glittering silver letters.

Platinum Level tickets.

I pulled in a long breath.

"It's frigging real?" I asked. My knees actually felt weak for a half-second. "There really is a Platinum Level?"

"It's real, all right. But we gotta leave. Like, now. Get in, girl."

I ran around her car and jumped in, slamming my knapsack into the backseat.

"This level's different, really different. Check it out." She handed me a computer printout to read as she drove away. I had a momentary snap of conscience as I realized I was ditching my little brother. He'd have to find another way home today. Then I remembered all the times I'd waited for him after school and he hadn't bothered to tell me he was going to a friend's house to play video games.

I scanned the paper. It contained a list of instructions for the event.

"It starts in an hour?" I asked, glancing at the map. "Can we get there in time?"

"Watch me. I've got mad driving skills." She laughed, a deep, throaty sound that made me laugh, too.

"And what's this?" I pointed at the page. "The only rules are there are no rules? Is that scary or exciting?"

She shrugged as we zipped onto the freeway, buzzing from one lane to another. "Maybe a little bit of both?" she said.

We had to get down to a sketchy neighborhood in Rosemead, somewhere off the 10, so Nicole and I focused our attention on the road, her slipping into tiny slots that opened up between speeding cars and me pointing out any open spaces I saw. It took about forty-five minutes before we were chugging along the 10, then swinging off an exit. Neither one of us had been down in this area before, a narrow industrial park wedged between Temple City, El Monte, and Rosemead, where most of the buildings were colored by graffiti and gang signs. We passed abandoned gas stations with broken windows, a drive-in theater, tiny stucco houses with bars on the windows, and strip malls where all the signs were written in Korean.

I read her the address again and we slowed to a stop, both of us staring at a building up ahead. A row of square windows was placed high up on cement walls. Smokestacks jutted out of the roof, and a big black and white sign said HALL FOR RENT. It was a large building, but there was no rave here, no thumping music. Only a few thick-waisted, heavily muscled men in white tank tops standing outside let you know this building was even open.

"You sure this is the right place?" I asked, looking at the paper again, a strange feeling twisting in my gut. All the other raves we'd been to had been crowded with thousands of people my age. That whole safety-in-numbers thing was ringing in my ears.

"Yup," she answered quickly, pulling her keys from the ignition.

"How'd you get these tickets and this printout?" I asked as we climbed out of her car.

"Found a manila envelope with my name on it in my mailbox this morning."

We walked toward the building, but that sense of

something being wrong wouldn't go away. "But nobody at Phase Two knows our names or addresses. Isn't that part of the rules? Only stage names, so we can be anonymous."

She laughed. "How hard would it be to ask someone we hang out with what our real names are?"

"But they could get kicked out for doing that—"

She shook her head, tossing a grin to the guys who surrounded the building. One of them smiled back and opened the front door for us. "It wasn't that hard for us when we were checking out Alexis, Shelby, Lacy, and Janie, back when we were putting our teams together."

"True."

"Besides, nobody would get kicked out if the guy who runs the show was the one asking the questions. Like that announcer guy with the Brooklyn accent."

I accepted her reasoning, a sliver of excitement charging through me as we walked down a long, narrow hallway. The building's interior was even more shabby and deteriorated than the exterior. Maybe this was an element all the rave locations had in common, something that had always been hidden because we only saw them at night, when the walls were smattered with colored lights and the floors were covered with dancing people.

"This *is what we've wanted from Day One, girl,"* Nicole breathed as we approached a pair of double doors. Loud cheering rumbled from the other side, something about it sounding different than all the Phase Two events. "To make it to the top. And since I got two tickets, we finally get to go, both *of us. We never had to break the rules or fight each other. We kept it clean."* She smiled an honest grin, the kind only a true friend could give you. She was the kind of friend you'd want to keep for your whole life, all the way through high school and college and even after you both had families,

still getting together for birthdays and still calling each other
in the middle of the night if something went wrong.

Next to Molly, she was the closest friend I'd ever
had, and we held hands as we walked through that door,
a blinding light shining down on us that washed away
everything on the other side.

I sank back in my car seat, the memory of Nicole
fading away, the parking lot and the school building
coming back into focus. My brother's books and gum
wrappers lay scattered about on the backseat, my shirt still
sticky and damp from Red Bull. An echo of the school bell
hung in the air, heralding the beginning of yet another day
at Lincoln High.

That was the last time I ever saw Nicole and it was the
same night I went missing.

She was murdered and I was kidnapped.

But something had happened even before that,
something I couldn't remember, and it had propelled me
toward that Platinum Level door—I'd broken up with
Dylan and lost my teammates and it had left me feeling
raw and wounded. And, despite what everyone thought,
I hadn't been *taken* at school. I'd gotten into Nicole's car
willingly, eagerly, more than ready to face whatever lay on
the other side of that Platinum Level door, beyond that
blinding white light.

Had whatever lay on the other side been too terrifying
for me to remember? Had I blocked it out and erased it?

Those questions jabbed and punched from the shadows,
fists reaching out to make me stumble as I grabbed an old
sweatshirt from my trunk. When I walked away from my car,
my footsteps were unsteady and my concentration limited.

PART THREE

The ONLY rule is There are NO RULES.

CHAPTER THIRTY-TWO

I did what I vowed I'd never do. But isn't that what always happens when things get tough? We run in the wrong direction, arms flailing, calling for someone, anyone, to help. We climb up muddy inclines and wave our arms as we walk across lanes of traffic, willing cars to stop, demanding strangers to rescue us.

We walk away from danger toward any bright light that flickers.

I shuffled down the school hallway, legs on autopilot as I headed toward first period. My body was willing to keep up the charade, to attend classes and nod knowingly when teachers asked questions. My mind, on the other hand, was doing that flailing thing, forcing my hands to scream for help.

My phone was out and I was texting Agent Ryan Bennet. I was telling him everything.

I'm not even sure how coherent my end of the conversation was, since I was continually interrupted by him texting me back for clarification.

You left school grounds with Nicole Hernandez?

That's what he wrote but I knew what he was thinking—Nicole, the dead girl, she left with the girl who got murdered, it's a miracle they both didn't end up dead.

Do you remember the address of where you went?

I didn't. The landscape of my past was full of holes, parts of it disappearing off the edges of my vision, as if only a few city blocks existed and everything beyond that was fantasy. And that blinding white light—it erased everything, it mesmerized and it destroyed. The other side of the door wasn't real. It was the edge of the universe, it was hell, it was the end of everything.

How did you get away?

Why wouldn't he let that drop? I got away because I got away, because somebody left a door open or because they didn't tie my ropes tight enough. I didn't know. I might never know. I only wanted to catch whoever killed Nicole and make him burn. Forever and ever and ever.

"Do you have the answer to the next problem?"

That was my algebra teacher, Mr. Buchanan, interrupting me while I was trying to work out a plan to destroy the network of thugs who were kidnapping and killing girls my age.

"Yes," I answered, slightly thankful that I had spent the past two nights working with a tutor. Now I could get through the day without my teachers knowing that I was only partly here. The other part of me was hunting monsters. I got out my worksheet, walked to the front of the class, and wrote the equation and the answer on the whiteboard.

When I turned around my gaze fell on Dylan.

We had broken up, right before I went missing. But I couldn't remember why.

What happened? I wanted to demand. *Why had we broken up and why had I felt like I didn't have any friends?* He saw something in my eyes, maybe anger or confusion or maybe the fact that I finally had a specific question to ask him, and he flinched.

You don't remember all the things I've done, things I regret.

Yeah, I thought. *Things that I need to know.*

I marched past him, refusing to look at him again. Once I got back to my desk I continued to text Agent Bennet. Before I knew it, class was over and the bell rang. Dylan stood next to my desk, looking like he wasn't about to let me leave the room.

"What's wrong?" he asked. "I tried to call and text you about a jillion times since Friday night—"

"Why didn't you tell me we broke up right before I went missing?" I asked as I stood up, my voice louder than it should have been. The teacher raised his head and looked at both of us. I stabbed a finger at Dylan's chest. "Why have you been acting like everything's fine and has been all along, except it couldn't have been, could it?"

A long beat passed, then a flicker of guilt settled on his face and his brows pinched together. "I—it—*you* were the one who broke up with *me.*"

"Why would I do that?"

"You don't remember?" A moment of relief flashed in his eyes. Then it disappeared because he knew this wasn't over yet. "We can't talk about it here." He tried to take my arm, but I yanked it away.

"Is everything okay, Rachel?" Mr. Buchanan asked from the front of the room.

"Oh, it's just peachy," I said as I huffed out of the room, Dylan a step behind me. I pushed my way into the crowds that shuffled down the hall, amidst students heading zombie-like to period two, half of them not even awake from the weekend yet. Dylan grabbed my arm again and pulled us over to the side of the hallway. "Nice," I said. "Are you going to give me some answers now?"

He glanced around us, a look on his face that said he didn't care who knew about our double lives anymore. I certainly didn't.

"Why did we break up?" I asked again. "What did you do and how did I end up without my team?"

"You didn't lose your team because of *me*. We were at the club and you were having the worst fight ever, so bad I thought about going up there and stopping it —"

"With who?"

"Cyclone, one of the Blue Hurricanes."

My brow lowered as I tried to figure out who that was. Then a girl who looked like Katy Perry appeared in my memory. It was Janie Deluca and she was slamming her fist in my gut, again and again.

"She was double tapping," he said, then explained what that meant when I gave him a blank expression. "She took two hits of Pink Lightning and turned into a killing machine, shoving you around. No matter what you did, she wouldn't back down. It was like she wasn't human."

My hands were on my hips and I tried to remember, but all I could see was one image, like a snapshot—Janie's eyes narrowed and swollen, her mouth dripping blood, a bruise darkening her jaw and her fist reaching toward me, sweat flying off strands of her blue hair—

"She was wearing you out," he continued, "and your fight had already dragged on for twenty minutes, way longer than you normally fight. You're usually done within five to ten. At that point you *had* to get serious—"

So far, none of this explained why Dylan and I had broken up. I got impatient, my left foot tapping the floor, my arms crossed. The school crowd around us thinned until only a few kids still lounged against lockers, some of them staring at us whenever our voices raised.

"You delivered one bone-crunching kick after another until, finally, she tumbled to the floor, a hot mess of blue hair and bruised skin, blood streaming from her nose. But—"

He paused and I could tell by his expression that whatever was coming up next was bad.

"She wasn't moving and she wasn't breathing."

It was like knowing the end of the story, but not the beginning. I knew that everything must have worked out because I had seen Janie alive since then. "What happened?" I asked.

"The announcer lifted your hand and proclaimed you the winner, but you pulled away from him. You got down on your hands and knees and started doing CPR on Cyclone. Not exactly what you're supposed to do—"

I stared at him with glassy eyes. I still couldn't remember what had happened, but if what he said was true, then I had broken one of the cardinal Phase Two rules. Never touch your opponent after the fight's been called. I'd risked everything to try and save her.

"Thankfully, Cyclone came to," he continued. "But the cheering stopped and a deadly silence filled the room. The cameras stopped panning the crowd and the rest of the fights that night were cancelled. Meanwhile, you and your patron got into a huge argument. When you were finally ready to leave, you were majorly pissed off and said you never wanted to come back. You even quit your team and told all your girls they were on their own. Zoe and I tried to talk you out of it, and then that turned into another fight—"

Flickers of our argument came back to me. I remembered screaming at him, telling him that he had to drop out of the club, too, or I never wanted to see him again.

"It didn't matter *what* I said." He stared at the floor, his jaw clenched shut.

Everything he said was true, yet it had a hollow ring to it, like there was more to this story. I kept getting flashes of those cars that I'd seen lined up at the rave Saturday night, and a horrible shiver ran over my skin, along with a sick feeling in my gut.

The two of us were running away from a stolen car, being chased by a cop—

I gasped and took a step away from him.

"We were stealing cars!"

He shook his head. "*I* was stealing cars, you only came with me once. You wanted me to quit, but I couldn't—"

"Why not?"

He lifted his shoulders, looking defeated. "The club's a different place for guys. They only give us Blue Thunder until we get hooked." For the first time I noticed a slight tremor in his hands. He must have been struggling with side effects, just like I was. "Once we're addicted, our patrons won't give us more, not unless we do what they say. For a long time, I just had to get new recruits for Phase Two. But once I had the Ravens put together, the rules changed. Stealing became a requirement—we had to bring them a car every week or two."

"Why didn't you just go to the cops?"

He laughed. "That's what you said before. Who would believe me, Rach? I don't even know who these people are. I tried to quit taking Blue Thunder on my own, more than once, but—it just didn't work."

I waited, wondering what else had happened.

"So, we broke up," he said, looking like he had ended up on the mat at the end of a long fight. "And then a couple of days later, you went missing." He was staring into my eyes now, a deep, soulful look like he hoped I would believe him and that he wouldn't lose me again. "I never told you how much I cared about you. Not before you went missing. And when you were gone, I couldn't live with myself. It felt like everything was my fault—"

I believed what he said—that we had broken up because he wouldn't leave the club—but there was still some other detail he wasn't telling me. I could hear it in his voice and see it in his eyes, almost like when he'd asked me out a few days ago and then wasn't sure if I'd say yes.

"But *something* else happened, didn't it?" I asked. "You're not telling me everything."

"You asked why we broke up and that's it. There isn't anything else."

"Yeah." I nodded my head. "There *is*."

But I could tell he was done talking. I frowned, disappointed, wondering why there was such a guilty look in his eyes. "I gotta get to class now," I said. "See ya later."

He tried to grab my hand, but I pulled away and headed down the hall. Alone.

Chapter Thirty-Three

I walked away from Dylan more confused than ever. There was a heaviness in my soul now, like I'd been kicked in the chest and knocked backward. The fact that he and the Ravens had gotten involved in stealing cars was worse than I'd expected. Had the Skulls and the Orcs and the other boys' teams been forced to participate in criminal activity, too, and if so, what? The more I found out about this underground fight club, the worse it got. Still, I wasn't going to give up, I couldn't. I had to find out what had happened to Nicole and this was only Round One.

That's what I kept telling myself as I shoved my way down the hall, from one class to another. I kept feeling like I'd missed something, like something was coming and I needed to be ready for it, like somewhere along the line I was going to get another clue. Then, when I walked into history, I saw that none of the Dragon Girls were in class today.

Had Sammy/Komodo been injured that badly during our fight?

Guilt mixed with the bewilderment I was already feeling.

Throughout history class, I kept getting brief memory flashes from the night Dylan and I had stolen a car together, how it had been exciting at first, but had turned terrifying when we almost got caught. Panic rushed over me when I realized he could end up in prison if he stayed in Phase Two. There had to be something we could do, some way to get him out.

But he wasn't waiting for me when class was over. When I got to lunch, I discovered he wasn't in the cafeteria, either. Or at least, I couldn't see him from the lunchroom door, because that was as far as I got. I paused, backpack in one hand, cell phone in the other when I got a text from Molly.

How was your weekend?? Never heard from you again.
Weird. Where are you?

A few seconds passed before a reply came.

Home. Asthma. Going to doctor.

I sank back against the doorframe, letting the throng of hungry teenagers pour past me. This was what it had been like throughout our childhood. If Molly ever got too stressed out, she got sick, really sick. Like she couldn't breathe and had to go to the hospital sick. You never knew what would trigger her asthma, either, because sometimes she'd have a small attack at first and then a worse one a few days after. I remembered how she had fumbled with her inhaler the other night when we were in my car, right after I'd kicked the crap out of Janie Deluca.

Molly was probably sick because she was hanging out with me again.

Leaving for doctor. Call me after dinner? she texted.
Yeah.

I was just putting my phone away when Lauren came out of nowhere, grabbed me and half-dragged me down the hall toward the girls' bathroom. All the way, she tried to shush me. I kept asking her the same questions over and over—*what's up?, what's wrong?, where are we going?*—but she wouldn't talk until the two of us were locked together in a stall.

As far as secrecy went, this place would have been at the bottom of my list.

People had seen us come in here. They could see us now with our legs poking out below the bottom of the stall, and once we started talking they would be able to hear us.

"This isn't exactly a cone of silence," I said when she finally released me.

"It is if we whisper," she said. "Look what I got!"

I probably shouldn't have been surprised. I mean, hadn't God and the universe and my own retrograde memory banks been preparing me for this moment? Still, the serendipity of it caused my eyes to widen and a loud gasp to come out of my lungs.

She held two black and silver tickets in her hand.

Platinum Level.

"It wasn't just a rumor." Her voice came out in a low, hoarse whisper.

I shook my head.

"So what do you think? You wanna go with me, don't you?"

I nodded. My words had evaporated. I kept seeing that door opening and the blinding light; I kept hearing the loud cheering that came from the other side, sounding somehow different from what we'd always heard during the normal Phase Two raves.

"Cat got your tongue, girlfriend?" Lauren laughed.

"I, um, yeah, I guess. Did you get any instructions or do you know where to go?" I didn't want to tell her too much, like the fact that I had just found out my boyfriend was a car thief or that I had gone to a Platinum Level event before, or that some really bad stuff might have happened there. I *had* to go to this tonight and I *had* to find out what was on the other side of that door. It was the only way I would ever find out what had happened to Nicole.

"I have the directions in my car," she said. "It's not anywhere they've held raves before."

"Any chance it's off the 10?"

"Yeah! How did you know? Did you get tickets, too?" A disappointed expression darkened her features.

"No, it's just somebody I know went to one of these once. I only remembered it this morning."

"Really? Did she say what it was like?"

"Nope. She was totally secretive, like, *I can't give you any details.*" I was going to Hell for this. I was lying to one of my friends and possibly putting her life in danger. "What if it's dangerous, Lauren?" I asked, giving her a chance to back out. "What if it's not what we expect, like we could get hurt or something—"

"That's why we're going together. Nothing can happen as long as we stick together, right?"

I swallowed nervously. Well, technically, we could both wind up beaten to death and dropped off by the side of the road, or we could end up missing like the other Lost Girls. I gave her a look that revealed all my concerns and doubts.

"You're not afraid, are you?" she asked. "You've never been afraid of anything."

"No. I'm not afraid. I want to go. I just wonder if maybe we *shouldn't* go. Not this time—"

She shook her head, sent that long, golden Rapunzel

hair spinning around her. "No way. I'm not giving you these tickets so you can go with somebody else. You're coming with me or not at all!"

There was a slender moment when I could have grabbed those tickets away from her and ripped them up. But it was almost as if she sensed what I was thinking. She pulled them back, then stuffed them in her Prada purse.

"What's it gonna be?" she asked, a cold expression in her eyes. "Me and you? Or me and somebody else?"

I sucked a long breath through my teeth, forcing myself to relax. I was still tempted to lunge at her and wrestle her to the ground and yank that designer purse away—which would be hard in this tight space. We'd probably smash our heads on the wall or the stall or the floor. If we were out in the hallway, or outside the building, it would have been easy to take her down. But in here, I might lose. Somebody might come in the bathroom, some teacher or janitor or administrator, and think they needed to break us up. They'd be wrong, of course.

This wasn't just about finding out what had happened to Nicole anymore—it was about stopping it from ever happening again.

I gave Lauren a reluctant grin, then raised one eyebrow. "If you go with anybody else, I might have to kick your ass. Here and now."

She laughed. "*That's* the Rachel I know and love. We have to leave right after school. In fact, if we could skip last period, that would be even better."

A lump lodged in my throat, like I'd swallowed a rock. We were leaving the safe haven of the Swan Girls, getting ready to swim out into deep water, away from our lake and into an adjoining ocean.

It was going to be a miracle if either one of us survived.

...

We climbed into Lauren's car at 2 p.m. and I still had no idea where we were going. She never showed me the paper with all the instructions and directions. Just like the compulsive control freak she truly was, she'd already pre-programmed everything into her GPS system and I couldn't see it from where I sat. I sent Agent Bennet a quick text. Maybe if I kept the FBI in the loop, everything would be safe. They could be our backup.

I didn't get a reply, but I was wearing that kandi bracelet.

I twisted my hands in my lap and bit my lip. I would have felt a whole lot better if Bennet would effing text me back and let me know he got my message. I hadn't heard from him since this morning, since before Dylan revealed his criminal side and Lauren showed me those tickets.

"You're pretty quiet for a girl who's on the way to her Ultimate Destiny."

"What?" I asked. That term sounded both familiar and creepy at the same time.

"That's what you used to say whenever we were heading to a Phase Two event. 'Get ready for your Ultimate Destiny, girls.'"

"Sounds pretty shallow," I said as I stared out the window. I tried to remember details of my previous journey to this place, but the fear surging through my veins prevented me from thinking clearly. Was that our exit up ahead?

"Sounds to me like somebody needs a hit of Pink Lightning."

"No. Absolutely, no way. Nada."

"You're just chicken because you don't remember what it's like. Trust me, it's *amazing*. And I have plenty. We could even double tap, if we wanted."

A shiver ran through me as I thought about what Dylan had told me earlier, about that fight I'd had with Janie Deluca. "Have you ever double tapped?" I asked.

"Not yet, but I've always wanted to. Ever since—" Her voice trailed off.

"Ever since my last fight with Cyclone?"

"You remember that?" She shot me a startled glance.

"Yup."

"And you, uh, remember *everything*? Like what happened afterward, too?"

"I remember that I quit. Then Dylan and I broke up. And I got kidnapped—although I don't really remember that last part."

"Yeah." Sweat beaded on her forehead. She flashed me a look that was probably supposed to be empathetic, but was a complete fail. "That all sucked. I'm really glad you're back and okay."

"Me, too. The only thing is, there's like this blank spot between me breaking up with Dylan and the day I went missing." I paused. "You don't know anything about what happened between him and me, do you?"

"Me? Nah. I didn't see you after the fight—I was out of school for a couple of days. Wish I had, though. I'd have told you that us girls were all still behind you, whether you were on the team or not. Wait, there's our exit."

I thumbed in the name of the exit and the direction we were headed, then pressed send, hoping that Bennet was getting my messages.

"Who are you texting? This is all supposed to be secret, you know," she chided me as we drove.

"I'm just letting my brother know he has to get another ride home from school," I said, staring out the window.

Everything looked like it had in my memory of Nicole this morning. There was that abandoned gas station, the windows still broken. Up ahead was the drive-in theater. The surroundings felt eerily familiar, like I was driving through a nightmare and was desperate to wake up. I shoved air down my throat and filled my lungs, reminding myself to breathe.

"You okay?" she asked. "You look like you might get sick."

"I'm just really, really excited," I told her, but in reality I was telling my stomach to settle down. It wasn't working. Was this event always held in the same place? If so, that didn't make sense. The whole rave culture was illegal, hence the reason for continually moving the location. Everything we passed looked vaguely ominous, from the bar-crusted windows to the power lines that choked out the sky, like these were all warning signs.

You're heading toward destruction.

I should have said, stop the car, turn around, run if you have to.

Instead, I texted Bennet again, sending the names of cross streets we passed.

"Hey, enough with the nimble fingers. Give me your phone." Lauren leaned over and grabbed my cell before I could react. "Come on, Rach, stay focused. We need to psych ourselves up. We gotta be at the top of our game."

I leaned back in my seat, reluctantly agreeing with her. Some of my texts *had* to have gone through and that kandi bracelet was supposed to alert the FBI if I did anything unusual. Skipping my last class and driving through a gang-infested neighborhood sure seemed to fit the bill.

Bennet would be here. I was counting on it.

...

Our car doors swung open, our feet crunched over gravel and we moved, dreamlike, over cracked concrete toward a building that looked like it had been abandoned since it was built in the '40s. My throat was dry and I craved a drink of water. That high-spirited demeanor Lauren had exhibited earlier was fading. Now every step she took was light-footed, her shoulders slightly hunched, her posture defensive. She swung a glance around us, taking everything in and still denying what she saw. That same group of tough guys guarded the entrance, although the doors hung open today, a thick, hungry darkness beckoning from within.

"Where are all the cars?" Lauren asked me. "This place should be packed."

The lot and surrounding streets looked suspiciously empty, just like the last time I had been here. But, once I'd gotten inside, I'd heard the emphatic shouts of a mob. Had all those people come on a bus or something?

"Hey, sweetness," one of the greasy-haired creeps called out to us. "You got an invitation?"

Lauren's head bobbed up and down as she slid those tickets out of her pocket, then lifted them so everyone could see. A couple of the guys chuckled, almost as if they could sense her apprehension.

"Platinum Level, huh?" I said in a loud voice, striding toward that open door with as much confidence as I could pull together. "That means there's gotta be a crowd inside. So, where are all the cars?"

One of the guys did a dramatic bow, which set the others laughing again. "Valets, at your service. We aim to please. No need to have looky-loos dropping by, right?"

"You sure you want to go through with this?" I asked Lauren, my voice low.

She nodded.

We walked through the front door together, side by side, heads up as if we were already inside and being watched by the largest crowd we'd ever seen.

"These raves sure look different during the day, don't they?" she said, pushing a short laugh out of her lungs at the end of her sentence.

"I don't think this is a rave."

"True. But this place still looks like a dive, just like all the others."

Our footsteps echoed down the long, narrow hall, a dull harmony of heel-toe, heel-toe. I swung a nervous glance over my shoulder, back toward that sun-drenched yawn of empty parking lot. Bennet wasn't here yet. I worried that he wasn't coming, that some other crisis had been more important. Maybe some other teenage girl had needed rescuing or maybe the traffic had been too heavy or maybe he never cared as much as he pretended.

I forced those thoughts away. Lauren and I weren't alone in this, we couldn't be.

"Give me my phone," I said. She slid it into my hand. That closed doorway loomed up ahead. Already I could hear the faint, whooping shouts of a large crowd on the other side, could feel the thunder of applause in the soles of my feet.

Some door guard was going to take away both of our phones soon. Someone was walking toward us now, coming from behind, heavy footsteps pounding on cement floor. I could feel him getting closer. At this point, I knew that Lauren and I no longer had the choice to turn around and leave.

My legs slowed me to a stop, like they just realized they

had somewhere else they'd rather be.

"If there's ever a problem, you can send me a text. Okay?"

It was too late to call my dad now—not with a Platinum Level guard a few feet away and getting closer with every breath—but I could send a text. I clenched my phone like it was a lifeline, punched in three buttons and pressed send.

9-1-1

I hoped he would know what it meant.

Sweat dripped down my neck as I prayed that this building got cell reception. The walls were made of thick cement blocks, probably reinforced with steel, just like Costco and Sam's Club. Mom and Dad would lose each other forever in those places because their phone calls wouldn't get through.

"No phones, no cameras, no keys, no purses," a gruff voice said behind us. "And no jewelry." One of the meatheads who had been lounging outside grabbed both Lauren and me by the arm. "Hand 'em over."

"But I have our gear in my purse," Lauren argued. "We can't fight in our school clothes—"

"We've got that all taken care of, sweetness," he said as he yanked away my phone and my kandi bracelet, tucking them into a large plastic bag. But in the process of reaching for Lauren's purse, that kandi bracelet tumbled out of the bag and when he took a step forward, it got crushed beneath his heavy boots. Before I could even react, he pulled the batteries out of our phones.

Had my text to Dad gotten through or was it lost in cyberspace?

"Inside, girls," the guard said with a smile that looked more like a snarl. He pointed toward the closed door that had been haunting me all day. "They're waiting for ya."

Chapter Thirty-Four

The door opened and the sweaty heat of a large crowd poured out. I blinked, temporarily blinded by the bright lights that focused on us. Then the lights swung away, beaming down on a fight that was already taking place in the center of the cavernous room. That guy behind us pushed, one broad hand on my back and one on Lauren's, guiding us both toward another door. We weren't in the main arena long, but in that amount of time I was able to see a lot.

This hall was bigger than anywhere we'd fought before.

And it wasn't filled with a crowd of cheering kids.

This place was crammed—wall to wall with barely enough room for a center aisle to walk down toward the stage—with screaming, jumping, cheering adults. Most of them were men who looked like the guys standing outside, muscles pumped, skin tattooed, faces stubbled and unshaven. They were all ages and races, from early twenties to late sixties, black hair to white, all with fists raised— the same way we acted when we watched our own fights.

But there was a chilling difference between this group of spectators and us. They leered and jeered and called out obscenities to the girls onstage. They licked their lips and they leaned forward, fingers digging eagerly into pockets for more cash as they shouted their bids.

It felt like I was at a slave auction.

Was that what went on in the Platinum Level? We were up for sale? A shudder ran through me, one that shook me all the way to my bones. If I was right, who was buying fighters and what were they planning to do with us?

I looked at Lauren, wondering if she understood what was happening. Fear glistened in her eyes, but she looked like she was fighting against it. She pulled her shoulders back and walked with a swagger. The indecisive girl in the parking lot vanished. If she kept this act up, she was going to get top dollar.

But I had no idea whether that was good or bad.

We were pushed through the second door where a small entourage of girls our age waited, all with doe-like eyes and heads that bowed when we walked in.

"Get these two ready for the next fight," the guy behind us growled.

"Of course!" One of them—an amber-haired girl with olive skin—hurried forward, her features both exotic and slightly familiar. She led us to a couple of chairs and gestured for us to sit down. Then she pulled out a makeup kit and started setting up her brushes and pots of color. "How do you want them? Innocent? Sophisticated? Trampy?"

I flinched when she said that last word and I shot a glance at Lauren. She swallowed but kept her head up as the girl started applying base foundation on Lauren's ivory skin.

"Innocent, like babes in the wood," he said, then he flicked a finger toward me. "But make sure this one draws everyone's attention. She's the leader of her group. And a real troublemaker."

I wished I could remember what I'd done the last time I was here. Clearly I'd been difficult. I gave him a haughty look, pretending this was what happened before every fight. "No men in the changing room. We won't be able to act innocent onstage if some meathead watches us change clothes."

The makeup girl let out a small gasp, but the rest of the room remained still. The guard took two quick steps until he stood in front of me, then he grasped my chin in one hand. "I could break your neck with a single snap," he whispered, leaning so close his rough cheek scratched against mine.

"You *think* you could. There's a reason why I'm the leader of my group and why I've never been defeated."

Time stopped and I held my breath, hoping he didn't notice my trembling lips.

He grinned, the expression in his eyes turning my stomach. "This one's got fire, I'll give her that much." Then he spoke to the girls who had already been in the room when we arrived. "Make sure they both wear matching costumes and that they are sleeveless. These girls have black-light tattoos that could bring a pretty penny tonight."

"How could our tattoos affect the betting?" Lauren asked. She still didn't understand what was going on here. "Lots of fighters have tattoos. The Skulls, the Ravens, the Dragon Tattoo Girls—"

He ran one hand over her hair, almost like he was petting her. "Wish I could take this one home for myself. Just for one night."

She froze, a frightened expression in her eyes.

"Remember to braid her hair and pin it up," he said. "Don't want it to get pulled out during the fight. Can't have damaged merchandise."

"I'm not merchandise," she said, pulling away from him.

He laughed. "Of course you're not. No need to get your little panties twisted up." He turned to look at the other girls, giving them instructions. "The first fight should be over in a few minutes. Make sure these two are ready when the announcer calls for them." Then the guy turned and left the room. It felt like he took all the oxygen with him. No one moved or said anything for half a minute.

Finally Lauren spoke up. "Rachel, what the hell's going on? I think we should leave. This place is giving me the creeps." She stood and pushed the makeup girl away from her. "Stop messing with my face!"

"Find them costumes, quick!" the makeup girl said while she kept trying to dust powder across Lauren's brow. All three of the other girls fumbled through a rack of clothing that I hadn't even noticed until now. I ran a quick gaze over the costumes, some flamboyant, some almost puritanical, some that were obviously made for boys. "You can't leave. Not yet," she said to Lauren. "They have too much money invested in your event. No fighter would walk away now." She paused, her brush in midair. "No good fighter, anyway."

"Rachel?" Lauren stared at me, her skin pale beneath her makeup.

"You're right, we should go." Then I turned to the makeup girl, noting once again that she looked like someone I'd seen somewhere before. "What's going on out there?"

She shrugged. "Platinum Level competition." There was a dead expression in her eyes, like she'd seen too many girls like me come through the door.

"Sounded more like an auction to me," I said.

The other girls shook their heads vigorously.

"No."

"Nothing like that."

"I've seen you before," I told her.

She shook her head. "No, I'm not from around here."

"Rachel, come on!" Lauren whimpered. She stood by the door, first one hand twisting the knob, then two. "Holy shit, it's locked! Is there another way out of here?" A thin layer of sweat covered her brow, and her gaze darted around the room as she searched for another exit.

"Relax, Swan Girl," the makeup girl said, her calm voice sounding like something from a horror movie. "It's not what you think. Come back and let me finish your makeup."

Her face tilted sideways and the light reflected off her cheekbones, the posture familiar—almost like a yearbook picture. That's when I knew why I recognized her.

She was one of the Lost Girls.

"You can do my makeup first," I offered. "I'm not as pretty as my friend, so I'll probably need more work anyway." I forced a grin as I sat in the chair beside her. I had a feeling she might be the only person here who'd be willing to help us—if I could convince her to trust us first. "You went missing, just like I did, didn't you? An FBI agent showed me your photo. What's your name—Madison, Haley, Brooke?"

She tried to hide it, but her head jerked backward, just a fraction of an inch, when I said Madison.

"How long have you been missing, Madison?" I asked.

She smudged foundation on my nose and cheeks, her own face reddening.

Meanwhile, Lauren ran around the room, still searching

for another way out. I could tell she was scared. I was afraid, too, but I had to push through this if I wanted to get the answers I needed.

"My name is Indigo," Madison said in a low voice. "If you call me anything else, they'll beat me."

"Okay. Indigo it is. How long have you been here?"

Lauren glanced at me, her eyes dark. Madison wore a long-sleeved top, one of the cuffs swinging loose, exposing bruises and long, thin scars that covered her forearm. She kept her gaze on my cheekbones as she applied blush, avoiding my eyes.

"Do they beat you often?" I asked.

She shrugged.

The other girls were pretending they couldn't hear us talking, all three of them pouring their attention over the costumes they had selected for us. Lauren settled into a chair beside me, but couldn't hold still. She kept tapping me on the arm, as if I didn't already know she was there.

"What do they do with us after the fight is over?" I asked. This is what I needed to know. What had happened to Nicole and me, and why? "Those people out there are bidding for us. Don't pretend they're not. But what do they do with us?"

"You really want to know? Even though you already went missing once?" Madison's eyes turned into long, narrow strips and her nostrils flared. "You fight. And you fight. And you fight. Forever."

Lauren frowned. "We already fight."

She gave us a grim smile.

"You fight for your new owner. In an underground club somewhere else, far away from your home and your family. You never see anyone you love again—"

"Indigo, don't!" one of the other girls said in a hoarse

whisper. "You know they listen in on us."

But Madison didn't stop. She continued to apply my makeup and she continued to talk, despite the single tear that began to trickle down her cheek. She looked eerie, her eyes emotionless, her voice flat, that tear the only sign that what she was saying might actually be true.

"You live in a cage or a closet and you wish you had a blanket when it's cold or a glass of water or a change of clothes. They only wash you before a fight and they only feed you when they remember, when they aren't too drunk or high. They use you like an animal for whatever they want, whenever they want—" She paused to look into my eyes for the first time, revealing the hollow emptiness inside. "You fight and you fight and you never get away. No matter how hard you try."

Lauren got up and frantically put on her costume, almost tearing the bodice in the process. One of the other girls was braiding and pinning her hair.

"I'm going to get away," she mumbled. "As soon as that door opens, I'm running—"

But the door was already open and two burly guards stood there, watching us, barring the only exit. They walked inside the room and locked the door behind them.

"Shut up!" one of them said as he grabbed Madison, then punched her in the face.

I flinched. Lauren let out a scream.

Madison crumpled to the ground, unconscious.

"And you"—the guy shot a dagger-like finger at me—"get dressed. Now! Or you won't even make it as far as the stage. You'll have your last performance right here." He grabbed his crotch with one hand and gave me a dark grin.

I glared at him, but I knew I was outnumbered.

So I put on my costume and got ready for my fight.

Chapter Thirty-Five

One wall in the dressing room was covered with floor-to-ceiling curtains. Behind that stood a two-way mirror that overlooked the fight and the undulating crowd. A guard had opened the curtains and turned on a loudspeaker, broadcasting the fight into our room. The familiar sounds of *oof* and *uuh* flowed into the room as two girls slugged and kicked each other on the distant stage.

"Who's fighting?" Lauren asked. She stood beside me at the window. We were both trying to ignore the people behind us, the guards and the girls who were what we could become, if everything went as planned.

I stared through the glass, squinting, my hand shading my own reflection. The girls onstage were so far away it was hard to see their features. But I was sure I knew them. I recognized their fighting styles. "I'm pretty sure it's Cyclone and Komodo," I said. "And it looks like Cyclone's double tapping—"

"Triple," Madison said. She was awake again and she now sat in one of the chairs behind us, an ice pack on her cheek. Her words were slightly muffled, like her mouth was swollen. "Two Pink Lightning and one Blue Thunder. We have anything you want. E, Meth, all the usual stuff. Or if you want some espresso, we have that, too. Whatever it takes to get your engine purring." Despite the fact that she'd been beaten by one of the guards, she still treated Lauren and me like we were honored guests and she was our hostess.

"Who are we supposed to fight?" I asked, never taking my eyes off the stage. I could see a dim reflection of Madison in the window. She was watching me with curious intent.

"That hasn't been revealed yet," she said. "But I'm sure it will be a good match."

Lauren took my hand and spoke in a low whisper. "You tried to get me to change my mind about this place. I should have listened."

I matched her tone. "I just would have taken your tickets away. I still would have come."

"Why?"

"I had to know."

She hung her head and chewed on her lip. "You know what I did, don't you? I could tell by the way you acted in the car."

This must have been the time for absolution. Both she and Dylan were hiding something and I needed to know what. Instead of speaking, I released a heavy sigh.

"I didn't sleep with him," she confessed. "It just looked that way."

My head snapped up.

"We were all at Brett's party, two days before you went missing. You and Dylan were broken up. He got so wasted, he went into one of the bedrooms to pass out, and I followed him in. At first, he thought I was you—"

I stared at her, not believing what was coming out of her mouth. I wanted to stop the words, as if it could change the past.

"When you came down the hallway, he had just realized who I really was and he was leaving the bedroom—"

My chest tightened, my skin two sizes too small.

I could see it, Lauren with her arm around Dylan's shoulders, the lipstick on his cheek, her hair messed up and both of them staggering toward me, their clothes rumpled. He kept trying to push her away, saying things like, *enough already* and *get lost.*

But when her eyes met mine, I saw the true story.

She thought she'd finally gotten my boyfriend. When he was drunk and high and we were broken up and I'd quit the Swan Girls. It was like she'd been waiting for that moment since we'd become friends. She now had my boyfriend *and* my team. She'd beamed proudly, her chin lifted, her eyes half-closed.

I'd wanted to smash that pretty face with my fist.

Dylan had continued to shamble closer, unaware that I was just a few feet away. He licked his lips and tried to untangle the arms that were wrapped possessively around him. Then he lifted his head. Shock filled his eyes when he saw me, then sorrow, then shame, all within an instant.

I had spun on my heels and stormed out, leaving the party and my pretend friend and my former boyfriend behind. I didn't care that he was struggling with drug addiction and needed help. I only knew that they had both betrayed me and I never wanted to see either one of them again. I almost got my wish. I desperately needed to blow off steam, so when Nicole showed up after school, a pair of Platinum Level tickets in her hand, the primal urge to fight came back.

I had said *yes, hell yes.*

Lauren had become Odile to my Odette. She was my evil twin and the Black Swan. She had tried to steal the prince's heart, and it had driven me to destruction.

And I'd almost died because of her betrayal.

Now she stared at me, wanting forgiveness, hoping I would tell her that everything was okay. But it wasn't. It would never be okay again. Nicole was dead. And as far as I was concerned, it was all Lauren's fault.

"Go to Hell," I said and turned away from her.

CHAPTER THIRTY-SIX

A moment later, the fight between Cyclone and Komodo ended. Cyclone won, her hand held high above the screaming crowd, her blue hair drenched with sweat, a thin smile on her face and an insane look in her eyes. Komodo had been badly beaten, so many bruises on her arms you could barely see that dragon tattoo. She shouldn't have accepted the challenge today—she hadn't recovered from our fight the other night and she now sprawled on the floor, a mess of broken pieces that looked like they might never fit back together again.

Lauren tried to get my attention, her eyes pleading, her words fast and quiet because she didn't want the guards standing behind us to hear.

"You wouldn't leave me here, would you? We have to stick together. We have to get away—"

One of her hands touched my shoulder and I brushed it off. I wasn't sure how I felt about her anymore. She was the reason I'd gone missing. "No, I wouldn't leave you here," I said, although as soon as those words left my lips, I wondered if they were true.

Someone was escorting Cyclone off the stage, two large men in business suits. They weren't like the rest of the crowd. These guys had an Eastern European look with their high cheekbones, shaved heads and expensive tailored suits. Cyclone swiveled toward them, blue hair spinning around her, a confused expression on her face. She was shouting and struggling to get away, but since her microphone was shut off, we couldn't hear what she was saying. A twinge of pain centered in my chest, something I couldn't shake and I knew would never go away. She was disappearing into the night, just like Nicole. Cyclone, aka Janie Deluca, had been one of my competitors but I had never wished her this. I fought the moan that slid out of my lips when the two men lifted her off her feet and carried her down the stairs.

"She put on a good show and she got a good price," Madison said matter-of-factly. "She'll get good handlers. The best ones always do."

I knew what she was saying wasn't true. "What about Komodo?" I asked. She still lay, crumpled and broken on the stage floor, not moving.

Madison's reflection continued to watch me. She shrugged. "No one has made an offer for her yet. We will wait and see."

It was as if I was on the stage then, staring down at Komodo, at the blood and the broken bones. She faded away and the sounds of the crowd continued to thunder in the background, a song of violence that would never end. And, just like the other night when I had beaten her, I didn't see Komodo, the Dragon Girl, anymore.

I saw Nicole, the Pink Candi girl, my friend.

Something had happened here, but I couldn't piece it

together yet. The back of my skull started to ache, fissures of pain radiating downward, like my head didn't connect with my body. I rubbed my fingers over the base of my neck, all the while staring out at that stage where a girl's body lay, discarded and broken.

"Pink Lightning could fix that headache," Madison said behind me. "One hit and you'll be feeling great again."

But that was just one more stone in the wall of lies that I kept hearing. The pain in my head wasn't because I was craving some drug. It was caused by the battle I'd been fighting with myself since I'd been kidnapped, part of me wanting to know what had happened, the other part refusing to let myself remember.

If only I could push through —

The announcer's voice came over the intercom then, his deep voice echoing throughout the arena and being piped into the dressing room where we waited. "Just like I promised," he exclaimed, one hand waving over his head with theatrical flair. "We have something special for you tonight — a girl who's never been defeated in a fight, not once —"

The crowd roared and my eyes flared wide in response. They were talking about me.

"And she's going to be fighting someone from her own team, a girl who until a few minutes ago was supposedly her friend —"

This had never happened before. No one in Phase Two ever challenged anyone from their own team. It was wrong. We were supposed to have each other's back.

"Listen to what we recorded from their dressing room a few minutes ago —"

Another voice came over the loudspeakers, a hushed whisper amplified so we could hear everything she said. *You know what I did, don't you? I didn't sleep with him — it just looked that way.* It was Lauren. And a full second later, my voice followed. *Go to Hell.*

I wanted to say, *you frigging bastards*, to everyone in the room with me, Lauren included. But at that point, it became hard for me to focus. Two things took place almost simultaneously, and in my mind they merged as one event—

The first thing—and this was probably why everything got so jumbled in my mind—was when I felt a prick in the crook of my left arm. The notch of pain forced me to glance down and, when I did, I realized both of the guards had pinned me in place and Madison was giving me a shot of Pink Lightning. But she didn't stop with one. She gave me another and another, until my knees wavered beneath me and those guards were holding me up.

The room turned as bright as the sun, one of my hands tried to block out the light, my head slipping backward, but even when I closed my eyes the light remained. I groaned, a soft thud of pleasure surging through my limbs and my heart pumping out something that felt like pure lightning, like I wasn't made of flesh and blood. It felt like I was a god, standing on Mount Olympus, ready to fly, wings spread wide, all the humans around me tiny and insignificant. I shrugged off the guards who held me, kicking one of them until he fell against the mirrored wall, the force cracking the glass. I glanced at the mirror, my reflection splintering and fracturing until it looked like there were countless versions of myself staring back, all of them stronger and fiercer than I'd ever been before.

"Step away from her," Madison warned. "She's ready to fight now."

I was, too. I was ready to rip sinew from flesh, to crack bone and shatter skulls. I snarled at her and she raised her hand, palm up.

Then the second thing happened and it was even worse. The door opened, freedom calling from the other side, a waft of air that tempted me to run but before I could respond, a body was shoved toward me.

Barely breathing, bloody, arms and legs bound, and a gag in his mouth.

Agent Bennet.

He fell to the floor, unable to get up.

He was the one who was supposed to rescue us, but now it looked like he might not survive. Lauren and Bennet and I were alone, no one to help us. Unless, maybe, that text to my dad got through and he understood what it meant. Unless he knew how to find us and he somehow managed to get here in time and he had a small army with him...

"You're going to fight for me or this man and your friend, Lauren, will die. *Both* of them. Painfully and slowly. While you watch," a sinister voice spoke behind me.

If Pink Lightning hadn't been flooding my veins, giving me strength, I would have cringed. I recognized this voice. It was the man who bought and sold girls and boys like stray dogs. It was the man who had sent Nicole to her death.

It was the man I'd run away from, all the way down the mountain.

I didn't want to see his face. I knew that everything would come flooding back as soon as I looked into his eyes and I was too terrified to remember. But that didn't matter, because he took my face in his hand and turned me toward him. The first thing I saw was the row of new track marks on his arm. Four red pinpricks, so fresh they each still held a glistening bead of blood in the center. It was his way of showing he was stronger than me, he was the alpha, he

could crush me with one hand no matter how much Pink
Lightning I had taken.

I fought the trembling in my legs and the shudder
that blurred my hands. I didn't want to look at him and he
seemed to sense it. A coarse laugh bubbled up from his
chest, and he lifted my chin, feeding off my fear, forcing me
to lift my gaze.

He towered over me, shoulders broad, muscles pumped,
every inch of him screaming that he was in charge and he
could take down anyone who stood in his way. His eyes
were the color of slate, the color of a world without light or
hope, his skin and hair so pale they were almost devoid of
pigment.

"Rachel Evans from Santa Madre," he said, revealing
that he knew exactly who I was and where I lived, and I
remembered how my driver's license had been in my
pocket when I was found. He'd been sending me a message.
I know who you are and where you live. He watched me as
I processed all of this. "I knew you would come back and
I'm glad you did. You're worth twice as much as before. I
can't believe how many times your stupid patron ripped up
the invitations I sent him for you to attend the Platinum
Level. He won't be ignoring my instructions ever again."
He laughed again. "The only way we could get you here
was to invite one of your friends. It worked. Both times."

My muscles had grown strong enough to shake off his
grip, but the cold expression in his eyes kept me trapped. I
wanted to stop the memory that I knew was coming. But it
was like trying to fight a tsunami, a force of nature caused
by something that had quaked long ago and far away
and was much stronger than I was. Then the wave swept
over me, knocking me backward, a sensation so visceral
I couldn't tell whether it was a memory or whether I was

really being carried out to sea, right now, away from that lake where all the Swan Girls had been swimming together for too long.

I was here, but not back in this secluded dressing room…

I stood in a corner, watching Nicole as she fought, as she lost, horribly. Twice I tried to run up onstage and help her but, after the second time, two strong guards grabbed me and held me back. Meanwhile, Nicole lost consciousness—a sign that the fight should be over—but the other girl wouldn't stop. She must have been double tapping and, maybe nothing seemed real to her anymore, but she was close to beating my friend to death. The crowd yelled and screamed and gyrated as if this was a fantasy they had been hoping for, dreaming of—

The only rule here was there were no rules.

I stopped trying to break past the guards and fight my way toward Nicole. Instead I backed up, taking two cautious steps away from the guards, hoping they wouldn't notice. My fight was already over and I'd won, so maybe that would grant me a little grace.

I turned sideways—I had changed back into my street clothes after my fight—and I slowly slid my cell phone from my pocket. Head slanted down, I punched in one number, then another.

9-1—

One of the guards saw me before I could hit that last digit. He knocked the phone from my hands, while the other guard grabbed me and jammed a gag in my mouth. They dragged me out to a van that rumbled outside. There, someone tied my hands and feet. A few moments later, one of them tossed Nicole in beside me, her body landing with a dull thud. It took a full minute before I realized she was still breathing. I dared to hope we might find a way to escape.

Up until a few minutes ago, I'd thought we were at a normal Platinum Level fight. But when she lay beside me— her eyes fluttering open, her lungs gasping for air—I knew what was really happening.

We were being kidnapped.

I tried to scream, I tried to talk to Nicole, I tried to comfort her, to tell her everything was going to be okay, she just needed to wake up, please, wake up. But everything I said came out muffled and unintelligible. The guys driving the van looked back and laughed at me.

That was when I realized there were other girls and boys in the van with us, all of us bound and gagged. Most of them were like me, with just a few cuts and bruises. Nicole was the only one who looked like she'd been crammed through a meat grinder, her flesh cut and dark with purple bruises, bones poking out of the skin on her left forearm and her right shin. I winced when I looked at her, my eyes never leaving hers as if I could magically transfer my strength to her. Tears slid down my cheeks, but she didn't cry. She stared straight ahead, a glazed expression in her eyes, the light fading with every slow-motion thud of her eyelids.

"She's not gonna make it," one of the guys in the front said. "And nobody made any bids on her."

"Take 'em up to the cabin, that's what you said we should do," the driver said.

"Changed my mind. We should get rid of her. But we don't want any bodies laying around in the woods, drawin' attention to our tradin' spot."

"True."

"If we dump her in the city, it'll look like a normal kidnapping."

"Except she's not dead yet. She could still talk if somebody finds her," the driver argued.

"I can fix that."

The van slowed and the whole time I was screaming, but it was a sound no one heard but me. Don't hurt her, don't leave her here, let us go, we won't talk, we promise—

They were dragging her out into a thicket by the side of the road. She lifted her head one last time and glanced back at me, terror in her eyes. I wept and screamed until my throat was raw and I could only whisper, still I cried out.

One of our captors—the burly one with the slate-gray eyes and the pale skin—kicked her again and again. In the face and in the gut and in the chest. Until her frail body slumped back and forth like a duffel bag. Then, when she didn't move anymore—when I still hoped that maybe there was still a flicker of life hiding inside somewhere—then they rolled her into a ditch. They wiped their hands on their shirts and they scraped their boots in the grass.

They were trying to wipe away her blood, but as far as I was concerned, it would never come out.

I saw their faces clearly then, in the headlights when they came back toward the van.

One, tall and slender, with pock-marked, bronze skin and thinning black hair.

The other, broad-shouldered, with pale skin and eyes like a tornado.

They were demons who needed to be sent back to Hell.

They kept me, helpless and bound, as they drove all of us up into the mountains, to a small hunting lodge where it took me two days to escape. Then it took me almost two weeks to climb down the mountain, careful to stay off the main trails and roads, knowing that they would be looking for me and that they had made a good deal for me—they were planning to sell me for more than any of their previous victims. I heard them bragging about it after the deal was made and my buyer was on his way up the mountain.

But my memories began to fade away as I blazed new trails across the San Gabriel valleys and crests, on my way home. No matter what happened, I knew I had to get home. But, as hard as I tried, by the time I made it to that ditch, that gully where I collapsed, too weary to climb onto the highway, even the thought of getting home was temporarily erased.

I collapsed in a ravine, just like Nicole, my body bruised and worn out, my clothes torn and bloody, the soles of my shoes worn out, and when that rain fell it washed away everything. At that point, the memory of Nicole's death and our kidnapping and my escape were too horrific for my mind to hold on to. It all slipped away, like a shadow in the mist, waiting in the dark, until just the right moment to loom back into my line of sight.

Tonight was that moment.

Here and now.

When I remembered everything.

A long, deep breath pulled through my lungs, all of me feeling raw and bleeding and mangled, my soul black. But my mind was clearer than it had been in a long, long time because of that Pink Lightning.

I turned around slowly, away from that two-way glass and the visage of a stage that would be mine soon. Madison sat on a chair, her face bruised, her nose possibly broken. She lifted her chin, staring at me as if she wanted to know what was different about me now.

I ran my gaze over those two guards in the room with us, from one to the other, taking everything in. One of them I didn't recognize. The other one had been in that van—he was slender, with dark, pock-marked skin, his hair black and his eyes darting away from the knowledge he saw inside me. And the man who had walked into the room last, the broad-shouldered brute with steely eyes—he kept his gaze steady and even, a grin widening on his face, as if he'd been waiting for this moment all along.

This was the moment we had all been waiting for—my therapist, my parents, my friends—when I would remember what had happened when I went missing. But none of us had expected it to happen when I was standing in the same room as the man who had murdered one of my closest friends.

CHAPTER THIRTY-SEVEN

The world was beautiful and horrible, every inch of my body ready for battle and every synapse in my brain firing like it never had before. Step by step, I was being led toward the arena stage, Madison at my side. Lauren and the Man Who Had Murdered Nicole were somewhere behind me, their footsteps in tandem. The crowd cheered my name, my Swan Girl name, and clouds of white smoke billowed from the edges of the room.

Stars fell and worlds collided and civilizations were destroyed.

My body felt like it belonged to someone else, like it was being manipulated by remote control, like I was some kind of hero action figure being sent into a skirmish.

The worst part of it all was that I couldn't *wait* to get up on that stage. I wanted to fight, I wanted to tear holes in the fabric of existence, I wanted to do surgery on Lauren's face with my knuckles, I wanted to clutch her throat in my fist and watch as all her dreams slipped away, beat by rugged beat.

I wanted to leave her in a pool of her own blood, no

one to help her.

Just like she had done to me.

A growl surged from my chest. I was a beast. I was exactly what they wanted me to be. I soared with swan wings, head lifted high, past adoring subjects. I was the Queen, I was Odette.

I was horrible and I was beautiful and there was a good chance I was about to kill a girl who had pretended to be my friend.

A cool hand touched my arm and I snarled, ready to break the fingers off the hand.

"I am expendable," Madison confessed, her voice low, her head turned toward me. "That is why I was given the task to walk you to the stage. If you hit me, even if you kill me, it will only make the crowd more excited. No one will care."

The fire in my chest quelled, just a bit.

"I couldn't do anything before," she continued. "Not until you got your Pink Lightning. But now, you can do whatever you want. There are many ways you can still escape." She paused, maybe weighing the danger of what she was about to say next. "I'll do whatever I can to help. And I will be assisting you during your fight. If you need anything, an ice pack or a towel or another shot of Pink Lightning, all you have to do is nod. I'll even sneak you a shot of Black Skies, if you want to put Lauren down. The only rule here is there are no rules."

She bowed gracefully as we neared the stage, sweeping her arm toward the stairs.

"I am here to make sure you win," she whispered as I passed her. "And if that means you escape, then so be it."

I soared past her, not sure if I believed her words. But I found unexpected solace in knowing that I wasn't as alone as I felt. Someone had my back.

...

The stage became my kingdom, my feet barely touching the floor. I felt like I could walk on water, like I could sail across the room, granting wishes to the swarthy crowds, a beatific smile on my face. They were chanting. I couldn't hear it—I had entered into that magical silence that exists when you're in the ring—but I could feel it, a steady push of sound that thrummed against my feet and chest.

The steady vibration gave me energy; it gave me life, it gave me a reason for being.

I was adored and worshipped, and I would do everything in my power to give pleasure to my subjects.

I faced Lauren, my opponent, fire in my eyes, and she must have been able to see it. Maybe she could even feel the heat radiating from my skin, see the steam billowing out of my mouth when I spoke. "You bitch," I said and I took a threatening step closer. Lauren must not have expected anger to factor into this fight.

If she had, she wouldn't have confessed her deepest secrets to me. Not tonight. Not right before someone pumped me full of drugs that could turn almost anyone into a killer.

She blinked, probably calculating what was going on inside my head, and how much survival time that gave her. Fists raised, she stumbled backward, on the defensive, knowing I wasn't going to pull any punches. Not now. Not ever.

My game was different from most of the other fighters. It was more elegant, more precise and much faster. I usually ended a match within five to ten minutes, a fact that constantly irritated my patron. He always complained that

I should drag it out, make it look like I might lose—then he'd be able to get better odds.

Today might have been that day.

I didn't want this fight to end quickly.

My mind was able to think five steps ahead of what happened around me. It was almost like Lauren and I were playing chess, rather than fighting for survival. The moment she clenched her fingers into a fist I knew exactly what she planned to do next and I was not only able to block her punch, I was able to follow it up with a one-two fist slam to her sternum, knocking the breath out of her chest, and making her slump forward, ready for another duo of punches, this time to her pretty face.

Black eye number one, black eye number two.

In between making the crowd roar and Lauren whimper, I figured out how to escape, just like Madison had promised. To the right of the stage stood a door, left unlocked, and it led to a long corridor, which in turn led to a parking lot behind the building. I knew all this because I'd been dragged down that corridor the last time I was here. Once outside, I'd been stuffed into a windowless van with all the other fighters.

All I had to do was let Lauren win the fight.

That was going to be the hardest part, since I really wanted to flatten her, to pound her until her bones turned to powder. The only thing I could feel was my anger and my fists connecting with her flesh. But if I could push aside my anger and let her win, then *I'd* be the one on the mat and all attention would be focused on her. I could slip away, through that door, down that corridor, across the parking lot, and into the night.

There was only one problem with that plan and it didn't bother me—not at first, anyway—not when my heart thudded to a slow, precise rhythm, a *boom-ba-boom-ba-boom* that reminded me of a funeral procession. Not when all her movements were in slow motion and her eyes were filled with so much fear. It didn't bother me at all.

Not until I saw something familiar in her eyes.

Clouds of white smoke curled from the corners of the room and the men in the front row laughed and catcalled. Shouts rose up from the cheering crowd and, in the midst of it all, there came the *whumpf* of bare knuckles against flesh, the wet sound as knees and feet hit ribs. A sticky spray of blood caught me on the side of the neck and, all the while, the shouts of the crowd made the floor vibrate beneath the soles of my feet.

Pink Lightning sparked through my veins, every muscle in my arms and legs was alive like never before, and her eyes—Lauren's eyes—they didn't look like *her* anymore. That fear, that sense of helplessness, I'd seen it before.

It was how Nicole had looked, right before those two men had carried her away into the night, right before they beat her to death.

I froze, my fist in midair, and the moment seemed to last forever. To everyone else it was probably just a millisecond, but in that amount of time I saw everything—

I could escape, but that would mean Lauren would be left behind. And not just her, but Komodo and Agent Bennet and Madison, too—all of them would be left here while I ran away. I knew how this group of kidnappers worked. As soon as they realized I was gone, they'd pack up and scatter. They'd be dust in the wind by the time I got back here with help.

Lauren would be sold, she'd be gone, she'd be another Lost Girl.

As much as I hated her right now, I didn't want that.

I finally followed through with my punch, but it wasn't as clean as it should have been. I'd paused too long and she had time to block me. It took a few more moves before I had enough momentum to do what I needed, before I could pin her in a headlock, my arm wrapped around her throat, her right ear positioned beside my lips. That was the first move where I was able to whisper my new plan to her, the one where I began to explain how *she* could escape. It took five holds, all of them different so we wouldn't arouse suspicion, before I was able to convince her it would work. Maybe she was just glad to hear that I didn't plan on killing her, since there were no rules, none at all tonight, but in the end she agreed to do exactly what I told her.

And that was good, because we both knew her only other option was to win the fight and go home with the highest bidder.

One final body slam and Lauren fell on the mat, a grimace on her face, her eyes closed. The fight was over. For a long, shuddering moment, I worried that I had actually knocked her out and that all our scheming would amount to nothing. Then she gave me a brief, almost unnoticeable wink.

Game on, you dirty, effing mothers.

I flashed a grin at Madison, then nodded at the spotlights. She punched the power switch and all the lights in the universe poured down on me. No more beams sweeping the crowd or the stage, nothing to illuminate Lauren when she rolled off the platform or when she crawled toward that door.

All eyes were on me, as they should be. It was time for my second act.

I spun, a sweet pirouette, left leg bent at the knee, all my weight on the toes of my right foot, arms over my head. I spun around and around while the audience chanted my name and then when I stopped, they realized the show was only beginning.

"Who's put up a bid for me? Anyone?" I called out. Cheers followed. I grinned, as if I couldn't wait to go home with my new owners. "Well, don't stop the bidding yet." I leaped across the stage, then pointed toward one of the meatheads in the audience. "Are you a brave man?" I asked. He nodded. "Do you think you can beat a seventeen-year-old girl?"

"Hell, yeah!" he shouted back.

"Come on," I taunted. "Let's see if you can go a full round up here."

While he was scrambling toward the stage and my handlers back in the dressing room were freaking out, I cast a quick look toward that door.

It was slamming shut.

Lauren was getting away.

My muscles relaxed for an instant, a bad move on my part for that goon from the audience was already looming toward me, beer on his breath, sweat pooling in the pits of his T-shirt. He swiped at me, fingers open, and I danced away, two short hops that made the audience laugh. Shadows were moving closer, two beefy guards and the Man Who Had Murdered Nicole all racing down the aisle. They had been watching the crowd, hadn't even realized *I* might be the threat.

I knew I could take this meathead opponent down with a snap of the neck. Problem was, if I did that he'd be dead.

So, instead, I spun around, kicking him in the crotch, in the gut, and in the chin. He fell with the first kick, and my foot was red with his blood by the time he hit the mat. I was pretty sure I broke his nose, there was so much blood.

Now other members of the audience began clamoring for a go at me. They all wanted their moment in the spotlight, they wanted a chance to take me down.

Come and get me, boys.

Guards were slamming fists in faces, Nicole's Murderer was grabbing the microphone, two new audience members had made it onto the stage, and I was fighting both of them at the same time. Meanwhile, I gave a quick nod to Madison and she ran toward the door that led to freedom, following Lauren.

Joy radiated from my chest. Pure joy like I hadn't felt in ages.

We were beating the brutes who had wanted to take us captive.

Kick to the face of Audience Member Number One, kidney punch to Audience Member Number Two, knee to the groin, elbow to the nose, and they were both down, one of them almost in tears with his right hand trying to stop the flow of blood that gushed from his nose.

I grinned and laughed and taunted. I could fight like this all night long, defeating one overweight, out-of-shape, wannabe wrestler at a time. I could have, but I didn't. Because Nicole's Murderer clambered his way onto the stage, then grabbed me and tossed me over his shoulder, an act that proved four shots of Blue Thunder trumped three shots of Pink Lightning. I'd known all along that this was how my escape scenario would end—someone would lasso me like a runaway colt, then either drag me back to the dressing room or drag me out to a car that rumbled in the parking lot.

Either way, my personal attempt to get away had failed.

A dark sadness enveloped me as I was taken through the screaming and cheering crowds. All along I'd been secretly hoping that I wouldn't need to implement this stage of the plan. I'd been hoping that my short 9-1-1 text had gotten through and that my dad would show up at any minute, a cavalry of ex-military soldiers at his side, all of them armed and stronger than Hercules.

But he must not have gotten my text. And a sharp pinch in my backside was all the warning I got that my reign as Supergirl was over. I saw Nicole's Murderer palm an empty syringe, dribbles of a black liquid inside, and my strength began to fade. My eyes struggled to stay open as my body fell limp. Two words were all that came to me as I slipped into a strange state of coherent unconsciousness.

Black Skies.

He had given me a shot of Black Skies, a knock-out drug so strong it could overpower both Pink Lightning and Blue Thunder.

So strong it could kill.

Chapter Thirty-Eight

Nicole's Murderer rambled on and on as he paced the dressing room, talking to his bodyguards and to himself. I struggled to stay awake, my eyes flaring open from time to time, only long enough to capture an image here and there. I had no idea how much Black Skies he'd given me. In my head, I was chanting, *don't die don't die don't die.*

All the girls were gone, but I wasn't sure where. The costumes had been packed up and the curtains that covered the large, two-way mirror still hung open. Fistfights and threatening arguments were scattered around the slowly emptying hall. Most of the fights were between two or three men, but one was a mass of punching arms and kicking legs and flying beer bottles, possibly fifteen men in all, with their testosterone spiking and voices bellowing.

"You're not worth the trouble you cause," he said, pointing a thick finger at me. "Phase Two is *good* for the community. We keep kids off the streets and out of gangs. But you come along and now we've got the FBI poking into our business. Four bodies!" He tucked his thumb into his palm, then held up four fingers and wagged them in my face. "Four! That's how many people we have to get rid of tonight because of *you*—"

I blinked and forced myself to sit up straighter, all of my muscles screaming at me to stop. "Who are you getting rid of?"

His eyes glistened with something that looked like excitement. He'd been waiting for me to wake up enough to tell me this. This was his revenge, I could feel it. "They're all out in the van right now and my boys are just waiting for me to give them the go-ahead. You want to know who they are? I'll tell you. Komodo, because you beat her so bad the other night she was completely worthless onstage. That FBI agent, because you told him to come here. Madison, because she tried to help you. And Lauren, because you told her how to escape."

An arrow of pain shot through my chest. Neither Lauren nor Madison got away?

He laughed. "They'll all be dead within a few hours, but those girls could have been sold. If *you* hadn't gotten involved." He leaned nearer and pulled something from his pocket to show me, holding it in front of my face. My iPhone. "You thought Daddy was coming, didn't you?"

A sick feeling twisted through my stomach and I thought I was going to throw up.

"Wanna see the texts we sent your precious papa? Look. First we said, *sorry, didn't mean to send that*—after you sent that stupid 9-1-1 message. He replied, *are you okay?* We said, *yeah, but I'm gonna spend the night at Lauren's. K?* We even matched your misspellings and abbreviations. He never suspected a thing. So, your parents won't be looking for you until after school tomorrow." He paused to study my expression, his gaze lingering on my lips just long enough to make me wish I could slug him. Then he held up two Platinum Level tickets. "Guess who these are for?"

I shook my head, a gesture that took all of my strength but was almost unnoticeable. Outside the room, the lights in the arena flickered on, then off, then on, but dimmer than before. I couldn't hear what was going on because the intercom had been shut off, but some of the fighting men turned around, looking at something I couldn't see, something in the corner of the room.

"These tickets are for your little friend. Zoe."

"No." All I could do was whisper, although I wanted to scream. Not her. She wasn't strong enough for this place. She wouldn't survive. I wanted to lunge at him and rip out his throat, my fingers on his windpipe to stop him from talking. The lights outside the room blinked off one final time. The only light left on came from the EXIT sign and the cherry glow of cigarettes that seemed to hang in the air like angry fireflies.

Nicole's Murderer cocked his head, then traced one finger along my jawline. I shuddered. "We're going to invite Zoe to Platinum Level. We'll get her tomorrow night and that'll help pay for all the damage you've caused. Maybe I'll even set up a little fight between you two, after you've been worn down so far you don't recognize her. I think the crowds would love a duo like that. Maybe I'll take you both around the country." He leaned even nearer, his lips close enough to touch mine. "That is, until one of you dies."

Tiny pinpoints of fire flared back in the arena, on the other side of that two-way glass. I couldn't hear it, but I imagined it sounded like sniper rifles firing rubber bullets, stuff used to control crowds during a riot. Those cigarettes fell, one by one, a puff of red and then the outline of bodies falling to the ground. Someone, probably one of the guards, flicked on a flashlight and for a brief moment, before the light was extinguished, I saw a team of men, all dressed in camo, their faces and skin painted with stripes of black and olive green. Then they turned into shadows again and everything out there was still.

A brief glimpse of a face, a familiar face, appeared close to the mirror, as if trying to look inside.

It was my father. Even disguised in camo and in an unlit room, I knew who he was.

"Zoe won't accept your invitation," I said, my words slurring.

"Why not?"

The door to the dressing room slammed open, the hinges taken off. Four men shuffled in, all with rifles pointed at the Man Who Had Murdered Nicole. He stumbled backward, but not quick enough, not before two of them had him by the arms.

"Because my dad's here, that's why not, you fucking monster!"

And then my father was there, arms around me, asking if I was okay, had that man hurt me, was I drugged, could I walk. I could barely answer him, so in the end he carried me out, into the midnight air where a caravan of police cars and ambulances waited, where all the men who had been inside were getting cuffed with plastic cable ties.

"They got Lauren," I managed to say. "They're going to kill her."

Dad said something I couldn't hear.

My head slumped onto my chest. I was losing consciousness, that drug they had given me was too strong. I couldn't fight it.

"Hang on, you're going to be okay," he said as he leaned closer, then he waved toward one of the paramedics. "Hey, get over here and take a look at my daughter! Make sure she's all right."

Dad stayed with me. I could sense his presence, despite the black clouds that rolled in and engulfed everything. His hand was in mine when I got in the ambulance, he walked beside me when I was carried on a stretcher into a hospital.

And when I started to black out, the world fading into muted sounds, I knew if I survived, he would be there when I woke up.

Chapter Thirty-Nine

I slept for a long, long time. I sailed through black heavens where flickers of lightning sparked, craggy and pink, and where every boom of thunder turned the skies blue. I thought I heard voices calling me, crowds chanting my name. But it wasn't my name, was it? It was the name of a character in a story.

Odette—Odette—Odette.

I'd lost everyone I wanted to save, they had all ended up like Nicole, broken and bruised and left by the side of the freeway like trash.

My eyes flared open now and then—in the midst of a series of unending nightmares—and I saw an IV snaked into my arm. The world was softer than I remembered, all made of cotton and pastel colors and voices that whispered. I saw my dad once and my mom. Another time I saw Kyle, pacing back and forth, running his fingers through his hair. As soon as he noticed I was awake, he stopped, a haunted look in his eyes.

"I didn't know," he said, his voice hoarse as if he'd been

crying. "Or else I *never* would have gotten in a fight with you that morning. I should have known something was up when I didn't see you at lunch. I should have gone looking for you." He moved closer, one hand reaching out to touch mine. "I'm so sorry, Rach—"

"It's not your fault." That's what I tried to say, but I wasn't sure if the words came out of my mouth or if they stayed trapped in my mind.

Once, I woke up and Molly was in the room. The only problem was, she had on a long *LOTR* cosplay gown and wig, and for a minute I thought I was hallucinating. It didn't help that she would only talk to me in J.R.R. Tolkien quotes or that she claimed to have elven 'lembas' bread and that it would heal me. I finally realized who she really was when she broke character and started crying.

"You can't keep doing this," she said. "You can't keep ending up in the hospital, half dead."

"I won't," I promised.

She stayed with me until I fell asleep again.

The next time I opened my eyes, it was morning. But I didn't know if it was the first morning since I'd been here or the third or the fifth. Light washed the room, pouring in from the window, making the sterile space a little more friendly. Hunger gnawed at me and I wondered how long it had been since I'd eaten.

I couldn't remember what had happened. Had my dad really come to save me or had that been a hallucination? Thoughts of fear jumbled through my head, knocking open doors that led to more corridors and more horrors. Remnants of the drugs that had been pumped into me made my mind work differently than it usually did. I couldn't seem to focus on anything. My thoughts kept jagging off on semi-related tangents, all of them frantic.

Where was Lauren, was she safe, and what about Madison and Komodo, and was Agent Bennet still alive?

Then a silhouette appeared in the doorway to my room, a man, hunched over and moving awkwardly, as if in great pain. He paused and looked in at me, his features still hidden in shadow. One arm was held close to his chest, the other leaned on a crutch.

"May I come in?" he asked and as soon as he spoke I recognized his voice. It was Bennet. A tear slid down my cheek as I nodded.

It took him a while to make his way into the room, to sit in the chair beside my bed. I winced as I looked at him, his injuries revealed now that he sat in the light—purple bruises on his face, a swollen eye, a broken arm, and a cast that went from his left foot to his hip.

"Are you all right?" he asked.

I was crying then, unable to talk for a long time. "I'm so sorry," I said at last. He reached out, just like Kyle had, and took my hand in his.

"Don't be sorry," he said with a crooked grin. "We won."

"Is Lauren—is she—"

"Lauren's fine. Some injuries from her fight, but she's—" He paused. "I was going to say she's at home, but she's actually been staying at your house. During our investigation we found out what has been going on with her father. Your mother's been working with child protection services to get her set up with one of Lauren's aunts in Riverside."

I glanced down at the blanket that covered me, wondering if Lauren had been sleeping in my bed, beneath that afghan Grams made me. A sliver of jealousy trembled from my shoulders down to my fingers. Obviously Lauren and I still had issues. Maybe we always would. But at least she was safe.

"Did you find Madison?" I asked.

He nodded, then grimaced in pain and closed his eyes. "We found most of the girls. Madison, Haley, Emily, Hannah, Sammy, and Brooke, plus some others we didn't even know were missing—"

Sammy. Komodo. The girl from my history class with the dragon tattoo. I sighed, and leaned back against my pillow.

"We found documents on a laptop that led us to most of the missing girls, all the way to a network of underground fight clubs that had been set up in Seattle, Detroit, Miami, and Houston. We're in the process of shutting those down, just like we did with the ones here in Los Angeles."

That was good news. No, it was great news. Still, there was something in his expression, something he didn't want to tell me and there had been one name he hadn't mentioned.

Janie Deluca. Cyclone.

I saw her again, blue hair spinning around her as those European-looking thugs had dragged her off the stage.

"What about Janie?" I asked, my mouth dry.

He stared past me, like he was looking for another answer, a better answer. But there wasn't one. He shook his head. "All evidence pointed toward the club in Detroit. That was where she was supposed to go. But that's not where they took her." His voice cracked and his eyes glistened and once more I wondered if he had lost someone once, some younger sister or niece. "I'm sorry. We'll keep looking, but I don't know—"

I saw her on her front porch with that bat, and in the club lifting her chin when I smiled at her, as if some measure of self-confidence had been restored. But I realized that I might never see her again. She'd gone into the midnight deep, just like Nicole. She was lost and she might never find her way home again.

"We wouldn't have rescued any of those girls if it hadn't been for you." Green eyes searched mine, probably hoping that this would be enough—shutting down clubs in five cities, putting the men responsible behind bars, and saving twenty-four girls. I found out later that was how many kidnapped girls had been rescued in total, plus almost as many boys.

Almost fifty lost girls and boys. It should have been enough.

But for me, it was a hollow victory.

I hadn't wanted to bring *some* girls back. I'd wanted them all.

"You were brave to do what you did," Bennet said as he stood up. "I know how it feels...to not bring everyone home. And I know you still have to finish high school and college, but if you're interested, you might want to consider a career with the FBI." A boyish grin revealed dimples I hadn't even realized he had. "We'd be honored to have someone like you working on our cases." He put his business card on the table beside my bed. "If you decide you ever want to work with us, or if you just want to talk, call me, okay?"

I nodded.

And then he was a shadow again, walking away from the light that poured in the window, heading out the door and into the hallway. Disappearing, as if he'd never been here, as if he had never risked his own life to save these girls. Or to save me.

. . .

It was another day before I was ready to go home from the hospital. I kept slipping in and out of a thick, suffocating sleep, waking up only occasionally. Sometimes my room was empty, nurses shuffling papers in the hall, carts rattling over linoleum floors. Those were the good times. I could be myself. I could cry and struggle to focus my thoughts; I could look forward to the day when I would be back in my own room, curled on my side, cocooned in my afghan, blocking out the world that tried to smother me with all its smells and sounds and bright lights. It was all too much right now.

The bad times were when I woke up and someone was in my room, staring at me, waiting for me to say something brilliant or profound.

My therapist appeared beside my bed once, looking like Cruella De Vil with her red lipstick and designer sunglasses. All she needed was a coat made from Dalmatian puppies to complete the picture. We didn't talk long. I didn't want her to see the darkness seething inside me. That was my secret. I'd already realized that I couldn't blame anyone else for what had happened to me. I'd gone to those clubs willingly, excited to find someplace new to fit in, to be a star. I just needed to find another way to feel special now, although I wasn't sure whether that would ever happen.

Another time I woke up and Lauren was here. Sitting in the chair, wearing a pink dress, her hair in long braids, like she was Heidi or something. Like she was completely innocent and all was forgiven.

We didn't talk long, either. I gave her a grin, asked a few vague questions, then acted like I couldn't hear her when she kept apologizing.

I was probably going to forgive her someday. It just wasn't today.

The worst of them all was when Dylan showed up, standing in the doorway as if hesitant to come in. He looked even more gorgeous than before, despite the fact that there were dark circles under his eyes and his hands were trembling. I'd been thinking about him a lot, when I had coherent thoughts, and now that he was here I didn't know if I could do what I needed to do.

"Hey," he said from the doorway, like a creature of the night hoping to be invited in. He didn't wait long enough to hear whether I wanted to see him or not. He made his way across the room, his eyes always on mine, his lips parted slightly like he wasn't sure whether he should talk or take a chance on kissing me.

He settled for talking, which was the better choice.

"I'm really glad you're okay," he said as he sat on the edge of the chair, his fingers tugging at a small rip in the hem of his jacket. A long pause followed and I tried not to look in his eyes, at the person deep inside who had revealed so much of himself to me, the person I had fallen in love with when I wasn't paying attention. Somewhere between that middle-school crush and finding out the truth about Phase Two, I had fallen for him. Deeply. Madly. And it was making it hard to breathe.

"I'm going through a detox program. It's been pretty rough..." he admitted finally, his voice trailing off as he tucked his hands in his pockets to hide the tremors. "And I'm going to testify against the leader of the club, that guy with the Brooklyn accent. But I'll still have a lot of community service to do, to get the car theft charges dropped. Your friend, Agent Bennet, is helping me and the other Ravens get everything straightened out." His gaze flicked away, as if he couldn't bear to look in my eyes. "I know you're starting to remember things—"

"I remember you hooked up with Lauren." I hated the bitterness in my voice, but for some reason, that betrayal had hurt the most.

He nodded, biting his lip. "Yeah, I figured you knew about that. Although, it wasn't really a hookup. I didn't, I mean, I couldn't, even though we were broken up—" There was a guilty expression in his eyes that wouldn't go away, something that bothered him a lot more than what had happened with Lauren. "Look, everything that happened to you is *my* fault, okay? I had no idea the people in those clubs were kidnapping people. If I did, I never would have asked you to join. I was the one who took you to Phase Two. I'm the reason you got involved in all of this. I trained you in the beginning and taught you wrestling moves. Then you started figuring out other moves and kicks on your own. At first, we always went to the Silver Level together—"

He was talking, but I was watching a movie in my head—us walking through the door, me not knowing anyone, but the energy and the thrill making it feel like a party where everyone was always high. You could taste it in the air, you could breathe it in, and then when you finally got up on that stage, oh, wow, there was *nothing* like it. Not even getting the lead role in Swan Lake had been like this.

"And then, we started going by ourselves, on different nights," he continued. "That was when we started forming our own teams and when you cut your hair and when we both started wearing black clothes all the time. We both changed—"

I saw myself laughing, hanging out with Nicole, her suggesting I bleach my hair and me telling her to add pink to hers. I saw us standing at the edge of a stage, sweat beading on our foreheads, our fists pumping air as we chanted and screamed and cheered, both of us longing for the day when it would be us up on that platform.

"None of this would have happened, if I never, if I hadn't—" Dylan paused, staring out the window, at the world outside that didn't seem to care that we'd been burned and shattered and nearly destroyed. I knew what he was going to say and I knew they were the right words, but they were also the worst words ever created. His eyes were focused on me again, the boy inside as defeated as Nicole had been. "If I hadn't fallen for you, none of this would have happened to you. I'm not good for you, Rachel."

That was the horrible and beautiful truth. I hated it. And I hated him for making me admit it. I had planned on breaking up with him, asking that we take some time apart, so I could figure out who I really was and so he could give up Blue Thunder. But maybe that had never been an option. Maybe we had both been ripped and shredded too badly. I wiped away the tears that were forming in the corners of my eyes, I fought the trembling in my lips. I couldn't show that I was weak, not now. I had to be brave and strong if I wanted to survive.

"I don't think we should see each other anymore."

His words.

Right cross to my jaw.

Him walking out the door.

Me falling to the floor.

It was a knockout. The girl who had never been defeated, not once, was flat on her back on the mat, staring up at the ceiling, at the black skies and the bolts of pink lightning, she was listening to the earth-quaking boom of thunder that temporarily turned the entire world blue. She was crying, glad she was alone, a lake of tears forming around her, a lake that would soon be deep enough to drown in.

Chapter Forty

It was the second Saturday after I was released from the hospital and we were on a mission. Zoe had borrowed her mom's car and we were spending the day exorcising my demons, Molly in the backseat, me riding shotgun. Earlier, when the sun merely tickled the freeways with fingers of light, we had driven down to Orange County, then on to Compton, and finally back to Santa Madre.

I talked to the remaining girls on that list from my closet. I met Alexis, Shelby, and Lacy, and found out that I had fought all of them, back in the Silver Level when I was putting my team together. But the good thing was, they were all still alive.

It was now almost three o'clock and we were nearly done with our first objective.

"Saturday traffic sucks. Don't these people have someplace better to be than on the freeway?" Molly slurped down the last of her Mocha Frappuccino, then pointed out the window. "Turn here. Don't listen to the GPS, this way is quicker."

Zoe gave me an indulgent grin as she followed Molly's instructions.

We had several goals today.

Our second objective had been accomplished along the way. We vowed to do it every Saturday, forever, until we finally got results. Whenever we weren't on the freeway, we'd stop every couple of blocks and hang up a poster.

Missing Girl. Janie Deluca.

A color photo of Janie was front and center. Below it was a description of her height and weight, where and when she was last seen, plus an 800 number to contact with information.

As we hung the posters, blue bracelets would slide down our wrists, bracelets that proclaimed FIND JANIE. Everyone we knew was wearing these bracelets, our parents, our siblings, our friends at school. And there was a memorial down in front of that hall in Rosemead where she had gone missing, with a big cross, candles and bouquets of flowers.

But the hardest thing I had to do was up ahead.

Molly set down her empty Starbucks cup, while Zoe slowed the car and parked at the curb. We all stared at that house, that very nice house surrounded by flowers and hedges, with shutters on the windows, that house that looked like it should have been in an animated fairy tale but accidentally got cast in a horror movie instead.

Nicole's house.

It still whispered for her to *come home, come home, please, I miss you, I love you, why did you have to go away...?*

I swallowed with difficulty, my limbs wooden as I climbed out of the car. Zoe and Molly opened their doors and I turned toward them. "You don't have to come with me."

"Yes, we do," Zoe said, her tone sweet but firm.

"Damn straight," Molly said. "Would Boo-Boo let Yogi go into the forest alone?"

I shook my head. "Probably not."

We walked together up that stone walkway, past palm trees and birds of paradise and bougainvillea. It felt wrong and right at the same time.

The door opened as soon as I knocked, as if Nicole's mother had been waiting for me. She gave me a smile and I tried to echo it but couldn't. She invited us in, gave us cookies which I couldn't eat—I tried, but I just couldn't swallow. That smile she had given me faded, inch by inch, as I told her my story.

I told her everything.

It's what I would have wanted someone to tell my mom. I would want her to know.

She was weeping, quietly, before I finished and she didn't stop. I wanted her to yell at me, to beat fists against my chest. But she never got angry. She merely got up and made me another bag of cookies, tucking another photo of Nicole inside.

This photo showed Nicole grinning, holding a teddy bear. She was nine years old and her whole life was before her. It sparked in her eyes—all those dreams she'd had, dreams of college and marriage and children, dreams of vacations in Hawaii and a nice house down in Huntington Beach and a career where she'd make a difference in the world.

I put that photo on my bulletin board, next to the other photo Nicole's mom had given me, and I looked at both of them every day. They hung next to an extra blue wristband that said FIND JANIE.

Dreams could be lost too easily. I knew that now.

So I dreamed that one day, one of us would bring Janie back home.

...

The months after I got out of the hospital went by quicker than I expected. Ms. Petrova and the students in my ballet class became like a second family. I found myself attending several sessions per week and, even though I was no longer taking Pink Lightning, I somehow landed the role of Titania in a production of *A Midsummer Night's Dream*.

School hadn't been a good fit, though—I still had too much stuff to sort through, too many emotions and nightmares and unexpected reactions to normal things, like hiking in the woods or watching someone get beat up on a TV show. So my parents got a special program set up for me, a cross between home schooling and independent studies, so I could finish the semester at home. That nerdy college kid down the street and Dad worked together to help me. By the time June came, everyone I knew, me included, was done with school and we finally had time to hang out, non-stop.

Sammy, aka Komodo, had gone through a transformation, almost like I had. She came over a couple of times a week. Her, Zoe, Stephanie, and I would spar in the backyard.

No reason to lose our skills. That was our new motto.

We even taught Mom a few moves, self-defense stuff, just in case. She ended up really liking it and signed up for a Tae Bo class at the local junior college.

Molly joined our kick-ass group, too, though we had to be really gentle and patient with her. More than once, Sammy wanted to knock Molly on her butt, to make her learn faster. But I reminded Sammy we didn't do things that way anymore. Molly would get it, sooner or later. For now, she was more of a mascot, knowing that we had her back if she ever needed it.

Lauren sent my mom and my dad cards on Mother's Day and Father's Day, since if it wasn't for them, she'd either be a pile of bones rotting in a ravine or a punching bag for her dad whenever he got pissed off.

The mountains didn't scare me anymore. That recurring nightmare finally faded away and now I could look at the peaks and valleys without getting short of breath. That didn't mean I wanted to take one of Dad's infamous survival hikes, though. Not yet.

I see Dylan every now and then, usually by accident, like at the mall or Starbucks. Like me, he's not Goth anymore, but he still wears a lot of black. It looks good on him. The last time I saw him we gave each other a hug, a long hug, and I didn't want it to end.

But it did.

Maybe good things are like bad things. They all come to an end sometime.

EPILOGUE

"You missed a spot."

"Crap. Somebody spilled paint on the carpet."

"Can you get me a paper towel? Hurry!"

We were painting my room, the last item on my Personal Transformation list. The dark burgundy walls were fading, one coat at a time, brightening to a pale turquoise. The shade of a summer sky or the ocean. Or a lake filled with tears.

I didn't want to forget what had happened. I wanted to rise above it. If that was really possible.

Sammy had splotches of primer on her chin, Molly's hair was speckled with turquoise, and Zoe's hair wasn't lavender anymore—it was almost the same shade as my new walls.

"We need to crack open that window. I'm dying of fumes here," Molly said. Then she stood there for a long moment, sucking in fresh air, staring down at my front yard as if something amazing was going on down below. "What the heck?"

But I didn't pay attention to her. I was testing out my new closet door, the one Dad had installed last night.

"Check it out, Moll," I said, opening and closing the door over and over. No creaks, no scary sounds, and definitely no monsters lurking inside. She grinned back at me.

"It's finally time for a sleepover, girl," she said.

Downstairs, Dad and Mom were making lunch. It smelled like lasagna and I was starved. It had taken me a while, but I'd gotten to the point where I didn't worry about my weight. Food tasted better and, the funny thing was, I didn't end up gaining much. Just a few pounds. Maybe the fact that I was working harder than ever in my ballet classes was paying off.

Zoe joined Molly and Stephanie at the window, all of them goofing off, staring outside.

"Is that who I think it is?" Zoe asked.

"Yup," Stephanie answered.

"Hey, we're never gonna finish if we don't keep working," I told them. Molly glanced over her shoulder at me, a big grin on her face.

Just then, Kyle knocked on my door, Game Boy in one hand. Sixteen years old now, his boy hormones kicked in when he ran a gaze across the room at all of my friends dressed in shorts and tank tops, all of them drenched in sweat and speckled in paint. I guess it was a turn-on, because he forgot why he was here.

"Is lunch ready?" I asked.

"No, uh—" He blushed, full-on red face, stuttering when Zoe flashed him a shy grin. "It's, um, you better come outside. There's something you need to see."

"Back in a sec," I said as I set my brush down.

"Take your time, girlfriend," Stephanie said with a wink.

I jogged down the stairs, wiping my hands on a paper towel I grabbed along the way, heading toward the front door that stood open.

"Tell him to come inside for lunch," Dad said from the kitchen.

"Tell who?" I asked with a frown, but I didn't slow down. I needed to get back upstairs and oversee those girls who were about ready to mutiny. There'd already been rumblings about quitting early to go see the new Liam Hemsworth movie. Paper towel scrunched up in my palm, I lifted my gaze, then slid to a stop.

The tree in our front yard, that one Dad planted last year, that one where Dylan and I had our first kiss—at least, the first one I really remembered, all the way from start to finish—was covered with paper notes, all swinging in the breeze, all tied with pink ribbons. I stumbled toward it, my feet catching on clumps of grass and decorative stones, my mouth hanging open.

"What's going on?" I asked, swinging back around to look at the open door where Mom and Dad stood, watching me. Up in my room, all the girls crowded around the window, trying to look down.

I took a couple more tentative steps toward the tree, realizing for the first time that this was one of those Japanese flowering cherry trees, just like the ones at school. I pulled down one of the notes and opened it, then I read it.

My eyes stung, tears threatening to fall.

It was a poem about me, about how I looked when I danced, how graceful I was, how beautiful I was.

It was dated two years ago.

I blinked as I moved from one note to the next, as I opened one poem after another. As I learned that Dylan had been smitten with me since we were both in seventh grade, long before the day I dropped my pen and he picked it up.

There was a poem about our first kiss. Another one about our first date. There was one about our first fight.

And another one about that day in the hospital when we broke up. I could barely read it, because my vision was blurred by tears. I couldn't see much, didn't hear him when he walked up behind me. Didn't realize he was standing right beside me until he spoke, taking my hand in his.

"Hey, girl," he said.

"Hey."

What do you say to the boy you fell in love with between middle school and the near-murder of one of your closest friends?

"I thought you weren't 'good for me.'" That's what came out of my mouth. I think it surprised both of us.

"I made some mistakes, but I can try to be better," he said awkwardly. His magic way with words faltered, but the expression in his eyes melted my heart. "Besides I...I haven't been able to stop thinking about you."

A breeze blew through that tree and the notes spun around me. I wondered how many of these poems were new, like the one about that day in the hospital, how many of these had he written since we broke up.

"Maybe we can start over," he said. "Wanna go for a ride?"

I glanced back at the house, at all the girls who were yelling *go*, and my dad and my mom who were nodding, and my little brother who was grinning like he had a clue what true love really was.

It was this.

It was second chances. And forgiving. Over and over.

"Yes." That's what I said, but inside, I was saying, *yes,*

always, yes, definitely, yes, and *why did you wait so long* and, *by the way, yes, so let's go, okay*.

And a few minutes later we were on his bike, my arms wrapped around his waist, my head nestled in his shoulder, the smell of his shampoo like sunshine. We were flying, faster and faster, wings spread wide. Together. We were together and he was here and he had been in love with me, even before I knew it.

Like ravens and swans, different but the same, wings spread wide, feathers catching the sunlight and the wind, we flew up one mountain road and down another.

He was back and we were together again.

And this was a day that I would remember for the rest of my life.

Acknowledgments

If you've already read this book, then you know that much of the story in *Lost Girls* is about friendship and family. The fact of the matter is, we all need someone to lean on when the going gets rough.

The list of people who have influenced/helped/cheered me on while writing this book is nearly as long as the book itself. I am always thankful for my talented agent, Natalie Lakosil, for her insight and input that truly shaped *Lost Girls*. She gave me expert advice when I had about a third of the book written. Someday I'll tell the tale about what I had planned to write versus what the story became.

All the hearts and flowers go to the Maester of Stories, my Entangled editor, Heather Howland. She's the one who transformed The Book That Was into The Book That Is. She found magical ways to deepen the story and enrich the characters, and she even helped make Dylan hotter than he already was. (Yay!)

Some books have a very unique journey. This happens to be one of them. When I wrote *Lost Girls*, I was going through one of those Dark Nights of the Soul that writers often go through, and I seriously considered quitting writing. A dear friend and fellow writer, Rachel Marks (you have to check out her Dark Cycle series!), continually encouraged me and prodded me to finish this story. We had many long conversations and emails and face-to-face chats where she was adamant.

I. Had. To. Finish. This. Book.

I'm so glad I did and I'm so blessed to have a friend who wouldn't let me give up. I hope everyone reading this book has at least one friend like that. Someone you can call when you're discouraged or when you're lost.

Another person who believed in this book and in me was Rebecca Luella Miller. Thank you, Becky! I sincerely appreciate every kind comment, as well as every red pen editor's mark on the page. You, Rachel, Paul Regnier and Mike Duran—members of our Panera writing group—gave me the courage to continue. I'm also grateful for the support of OC Writers, a group that gets together to both write and chat about books. I treasure those quiet times, when we all sit together and bang away at our keyboards. I'm also encouraged by the family atmosphere of the Barmy Drapers Writing Group. Eddie Louise Clark, Chip Clark, and Amber Theresa Morrell have made me feel completely at home from Day One.

Finally, but not lastly, thank you to my husband, Tom, for loving me and supporting me and helping me to pursue my dream of writing, and to my son, Jesse, who inspires me to be a better person, and to my God, who always loves me, even when I make mistakes and get lost along the way.

Author's Note

I may not have done all the things my main character, Rachel, did in this book, but I was definitely a Lost Girl when I was a teenager. I got drunk, took drugs, skipped school, ran away from home, hitchhiked to different states, and was put in juvenile three times. Being wild can seem like a lot of fun at the time, but quite often the consequences aren't fun at all.

There are many ways to be lost. You might have a family who doesn't understand what you're going through, or you might have a best friend who slept with your boyfriend. You might be bullied at school for being different, or you might be embarrassed because your parents don't have much money, or because they're alcoholics or drug addicts.

The fact that you feel lost doesn't mean you're alone or that nobody cares about what you're going through. I care. I care a *lot*. That's one reason I wrote this book. And I want you to know that there are people and organizations out there that care about what you're going through, too.

Please remember, it helps to talk to someone—a friend, a parent, a high school counselor, or perhaps someone from the list below.

- National Runaway Switchboard:
  Website: www.1800runaway.org
  Phone: 24-Hour Crisis Line: 1-800-RUNAWAY
- Safe Place:
  Website: NationalSafePlace.org
- Teen Health and Wellness:
  Website: TeenHealthAndWellness.com
  Phone: Suicide Hotline: 800-784-2433
  Immediate Medical Assistance: 911

Crisis Call Center: 800-273-8255 or text ANSWER to 839863

GRAB THE ENTANGLED TEEN RELEASES READERS ARE TALKING ABOUT!

LOVE ME NEVER
BY SARA WOLF

Seventeen-year-old Isis Blake has just moved to the glamorous town of Buttcrack-of-Nowhere, Ohio. And she's hoping like hell that no one learns that a) she used to be fat; and b) she used to have a heart. Naturally, she opts for social suicide instead...by punching the cold and untouchably handsome "Ice Prince"—a.k.a. Jack Hunter—right in the face. Now the school hallways are an epic battleground as Isis and the Ice Prince engage in a vicious game of social warfare. But sometimes to know your enemy is to love him...

THE REPLACEMENT CRUSH
by LISA BROWN ROBERTS

After book blogger Vivian Galdi's longtime crush pretends their secret summer kissing sessions never happened, Vivian creates a list of safe crushes, determined to protect her heart.

But nerd-hot Dallas, the sweet new guy in town, sends the missions—and Vivian's zing meter—into chaos. While designing software for the bookstore where she works, Dallas wages a countermission.

Operation Replacement Crush is in full effect. And Dallas is determined to take her heart off the shelf.

CHASING TRUTH
BY JULIE CROSS

When former con artist Eleanor Ames's homecoming date commits suicide, she's positive there's something more going on. The more questions she asks, though, the more she crosses paths with Miles Beckett. He's sexy, mysterious, *arrogant*... and he's asking all the same questions.

Eleanor might not trust him—she doesn't even *like* him—but they can't keep their hands off of each other. Fighting the infuriating attraction is almost as hard as ignoring the fact that Miles isn't telling her the truth...and that there's a good chance *he* could be the killer.

NEXIS
BY A.L. DAVROE

A Natural Born amongst genetically-altered Aristocrats, all Ella ever wanted was to be like everyone else. Augmented and *perfect*. Then...the crash. Devastated by her father's death and struggling with her new physical limitations, Ella is terrified to learn she is not just alone, but little more than a prisoner. Her only escape is to lose herself in Nexis, the hugely popular virtual reality game her father created. In Nexis she meets Guster, who offers Ella guidance, friendship... and something more. But Nexis isn't quite the game everyone thinks it is. And it's been waiting for Ella...

Romancing the Nerd
by Leah Rae Miller

Until recently, Dan Garrett was just another live-action role-playing (LARP) geek on the lowest rung of the social ladder. Cue a massive growth spurt and an uncanny skill at basketball and voila...Mr. Popular. The biggest drawback? It cost Dan the secret girl-of-his-dorky-dreams. But when Dan humiliates her at school, Zelda Potts decides it's time for a little revenge—dork style. Nevermind that she used to have a crush on him. It's time to roll the dice...and hope like freakin' hell she doesn't lose her heart in the process.

True Born
by L.E. Sterling

After the great Plague descended, the population was decimated...and humans' genetics damaged beyond repair. But there's something about Lucy Fox and her identical twin sister, Margot, that isn't quite right. No one wants to reveal what they are. When Margot disappears suddenly, Lucy is forced to turn to the True Borns to find her. But instead of answers, there is only the discovery of a deeply buried conspiracy. And somehow, the Fox sisters could unravel it all...